Forest City
to
Ascension

Randall Probert

Forest City to Ascension

by Randall Probert

www.randallprobertbooks.net
email: randentr@megalink.net

Art and Photography credits:

Cover photo background is the author's,
and the character is from iStock.com

Author's photo on back cover by Patricia Gott

Disclaimer
This book is a work of fiction, as are all the characters and any association with Irving Oil.

ISBN: 979-8357331779

Published by
Randall Enterprises
P.O. Box 862
Bethel, Maine 04217

Acknowledgments

I would like to thank Amy Henley of Newry, Maine, for her help typing this and for the rewrites and her advice. I would also like to thank Laura Ashton of Woodland, Georgia, for her help formatting this book for printing, and for her help and advice.

More Books by Randall Probert

Chapter 1

"Charles, go watch the early news, or go out to the shop; you're driving me crazy with your pacing?"

"I wish April would have come last evening, like she was supposed to, Liz."

"She'll be here, Charles. Now go watch the news and let me finish breakfast. You might make sure Gary is up and dressed."

Charles walked over to the upstairs stairs and hollered up, "Gary, are you up?"

"Yes, Dad, and I'm dressing."

"Hurry up, your mother said breakfast will be ready shortly."

Charles turned the TV on and sat down. The weather report was already on. When that was over, he went back to the kitchen. "According to the weather report, Liz, we'll have good weather for our trip to Tomah all weekend."

"That's good, Charles, now go back to the living room."

He sat down again and instead of listening to the news, he began reliving his life. His grandfather, John Henry Newman, in 1910 bought 500 acres on the right side of the East Madison Road in Skowhegan, from William Spears. Spears had lumbered and cleared three hundred acres of land with the intention of farming. But after the house was built and the land cleared, he had had a stroke and was never able to use his left arm again. Well, a farmer needed two arms and a rugged back, so he was forced to sell out to John Henry Newman.

John was a hard worker and he built a large cow barn with hay storage above the tie-up. He had fifty milking cows, pigs, chickens and, of course, two work horses. He built a large smoking room to cure ham and bacon which was sold to stores, as well as pork, eggs, milk and he would butcher three of the older milkers each year. Farming was a lot of hard work, but the family lived good and seldom went without.

"Gary, go see if your father fell asleep watching the news. I've hollered to him twice and no answer."

"Dad," Gary said, "you sleeping or what?"

"Ah—no," and he stood up and stretched.

Out in the kitchen, Liz asked, "What, had you fallen asleep, Charles?"

"Nah, just daydreaming."

"What about? Our trip to Tomah?"

"Actually, I was thinking about when Granddad started this farm."

Just then the kitchen door opened and their daughter April said, "Good morning, all. Mom, I could smell the bacon outdoors and I'm hungry."

April was in her first year of nursing at the University of Orono. Liz was also a nurse and now she was the nursing supervisor at the Redington-Fairview General Hospital there in Skowhegan. April had wanted to be like her mother ever since she could remember.

Liz had taken a week of vacation for this yearly trip to their camp on Tomah Stream in Forest City. April was allowed to skip two days a month from her classes as long as she maintained a 2.7 grade average.

Gary was on February school vacation. He was 14, five years younger than his sister April. His friend Galen Merrill was also 14.

Charles was taking a long weekend from work.

"Sit down, sweetheart; we just sat down," Liz said.

"I'm sorry I couldn't make it home last night. We had our midterm tests this week and I wanted to stay and find out how I did before leaving. The grades weren't posted until 6 o'clock."

"How did you do?" Gary asked.

"I aced the practicals and a 90 on one written and a 92 on the other."

"That's good, isn't it?" Charles asked.

"Yes, I'm happy."

"I have to eat in a hurry so I can pack a few things. Is Galen Merrill coming, Gary?"

"Yes, we'll stop and pick him up."

April swallowed the last of her scrambled eggs and picked up the last piece of bacon and raced upstairs.

"Gary, are you all packed?"

"Yes."

"Okay, help your father load the pickup and I'll clean the kitchen," Liz said.

Everything was loaded in back and the pickup cap closed. Charles said, "Let's go."

The Merrills only lived two houses below them towards town and Galen was ready and waiting. Gary put his pack in back and they were on their way.

As they were leaving Skowhegan, Liz said, "There sure is a lot of traffic so early on a Friday morning."

"Most people, I suppose, are going to work."

"How come you didn't put the plow on, Charles? Are we going to have to snowshoe into the camp?"

"Georgia Pacific has a crew lumbering in beyond the camp and I've had the woods boss, Arnold, keep the camp plowed out."

* * *

By the time they reached I-95 in Newport, the conversations had died off. Liz was napping and Charles looked in the rearview mirror and the three kids were also asleep. As he drove along, he began thinking about his dad, his granddad and the farm.

7

Both his grandfather and father had died at an early age of sixty. They were hard-working men and they simply had worked themselves into an early grave.

With the evolution of electricity, milking machines and tractors replacing the horse and wagon, life and farming was easier and more productive. But on the other hand, they had to increase the herd to pay for the equipment. And his father still worked as hard.

Charles and Liz had married as soon as she had finished college. But they waited five years before having April and then another five years for Gary.

Charles was pretty much running the farm and his dad would help milk in the afternoon, but that was all.

In time, it was becoming too expensive to continue farming, with the cost of grain and gasoline. The profit the farm should be making was now going to substantiate a way of living. There was nothing left for the future. So one day after his dad, Charlie, had died, he made the decision to sell off the cattle and equipment, except for one tractor.

Liz hated to see their farm life come to an end, but she, like Charles, could see the writing on the wall.

Charles had always been a good carpenter and one day he was asked to build kitchen and bathroom cabinets in an expensive mansion being built by a local contractor.

When other contractors learned of Charles' expertise with cabinetmaking, he began working fulltime. Then one day Liz had asked why he didn't build a shop in the barn and build cabinets to sell retail.

It took him a year of working only on weekends transforming the barn to a cabinet factory. Once complete, he had to hire three men fulltime to keep up with the orders.

Transforming the barn to a cabinetmaking factory was costly and he sold off four hundred acres of land, leaving a hundred acres for them. After the first two years, he had doubled the size of the building.

The business was doing so well, that two years ago he had purchased the camp at Tomah Stream in Forest City along with five hundred acres of recently cut-over woodland.

* * *

As they were driving through the Argle Swamp, Liz woke up. "Did you have a good nap?" Charles asked.

"Yes, I guess I needed it."

"I think the kids have been sleeping, too. They've been pretty quiet."

"Every time we drive north of Old Town, it's like entering another world. The houses have disappeared and all there is is woods."

"And practically no traffic, but us," he said. "We're making good time. We'll be at the camp before noon."

"How are you doing? Are you getting tired?"

"I'm okay. I think when we get to Lincoln, before we stop at the IGA, we should stop at Dunkin Donuts."

There was a chorus of, "Yeah," from the backseat.

"There isn't much more snow here than at home," Liz said.

By the time they were beyond the Howland exit, there was a noticeable difference in the height of the snowbanks.

"What does the dash thermometer say, Charles?"

"30°. Not bad for February."

"It sure is a nice day for traveling. And I'll be glad when we get there."

"Well, it's only another mile to the Lincoln exit."

"Yeah!" April said excitedly. "And Dunkin Donuts. I'm hungry again."

Gary and Galen both chimed in agreeing they were hungry, too.

"Are you still trying to build your own computer, Galen?" April asked.

"I finished it last fall and it works better than most computers."

"What are you working on now?"

"I am trying to write a security program. I'm finding it more difficult than building a computer," he said.

"That's remarkable, Galen. You're only 14 and you built your own computer and now you're writing your own security program. When do you find time for fun?" April asked.

"It's fun, April. At least it is for me."

"Some day, Galen, it wouldn't surprise me if you come up with something in the computer field that'll astound the world," Charles said. This statement surprised everyone. Usually Charles was quiet and had very little to say.

At Dunkin Donuts, they each had one donut with coffee and Charles bought a dozen plain donuts to take with them. "I'll drop you off, Liz, at the IGA and I'll fill up with gas."

* * *

With food and a full tank of gasoline, they left Lincoln heading east on Rt. 6. This was old farm country, now desolate and thinly populated, a true wilderness. Many houses were now vacant, except for summer visitors and the few living along the highway were probably older people who worked in the woods during the heyday of the lumbering industry, before the advent of mechanical harvesting. Three men and three pieces of equipment were now harvesting as much each day as eight, two-men crews used to.

This was a prime example where technology actually worked against the personal welfare of many wood cutters.

"This road with the high snowbanks reminds me of a tunnel," Liz said.

"With this much snow, I sure hope Arnold has kept the camp plowed out," Charles said.

"Yeah, or we'll have a lot of shoveling today," Gary added.

"Everything is so quiet out here," April said. "People have to travel a good distance to grocery shop. I don't think I could ever live out here, but I do enjoy this trip."

After leaving Topsfield at the Rt.1 junction, the snowbanks were not as high. The sun was still shining bright and the dash thermometer now was reading 35°. "I think this is going to be a good weekend," Charles said. "It won't be long now."

Six miles later they turned onto the Forest City Road in Brookton.

They turned onto the plowed woods road before the railroad at 10:45. The camp driveway was plowed and there was a cleared path to the door. "Look boys, the roof will have to be shoveled off. While you four unload the truck, I'll get a fire going in the cook stove and fireplace."

"Brrr, it's cold in here," Liz said.

"Yeah, but with the fireplace and stove, it'll warm up quick."

He wasn't long getting both fires going. Then he turned on the propane gas and lit two gas lamps. "There that is more like it, already," he said.

"Gary, would you start shoveling the roof off before the heat starts melting the snow and the water freezes on the eaves. Then I'll bank around the camp."

While the boys were doing that, he tried the handpump at the kitchen sink. After two minutes he had water.

"I'll go shovel a path to the outhouse," he said.

"Good, I have to go," April said.

"Me, too."

"I'll hurry," He always kept a third shovel by the side door.

While he was doing that, Liz said, "I can feel the heat from the fireplace already."

"It feels good. I'd like to drop my pants and back up to the fire with my bare butt," April said.

"April," that's all Liz could say.

April grinned knowing her mother would have something to say about her comment.

After the groceries were taken care of, Liz and April made

soup and sandwiches.

"Charles, would you call the boys in for lunch?"

He went outside and asked, "How are you doing?"

"This side is almost done," Gary said,

"Good, lunch is ready."

"Let's finish this side first, Gary," Galen said.

"The boys want to finish that side of the roof, then they'll be in."

When the boys came in for lunch Galen said, "Ummm, that sure smells good, Mrs. Newman. What is it?"

"Thank you, Galen, but April is cooking a pork loin for supper."

"Ummm, pretty and cooks too." Everyone laughed.

"How much snow is on the roof?" Charles asked.

"Oh, maybe two and a half feet."

"I'll be glad to get it off the roof."

When lunch was eaten, the boys started on the other side of the roof and Charles started to bank the side that was already clear.

Liz fixed a cup of tea for herself and April and talked about April's nursing studies. "Do you enjoy it, April?"

"Oh yes, Mom, and I think I'll enjoy nursing more once I'm really helping to care for patients. And I'm learning so much about the human body."

"That's how I felt, too, when I was studying.

"Any idea where you'll want to work once you graduate?"

"Maybe where you work, Mom. But then you'd be my boss, wouldn't you?"

"Would it be that bad if I was your boss?"

"Of course not, Mom. But some time I'd like to get out from under Skowhegan and see something different."

"How about the military?"

"Hmm, that's an idea. I'll work on it."

There was more snow on the north side and by the time the

boys were done, they were tired and their clothes were wet with sweat. "You two change your clothes before you catch cold." There was only the one room. At first, Galen was a bit reluctant with both Liz and April in the same room.

"Come on, Galen, aren't you going to get out of your wet clothes?" He saw Galen looking at his mom and sister in the kitchen and said, "Don't worry about them, Galen."

Charles came in just as April was hanging up their wet clothes on a clothesline stretched across the front of the fireplace. "I could use another cup of coffee."

Liz was already pouring it. She knew her husband that well.

"That tastes good, Hon. Thank you."

"Are you tried?"

"A little—I'll sleep good tonight."

* * *

It took longer to roast the pork loin than either Liz or April thought it would. Finally, at 7 o'clock they sat down for supper.

"This was worth waiting for."

Everyone agreed it was good.

After supper and everything was picked up and cleaned, they sat in the living room and Liz opened a bottle of wine. The boys were only allowed one juice-size glass.

When the wine was gone, they started playing cribbage. There were two boards. Charles and Gary were one team and Liz, April and Galen played three handed cribbage.

Everyone was getting sleepy after several games and they all agreed it was time to go to bed. Charles and Liz had a double-size bed and April had a bunk above them, and along the same wall Gary and Galen had bunkbeds. The gas lights were turned off and Gary lit a kerosine lantern on the table and turned the wick down on low, enough to give the interior a warming glow.

This wasn't Galen's first trip to the camp and he knew everyone slept in their underwear—took their clothes off and then crawled into bed.

* * *

In spite of Charles' snoring, everyone slept soundly and it was a rush to the cold outhouse in the morning.

The camp was cool but not cold. Gary started the fire in the stove while Charles started the fireplace. There were a few coals left.

April came back in from the outhouse and said, "It isn't as cold out as I thought it would be."

"What is the temperature?" Liz asked.

"20°."

While Liz and April were making coffee and breakfast, Charles shaved. Gary and Galen went outside and tested the snow to see if it was walkable. There was four or five inches of powder on top of a walkable crust. "This is good, Galen. Maybe we'll go for a hike after breakfast."

Breakfast of bacon and pancakes was ready and everyone sat down. There was very little conversation. After eating and still sipping their coffee, Gary said, "Galen and I are going for a hike down the stream."

"I want to go, too," April said.

"Okay, Sis."

"The snowshoes are still in the shed," Charles said.

"I don't think we'll need them, Dad. Earlier Galen and I did some testing and we could walk on the crust under the powder just fine."

"Where are you going?"

"Down to the stream and then downstream to the beaver dam."

"Okay, be careful. Your mother and I are going to drive to Danforth. You'll probably be back before we are."

By the time the three were dressed and out the door, the temperature had risen to almost 30°. "This is going to be a nice day for a hike," Galen said.

"It's so nice and peaceful out here," April said.

"If that beaver dam doesn't wash out come spring, there'll be some great fishing," Gary said.

All of a sudden, a partridge exploded out of the soft powder directly in front of them. They all stopped and April said, "Boy, did that ever jump me. What was he doing under the snow anyhow?"

"Probably keeping warm or hiding from a predator bird."

"Come on, April, I'll protect you," Galen said. But he had jumped with surprise, too.

In a short distance, April said, "Look, dog tracks. What is a dog doing out here alone?"

Galen said, "I think those are coyote tracks."

"Maybe that was what the partridge was hiding from," Gary added. "Come on, let's go."

"Will coyotes bother us?"

"No, they aren't as big as a wolf or a German Shepherd dog."

Just back from the edge of the stream there were two otters playing on the narrow strip of ice in the middle. "They play like two small children," April whispered.

Both otters stopped playing and turned to face them, sitting up. Then they headed downstream. Playtime was over.

Out on the frozen stream, they started following the narrow band of ice in the middle. The ice was frozen slush and not slippery at all. But they were being cautious. Around the first bend and downstream about two hundred feet, there were several deer feeding on cedar boughs and they stood in silence watching.

The deer seemed oblivious to their nearness, until a sudden breeze blew their scent downstream. Then one lone buck lifted his head and turned into the breeze and stomped his front leg and all the deer ran off.

Gary was anticipating her next question, "The breeze blew our scent down and the lone deer, probably a buck, was alerted

15

and he signaled the others when he stomped his left—hoof on the ground."

"That was interesting."

They continued on downstream. At the last bend before reaching the beaver dam, a flock of ravens took to the air. "What was that all about?" April asked.

"There's probably a coyote killed deer there they were feeding on."

As they walked closer, there wasn't much left of the remains to see. Galen took two steps off the middle strip to go over and look at the remains when suddenly the ice under the snow cover broke up and Galen disappeared in the water.

They both saw Galen go under and Gary hollered, "Galen!" and he jumped in after his friend. Galen never learned to swim.

April saw her brother disappear below in the water and she screamed, "Gary! What are you doing?" and she began to cry.

The water was deep and Galen had gone right to the bottom. Gary grabbed the collar of his jacket and pointed up to the opening. Galen knew what he meant and he nodded his head. Gary swam up to the ice hole bringing Galen behind him. When he poked his head above the water and then Galen's, April was still crying. "Jesus, Gary, you scared me when you jumped in!"

Galen said, "My head is getting cold in the cold air."

"Yeah, me too," Gary replied. "April, I can't get him out of here by myself."

"What can I do to help you?"

"You're going to have to lay flat on the ice, to disperse your weight and crawl out to the edge and grab his collar and pull him out. I'll be pushing. Hurry, April, I don't know how much longer we can remain in the water."

As April crawled out to the edge of the ice hole, she was now completely wet on the front part of her body. She reached out and grabbed his collar and began pulling. Gary was helping all he could and eventually Galen was out and laying on the snow-covered ice.

April crawled back to the hole to help her brother. There was no one to help push him up and she was a bit longer getting him onto the ice. All three just lay there for a moment, then Gary said, "Roll in the snow before the water freezes to our clothes." He actually had to roll Galen and brush snow onto him, "Come on, April, roll in the snow."

"I'm almost as wet as you two are."

Gary began rolling. When he had finished, he said, "Come on, we need to get to the camp."

They had to help Galen stand, and for a short distance they had to support him on either side. "Walking will get our blood flowing again and it'll keep us from freezing," April said. "Gawd, I'm cold."

"We all are, Sis."

"I'm getting colder," Galen said.

"We can't stop. If we do, hypothermia will set in and we'll die," April said.

Just as they were leaving the stream April broke through some slush and snow and the water now filled her boots and she lost her balance and sat down in the slush. Now she was as wet as the two boys. Gary helped her to stand and brush snow on her backside to soak up the water.

"That's enough, Gary. We need to get to the camp as fast as we can."

All three were beginning to feel the effects of hypothermia setting in. Their pace had slowed and their face, hands and feet were extremely cold.

"We're almost back. There's the camp," Gary said trying to cheer them up.

Galen could no longer stand on his own and Gary had to hold on to him while April opened the door. Her hands were so cold she had a difficult time turning the doorknob.

Once inside, April said, "Gary, we need to take our wet

clothes off and stand in front of the fireplace. We're all three chilled through to the bone. Help me set Galen in a chair and I'll start taking his clothes off. Can you put some wood on the fire?"

"I'll try." He discovered he didn't have much strength left. But he was able to put three pieces of wood on. By now April had Galen and her clothes off and was helping him to the fire. "Get out of your clothes, Gary," she said.

He did and April asked, "Can you steady him, Gary? These floors are so cold we'll never unthaw our feet. I'm going to double up a blanket and lay it in front so we can stand on it."

They were supporting Galen between them, directly in front of the fire. The first thing to come back was their speech; their words were not slurred. "This feels better," Galen said. "But I'm still cold."

"We all are, Galen."

Charles and Liz rode out to look at the lumbering operation instead of going to Danforth and they were back earlier than they had expected. "The kids must be back, look at the smoke coming from the chimney."

"I hope they made a pot of coffee," Liz said.

When she opened the door and saw the three naked bodies standing in front of the fireplace, her first reaction was, "What's going on here?" Charles didn't say anything. He was hoping for a reasonable explanation, though.

As Liz stormed through the camp towards the three naked bodies, she saw their wet clothes and boots on the floor. No one was trying to cover up. They were still cold.

Liz was now standing beside her daughter and said, "Well, what happened?"

April answered her, "Galen broke through the ice and went completely under and Gary jumped in to save him Then I got wet pulling them back onto the ice. We're still so cold, Mom."

"I'll get some blankets to wrap around them," Charles said.

"That won't help yet, Charles. The blankets would only

hold the cold in longer."

"My gawd, Liz, they look like icicles. They're blue around their lips and they're so white."

"It's hypothermia. Charles, heat up some water. But first give each a shot of your whiskey. This will help with circulation. Just water, no coffee yet."

"Can you three move your legs?"

They all said, "Yes, some."

"Good, walk in place. This will help the circulation." She put some more wood on the fire.

When the water was hot, Charles filled three cups and gave them each one. They held them in their hands warming them for a few minutes before drinking.

The cold was beginning to work to the surface of the three now, as all three began shivering and their teeth chattering. When this passed, all three were feeling better.

"How do you feel now, Galen?" April asked.

"Much better. I could almost put my clothes back on."

"Me, too," Gary said.

"Can you get us some dry clothes, Mom?" April asked.

Charles already had their wet clothes hanging up and drying.

When they were finally dressed, Galen said, "I have never been so cold in my life." That was a mutual feeling among the three.

"You two saved my life. Thank you."

"If April had not been with us, I don't know if we would have been able to climb out of the water and onto the ice," Gary said.

Charles had fixed a pot of coffee and they all sat in the living room drinking coffee and telling Charles and Liz the entire store.

* * *

After an early supper, they rode down the woods road to

19

the lumbering operation. The woods boss, Arnold, had told them that morning that if they were to drive out after dark they would see many deer. They began seeing deer in the road before they reached the operation. He drove slower so he would not run into any. "They're not at all afraid, Charles."

"Not as long as we stay inside. Look over behind the delimber. There's so many deer, it's difficult to count them."

"Probably the deer we saw on the stream are part of this group," Gary said.

"More than likely."

"They are so graceful and pretty I don't understand why anyone would shoot one," April said.

"Well, sweetheart, they are very good eating. And I suppose there are still families who depend on deer meat to see them through the winter."

"Well, maybe."

"I can't help but think about the dead deer we saw. I wonder how many deer the coyotes have killed here?" Galen said.

They spent an hour there in the log yard watching the deer under the headlights.

They eventually returned to the camp and Liz produced another bottle of wine and they all enjoyed sipping wine while sitting near the fireplace with good conversations.

"You three have had a very eventful day. You must have been terrified, Galen," Charles said.

"I was until I saw Gary had jumped in after me. Then I knew he would get me out. Actually, I was more afraid we would all die from the cold."

Tonight, Liz refilled the three glasses halfway. "You three have earned it. I'm proud of all of you and how you helped each other to survive.

"I must admit though how shocked I was when I saw you three standing naked by the fireplace." Then she laughed and the others laughed with her.

The fireplace was providing enough light tonight so the lantern wasn't needed. "Goodnight, everyone," Charles said. "We both are proud of you."

* * *

They left the next day after an early lunch. The ride back was not as quiet as the ride up. Everyone, including Charles, was in a talkative mood.

At Galen's house both Gary and April stepped out. Galen pulled his pack out from the body and set it on the ground. "Thank you, Gary, for saving my life." Then he turned to face April and he hugged her and said, "Thank you, too, April," and then he whispered in her ear, "and thank you for that show."

She stepped back and smiled and winked at him.

* * *

April didn't return to Orono until after lunch the next day. She and her mom enjoyed some mother-daughter time. Gary worked in the cabinet making factory. Every time Charles looked at his son, he couldn't help think how proud he was of him. The only time anyone would mention the event or talk about it, was when Charles and Liz were alone in bed. Even when Gary and Galen were together, they chose not to dwell on it. It was to them only something that had happened. But Galen did learn to swim that summer.

April went back to college and never said a word to anyone about the event. But she would often think about it. One night after her roommate had turned the light off April laid on her back reliving the experience and viewing the images of the three of them in the nude standing in front of the fireplace.

In her inner vision she could see the three of them in the nude warming themselves by the fire. She was naked standing beside two naked boys and she realized there never was a sexual overtone. But she did find it exhilarating and what was just as exhilarating was when the experience called for her training and knowledge. She knew what had to be done. And what was even more exhilarating was the fact that she had put herself in danger because Galen and Gary needed her help to get out of the water. She had responded without any thought of her own wellbeing. She had placed the wellbeing of the boys before her own.

And then seeing herself naked standing with two naked boys made her laugh. Her roommate Debbie asked, "What's so funny, April? Can you share it?"

"Sorry, Debbie, it is too personal."

She went off to sleep proud of herself for putting the wellbeing of the boys before her own.

* * *

At the end of her first year, Liz was able to get April a job as a practical nurse where she worked, on the graveyard shift.

Gary was working for his dad every day in the cabinet factory and banking his earnings.

By the end of that summer, Galen had perfected his new computer security program and he had consulted an attorney to help him apply for patent rights. The patent office was back-logged with new patent applications and he was told it would take approximately nine months.

In the meantime, his dad helped him to set up his own office above the garage where he could conduct his own computer business.

Galen's attorney was the only one outside the family that knew Galen had perfected his security program and because of client-attorney confidentiality, Galen knew he would not say anything. And then there was Gary. He was more like a brother and of course he knew, but not Gary's family.

Ten months after applying for patent rights, he had his patent and it was now filed in the patent office in Washington, D.C. During those ten months Galen was prepared now to put his program on the internet for sale and sold a thousand disk copies in his office above the garage.

After the first month, he had sold a thousand online programs and a thousand hard copies. He paid his attorney for his help and the extra equipment he needed for his business. His parents were extremely proud of their son.

Within three months his program was selling so fast, he had to rent a building in town and install automatic equipment to process the internet sales. Through his smart phone, he was able to monitor his business and answer calls when needed.

He named his new program Tomah Security and he had to have a company name for the IRS, sales tax and the bank; he decided on, *The Merrill Computer Service.*

Chapter 2

April graduated in June that same year as a registered nurse. She invited Galen to her graduation. Almost a year and a half had passed since falling through the ice. He had grown physically as well as mentally and now when he looked at April he could appreciate her beauty and friendship.

He went through the line offering congratulations to all of the newly capped nurses and when he came to April, he stopped and stood there looking at her for a few moments and then he hugged her and kissed her.

"You have grown taller, Galen, and you have filled out. Can you swim yet?"

"And you are more beautiful now, April, than I could have imagined. And yes, I learned to swim last summer."

"How old are you now, Galen?"

"I turned seventeen in March. And you?"

"I turned twenty-two in April."

The line was moving ahead of him and he was holding up the line behind him, so he moved on.

After the ceremony, they had dinner out, at the Governor's Restaurant in Stillwater. April already had her car packed so she didn't have to return to the dormitory.

Everyone decided on the fisherman's platter. Charles and Liz were certainly proud of their daughter.

* * *

Three days later, on a Monday morning, April drove to Bangor to talk with an Army recruiter.

"With your nursing degree, it is too bad you didn't enroll in the ROTC program, then you'd go in as a lieutenant. But once you are situated, you could still take an officer's training program.

"With your degree and in the medical field, your basic training would not be as extensive. You would be looking at four weeks Ms. Newman," Lieutenant Al Bickford said.

"Where would I go for basic training?"

"Fort Dix, New Jersey."

"When?"

"There is a class starting on July 1st and another on September 1st. My recommendation would be September 1st. It gets terribly hot in July.

"Do you need some time to think about this?"

"I don't think so. This is what I want. Providing I can have the September 1st date."

"If you sign your enlistment papers, you'll have the September date."

She signed and it was done.

"Be at the armory in Augusta on Western Avenue on August 30th at 0600."

"Thank you, Lieutenant."

On the drive home, she was excited about the possibilities of traveling the world and nursing. And there was a nagging supposition ... *Have I made a mistake?*

She wasn't sure how her family would accept the idea of her enlisting. And to her surprise, they all thought it was a good idea. "You got what you wanted, sweetheart," her mother said. "You'll be able to travel now and do what you have been studying to do. Where will you go after basic training?"

"I won't know that until after basic training."

"Any idea what you'll do next year, Gary, when you graduate from high school?" April asked.

"Yes, I've already made up my mind. I intend to study carpentry and drafting at the vocational institute in Auburn." He looked at his dad to see if there was any disappointment showing. There wasn't.

"Will you be an officer, Sis?"

"The lieutenant said if I had enrolled in the ROTC in college, I could have entered the service as a lieutenant. I'll work on it, though, once I get stationed somewhere."

"You'll have a good opportunity to see much of the world, sweetheart," her father said. He was very happy for her.

* * *

Until April had to leave she was now working in the hospital as an RN on the second shift and not the graveyard shift. She was happy.

"Gary," his dad said, "we are going to have to enlarge the shop if we are to keep up with orders."

"Okay, Dad, but there is something I want to say."

"Yes, son."

"When I finish college, I'm not going to work in the shop making cabinets. I want to build houses and I think we should consider it as our company. We build on spec, or custom building. I run the framing and finish work and you manage the cabinet shop."

"That sounds good to me, Gary."

That surprised him. He figured he'd have an argument with his dad.

"When are you going to quit smoking, Dad?"

"I keep trying off and on—but it isn't that easy to quit. Sometimes at the shop I'll just have the empty pipe to bite down on. It relaxes me."

For years Liz wouldn't let him smoke inside the house.

"Let's go look at the shop and come up with some ideas for expanding."

They looked over the shop layout for half an hour before

26

his dad asked, "Well, son, what do you think?"

"I think if we build an adjacent building for all of the materials, that would free up a lot of space for the actual construction. Then I would suggest another building for spraying the finishes. It would be dust free and no fumes in the shop. From the finishing building, the cabinets would go to packaging and the warehouse for shipping. All part of the finishing building."

"This sounds good, son. I would like you to put it on paper as soon as you can."

* * *

A week later, Gary showed his dad the plans he had drawn. Charles didn't just scan them, he perused them thoroughly. "I like these, son. This will be your project this summer. Hire as many men as you think you'll need.

"I like the idea of more and better ventilation. You get this project finished and we'll install some automated equipment."

"Thanks, Dad, for your support."

That afternoon Gary hired two more men and the next day they started forming a pad for concrete for both additions. While the help were taking the form planks apart, he went to the lumber supply and ordered a big load of lumber.

Charles stayed out of it. He wanted to see what Gary could do on his own.

Gary and Galen didn't see much of each other that summer. Gary was busy with the new additions and Galen was very busy with his computer business.

By the end of August, Gary and crew had completed the new additions and Charles had rearranged the shop to make work more efficient. And the three men Gary had hired to help with the construction, Charles now employed them fulltime as cabinet makers.

One day in the middle of July, April talked with her mother. "I have had good reports about you, sweetheart, from all of the doctors and Dr. Philbrick says in his opinion you should expand your medical interests and abilities. He thinks you should think about becoming a doctor."

"I have been thinking along those same lines, Mom. But there is one problem—I enlisted in the Army and I signed the enlistment papers. Three years, Mom."

"Well, maybe you could get some more training and earn some credits to further your medical field while you are in the Army.

"And then there is the G.I. Bill after you are discharged."

"You make me feel better, Mom. Thank you."

* * *

Time was getting short for April and she stopped work at the hospital a week before she would have to leave. "I hate to do this, Mom, but I want to make sure I have everything done before leaving."

"Understood, sweetheart."

After supper that evening, April drove down to the Merrill family home. "Hello, Mrs. Merrill. Is Galen home?"

"He is; come in."

"Hello, April."

"Hi, Galen. Would you like to go for a ride?"

"Sure, let's go."

As she drove towards the river and Rt. 2, she asked, "How is your business doing, Galen?"

"It's surprising but it is doing better than I ever could have imagined."

She pulled into the park between Rt. 2 and the river. "Let's go down and sit next to the water." They didn't have far to go.

They sat down on the grass looking out across the water. There were a flock of ducks looking for supper.

"When will you be leaving, April?"

"I have to be at the armory in Augusta on the 30th."

"Are you looking forward to going?"

"I was until yesterday when I was talking with Mom."

"What changed?"

"Since working at the hospital as a registered nurse, I've seen how much I enjoy the medical field and now I wish I had decided to continue studying to be a doctor."

"Can you ... not have to go into the Army?"

"Too late for that, I already signed the enlistment papers. I'm in now for three years."

"Well, that won't be so bad, will it?"

"Probably not, and I'll get to see more than Skowhegan, Maine. But after those three years I want to continue my studies. "What will you do, Galen, after you graduate next year?"

"I want to go to M.I.T. and major in advanced computer science and electronics."

"You have your own computer business now, Galen, I wouldn't think you'd have to do much studying concerning computers."

"Oh, April, there is so much more I don't know. And I have me an idea that'll require more knowledge than I have now."

"What do you have in mind?"

"I'd rather not say just yet. Not until I can have a better grasp on how to get started."

"Okay."

He put his arm around April then and moved over, hugging her. April was surprised. He had never showed any emotional attraction to her before. She liked his touch and she snuggled close.

She looked at him and he kissed her very softly at first and when she didn't pull back he kissed her again with more passion.

"When you finally get stationed somewhere, if you'd write to me, I'll write back," he said.

"I will," and she kissed him again.

The sun had set and it was time to leave. She had said her goodbye to Galen and she had thought this would make her feel better. It didn't. She suddenly realized how much she liked him since his falling through the ice. In three days she would have to say goodbye to everything she held close. *I'll be starting my life over.* She had to stop thinking like that. It was only making her miserable.

The day came and Liz drove April to the armory in Augusta. After a tearful goodbye, her mom said, "I'll walk in with you, sweetheart."

"No, Mom, I need to walk through those doors on my own. I'd rather we say goodbye out here."

As they hugged Liz said, "I have always had trust in you April. You have a good head on your shoulders. Call when you can, so we'll know you made it okay."

"Goodbye, Mom."

Two minutes later, the new recruits began loading the bus. April looked for her mother, but she had already left. She was really feeling lonely now. *Buck up, April,* she said to herself.

She found a seat with another young woman who was also looking as lonely. "Is it alright if I sit with you? My name is April Newman."

"I'd welcome the company. I'm Debbie Carpenter."

The bus made one stop in Portland and now the bus was full. There were six women and twenty-two young men. April felt really comfortable with Debbie and they talked until it was time to get some sleep as the bus rolled on. *Maybe this won't be so bad after all.*

* * *

Gary was so busy trying to finish the new additions before September 1st, there wasn't time to think about or miss his sister. While he and his crew were finishing the additions, Charles was rearranging the equipment in the main part of the shop for more efficiency. After the first week of operating like this, he said, "Son, that was a good idea you had. And this new assembly line is working so much better than I thought it would."

When Gary had to go back to school, his senior year,

Charles had to hire another three men, plus he kept the three that had worked with Gary during the summer. He now had twenty men working for him and every other day a truckload of cabinets was being shipped. Charles was so busy most days that after his first pipe full of tobacco in the morning, he would hold the pipe between his teeth most of the day, even though there would only be tobacco ashes in the bowl. But he was beginning to whiz, which he tried to hide from Liz and Gary.

Galen was a lovesick puppy for a week after he and April had said goodbye. Because of their age difference, he had never had any romantic illusion about April. She was a close friend and she seemed to keep it there.

But in all honesty, since standing beside her while they both were nude, he had had a few imaginative visions of her.

Once school had started again, he was too busy to be sad. His security program was still selling so fast that he had to hire a young fellow to work part time answering calls. He paid him well.

In two more years, he expected his sales would top a million copies. Most security programs required a renewal every year, but the Tomah program was good for three years. This became a tremendous selling factor, which other companies were not offering.

* * *

By the time the bus arrived at Fort Dix, New Jersey, because of her new friend Debbie, April was not apprehensive about her enlistment or homesick. She and Debbie were both nurses and they each were taking comfort with the other.

April ate hurriedly through breakfast and then telephoned her mother. "Hi, Mom, I am here and I'm okay." She told her mother about her new friend who was also a nurse.

"I don't have much time to talk, Mom. I have to go now."

It didn't take long for either April or Debbie to understand how unlike college this basic training was going to be. She had a difficult time at first with so much discipline. At home she was always able to come and go with the understanding that that came with responsibilities. Here they were told when to go to bed, when to get up, when to eat, when to shower and when to go to the bathroom.

She had made up her mind though that she would make it. If not for herself, then for her mom and dad.

Chapter 3

Galen Merrill was an absolute genius, but he never tried to hold anyone else up to his standards. The only thing apparently different was the fact he didn't go out for sports. He had a business to run.

And then again, Gary didn't go out for school sports either. He was always busy working in his dad's cabinet shop. He was a good student but not the same level as Galen. But this never came between them. Gary accepted his friend was brilliant and Galen never tried to flaunt it.

Galen never forgot that Gary had not hesitated, when he broke through the ice and went under. Gary had jumped in after him without thinking about himself. And neither had spoken about its since.

* * *

At the end of basic training, April had her choice of accepting a station in Pearl Harbor, Hawaii, or the Tori Army Base Station in Yomitan, Japan. And because she was a registered nurse, she was given a lieutenant commission. She chose Japan, knowing she would be leaving immediately. She only had time enough to telephone home. Gary had just gotten home from school and his mom and dad were still at work.

"Hello, Sis."

"Hi, Gary. I don't have much time to talk, I've been promoted to lieutenant and in a few minutes I'm flying to

Yomitan, Japan. I'll write a long letter once I'm settled there. Tell Mom and Dad I love them and I love you, brother."

"We're all proud of you, sis."

Gary didn't say anything until they were sitting down for supper. Both Charles and Liz were ecstatic about the news. "But why a promotion to lieutenant?" Gary asked.

"It is because she is a registered nurse, I would assume," Liz said. Charles agreed.

"How is business now, Charles, since the additions are finished and you hired more men?" Liz asked.

"I recently made Paul Giroux foreman and I put an ad in the newspaper for an accountant. The business is doing to much more production now, I just can't keep up with it."

"Business is that good?"

"Yes, it is beyond anything I have ever imagined."

"Dad, what about our yearly bird hunting trip to Tomah?" Gary asked.

"We'll try for the third weekend in October. I want to have a few days for Paul to feel comfortable as foreman and hopefully before then I can hire an accountant."

* * *

Paul Giroux had worked for Charles for fifteen years. First as a framing carpenter, then to finish work and now cabinet maker. The new accountant was different. Several had applied but not until the middle of the third week was Charles satisfied hiring Paige Allen.

"I won't be able to take the time off, Gary. Mrs. Allen needs more than a day to familiarize herself with the business before I take some time off. Why don't you and Galen go up?"

"Maybe we could drive up Thursday after school." He looked at his mother and she nodded her head it was okay.

"Tomorrow I'll put up some food for you," she said.

The next day Gary and Galen talked with the principal and because of their good grades he allowed them to take Thursday off at noon and Friday. That would give them two days of partridge hunting.

Charles was letting the boys have his pickup for the trip, as it was more dependable than Gary's older model. His mother was taking the time off anyhow and while the boys were in school she packed their gear and food.

At 12:30 they said goodbye to Liz and they headed north. As they were driving, Gary said, "I suppose your father isn't home now is he?"

"No, he gets calls sometimes in the middle of the night."

"I've asked you before what he does and all you have ever said was that he works for the government. So what does he do for the government? Or do you know, Galen?"

"All he has ever said is that he is an actuarial for a government employee insurance." Galen started laughing then and he continued. "I looked into his personal computer once and I found my answer. Now this is only between you and me, Gary."

"Okay."

"He is an analyst for the C.I.A. Before the company gets involved helping another country he and a team analyze the situation first and estimate what it would cost and human casualties."

"I see why he has to keep what he does a secret."

"Not a word to anyone."

"Not a problem. One question though."

"Okay."

"How in hell did you ever dare to hack into your own father's computer?"

"I needed answers and he couldn't tell me."

"What about your mother, Galen? Does she know what your father does?"

"I think she actually believes he is an employee insurance actuarial. It hasn't been easy for her with dad away so much. And I think that is probably why she buried herself in her position at the bank. It keeps her busy so she doesn't have so much time to wonder about my father's absences.

"You know she has a business management degree. When she and my father met, she was a teller now she is manager of the bank."

As they were leaving I-95 onto the Lincoln exit, Galen said, "I have an idea, Gary. Let's get a pizza and take it to camp and warm it up in the oven."

"Good idea, but let's get two."

"That smells too good to wait for camp. Go ahead and eat a slice, Galen. Then we'll trade places and I'll eat one."

It was still twilight when they drove into the camp driveway and two slices each. "I'll unload everything Gary and you get the fire going."

An hour later, they had finished the first pizza and had the second one half eaten when they heard a high-powered rifle shot. "That wasn't too far away." Five minutes later there was a small caliber shot. "That was probably the kill shot," Gary said.

"I wonder what they shot? Moose or deer?" Galen said.

"Whatever it was, it was illegal. They're night hunting and I bet they're on this property. Let's sneak out and see what we can see."

"Good idea."

They both pulled on a dark colored sweatshirt and Galen grabbed a flashlight and Gary the binoculars. "We'll have to be careful; there's only a sliver of moon tonight," Gary said.

"Yeah, let alone we'll have to be quiet," Galen whispered.

They hiked right along until they reached the logging road. Before continuing on Gary broke off a spruce branch and rubbed out the tire tracks. "Good idea," Galen whispered.

They had left one light on at camp and Gary turned to look and couldn't see it. "Shouldn't we close the gate, Gary?"

"Good point."

Now they started walking the road very slow and quietly.

They hadn't gone very far when they could hear two men talking. A little further and they could see a white pickup sitting squarely in the road and backed up to a slight bank. The pickup lights were off, and the engine. They stopped and Gary looked through the binoculars and then handed them to Galen. They both could see two men dressed in dark camouflage bending over a moose. "This is too much work, Den. I told you to shoot a couple of more deer. We'd have been loaded and out of here by now," Ben Wilber said.

"Stop your complaining. Didn't we see Bonney's pickup at his house and we ain't never see anyone else in here." He threw an empty beer can and said, "Give me another beer."

"I could use one too," and Ben threw an empty can and opened the back door of the extended cab and grabbed two cans from a red and white cooler There was enough light from the pickup's cab light so Gary had a good look at Ben.

"He hasn't any hat, red shaggy hair and beard."

Ben closed the door and went back to the moose and handed Dennis Bagley a beer. He stood up and stretched before opening the beer can.

They both finished that beer and thew the empty cans and went back to work. "While they're busy, Galen, let's sneak down and get the license plate number," he whispered.

They stayed inside the tree line and once they were in front of the pickup they waited a few moments and then on hands and knees they both crawled towards the pickup. Only close enough so they could see the license plate. "7731 HJ" Gary whispered. "You ready?"

"Let's get back in the woods."

Once they were back where they had been, Galen asked, "Now what?"

"I don't want them to see us on the road, so we stay here and watch and listen."

"Come on, Dennis, can't you hurry it up any. Somebody might have heard that shot. Hell, my ears are still ringing."

"What's the matter with you, Ben? You were never this worried before. Even when Bonney sent us up for ten days last time. Relax, we won't be much longer."

"I'm not worried about Bonney. He's an old man now."

"Maybe, Denny, but he got us two years ago."

"Yeah, tonight we know he is home."

Both Gary and Galen were having the time of their lives. This was exciting.

"Almost done, Ben. Get me an axe and the trash bags."

Ben had to open the rear cab door again and removed a box of plastic trash bags and an axe from in back.

Denny began chopping the lower part of the four legs off and then they put the four legs in separate bags. "Denny, what about that camp where the gate is?"

"I thought about that too, but I have never seen anyone there. Let's get these four bags in the truck. If anyone stops us they'll only think we're hauling trash," Denny said.

"Get one more bag, Ben, for the back straps. We'll fry those up tonight. I'm starving."

"Me too. Let's get the hell out of here, Denny."

"Let's go."

"What happens now, Gary, if they decide to check out the camp?" Galen whispered.

"Are you up for a fight?"

"If we're forced into it. The fight shouldn't be too bad. They're both half in the bag."

Ben and Denny left and Gary and Galen ran out behind them to the camp driveway. They drove past the driveway and didn't slow down.

"Now what do we do?" Galen asked.

"We go see Warden Bonny. We'd better turn the light off before we leave."

When they reached the Forest City Road, it was clear to see the poachers had turned left towards Brookton. Ten minutes later they pulled into Warden Bonney's house. His pickup was there. It was 10:30 p.m.

The outside light came on and a door opened and Bonney in plain clothes stepped out. Gary and Galen got out.

"What can I do for you? I'm on a regular day off."

"Mr. Bonney, I'm Gary Newman and my friend, Galen Merrill. We are staying at my folk's camp on Tomah Stream. Two men, Ben and Dennis, shot a bull moose tonight on our property and they left only about twenty minutes ago."

"Come in. This is my wife, Mary. While I'm changing into my uniform, tell me everything."

"We arrived at camp at twilight and we were eating pizza when we heard a high powered rifle shot in beyond the camp."

"What time?"

"8:20 p.m., Mr. Bonney," Galen answered.

"Five minutes later, there was a small caliber shot. Probably a .22 handgun."

"Then what?"

The two boys told Warden Bonney everything they did, saw and heard. "You said a white pickup. Was it a Ford?"

"Yes, it was," Galen said, "and the license plate number is 7731 HJ Maine."

They told him about the beer and the empty cans they threw and about checking out Bonney's house before going hunting.

"You boys were thorough. I'm quite familiar with Dennis Bagley and Ben Wilber and I know where to find them. I've always had problems with them. They aren't bad boys, they just can't stop poaching.

"Do you two want to go for a ride?"

"Hell yeah!" Galen said excitedly.

He kissed his wife and said, "Let's go, boys."

Bonney wasn't wasting any time. Good thing there was no traffic at this time of night. 11:10 p.m. "You said they planned on frying the backstraps tonight?"

"Yes."

"They'll still be up."

When they reached Rt. 1 in Brookton they turned south. There still was no traffic on the road.

"They live in Codyville about two and a half miles from Brookton in an old house trailer on the left."

A half mile away Bonney flipped several switches and turned off his lights and brake lights and turned the headlights off. "To answer your question, I want to pull into their trailer without them knowing."

"I take it you drive quite often at night without lights," Gary said.

"It takes practice. When we get there don't make a sound when you close the door. I want you two to come in and I'll introduce you as friends staying with us."

They rolled into the trailer yard without making a sound. Bonney pointed to the back of the white pickup. The four trash bags were still there. Then he motioned for them to follow. He walked up to the door and knocked. Someone opened it without any hesitation. "Denny, it's Game Warden Bonney," Ben said.

"Well, ask him to come in, Ben."

This wasn't going like the boys thought it might. "Late supper, boys. Boy does that smell good. Oh, I forgot, this is Galen and Gary. They're friends and staying with Mary and me."

"What are you doing here, Bonney, this time of night?" Denny asked.

"If I'm not mistaken, that steak you're frying smells like moose. Backstraps actually."

"What do you want, Mr. Bonney?" Denny asked again. He wasn't liking how this was going. *How in hell did he know?*

"I would think it would be obvious, Denny. I mean you are frying moose backstraps."

"What makes you think they are moose backstraps?" Denny asked. Had he underestimated this old game warden?

"Well, Denny, it's pretty obvious since you two have four trash bags in the back of your pickup, Ben, with four moose legs."

"Didn't I tell you, Denny, about Mr. Bonney," Ben was very upset. He knew they'd probably get months in jail this time.

"Where's your .30-06, Denny? Go get it."

Denny left to go into another room and came back with a Remington automatic .30-06 rifle and gave it to Bonney.

He handed it to Galen and said, "Put this in my pickup in the rack behind the seat."

"How did you know, Mr. Bonney? As far as we knew, you were home," Denny said.

"Well, boys, I might be an old man, but I sure as hell ain't dead yet."

Gary noticed the surprised expression on both Ben and Denny's face. As far as they knew now, Mr. Bonney was there.

"You got us over a barrel don't you, Warden?" Ben said. "Alright, you have us for that damned moose."

"That isn't all, is it, boys?"

"What do you mean?"

"Well, according to Ben and you confirmed it, that you have what is left of two deer. Now we can do this in one of two ways. One, you give us the deer meat now, or two, I get a search warrant. If I have to get a warrant, I'll go through this trailer with a fine-tooth comb and I'll probably come up with more than deer meat. As I said, it's your choice. Now what you two said while butchering the moose, you have meat from two deer. You give it to us now and I'll only write it up as possession of deer meat. As I said, your choice."

"Give it to him, Denny. We're in enough trouble as it is."

"I'll only be a minute. There's a chest freezer in the back room."

Five minutes later he came back with a big box of wrapped frozen deer meat. "Can you boys put the moose legs and this deer meat in the back of my pickup. And bring in my summons book. It's on the dash."

"Sit down, boys."

"Alright if we eat the steak before it is ruined?" Denny asked.

"Go for it."

It didn't take them long to eat the panful of backstraps. Gary brought the summons book in and then went back out to help Galen.

While he was writing out the summons, he never said a word and for some reason this seemed to bother Ben and Denny. The boys weren't long transferring the meat. Then they stood in the kitchen and watched as Warden Bonney wrote out the summons.

When he had finished, he said, "Court will be in Houlton on Thursday, November 21st. I've summoned each of you for night hunting. You shot the moose at 8:20 p.m. and the kill shot five minutes later. Another summons for illegal possession of moose, illegal possession of deer meat and last but not least, for littering. You each threw two beer cans. Now you need to sign each one right here."

While they were signing the summons, Bonney said, "You realize I could have arrested both of you tonight."

"You're a hard man Warden Bonney," Denny said, "but you're fair. I'm not going to say thank you."

Bonney looked at Gary and Galen and said, "You boys ready to go home?"

On the drive back, Galen asked, "Why didn't you arrest them, Mr. Bonney?"

"I would have had to drive them to jail in Houlton. That's the closest jail and you two would have had to drive their pickup so they would have transportation back after making bail. And neither of us would have gotten to bed until 4 o'clock tomorrow morning.

"I've had these two before and they have never failed to appear in court. Arresting them tonight would only rub salt in the wound. This way when they have time to think about it, I think they'll both plead guilty at arraignment.

"I was hard on 'em, but they also know I wasn't as hard as I could have been. And they'll remember."

"I'm surprised," Gary said.

"How so?"

"I figured they'd want to fight, by the way they were talking while butchering the moose."

"Well, I'm sure most of it was just talk. They're not bad boys, actually. They are both hard workers. One operates a mechanical harvester and the other a large grapple skidder. They just like to poach."

"Will they get any jail time?" Galen asked.

"Oh yeah, it won't surprise me if the judge would give them each a month or two in jail. They're also looking at at least $3000.00 in fines."

"Why did you say we were friends of the family and visiting you?" Gary asked.

"So they won't come looking for you at camp or burning your camp some time. Of course, if this goes to Superior Court you two will have to testify and the fat will be in the fire then. They may ask for a jury trial and if they do, it'll only be to buy time so they don't have to lose work this winter."

They pulled into Bonney's house and after he turned the truck off he said, "I certainly want to thank you both. I couldn't have done a better job myself with the quality of work you two did tonight. Have either of you ever thought about becoming a game warden?" he asked.

They both said, "No."

"Think about it. How long are you here for?"

"Just the weekend. We'll have to leave at noon on Sunday."

"Would you like the box of deer meat since it is frozen?"

"Maybe three or four packages, but the rest would probably spoil before we got home."

"Tomorrow morning, or maybe today at noon, I'll bring some deer meat down and I'll need your names and addresses and phone numbers. And I'll also need a written statement from each of you about everything you heard, saw and did tonight.

"It's 1:30 a.m., go back to camp and get some sleep. And thank you."

Galen and Gary returned to camp and after lighting the gas light and rekindling the fireplace they sat at the kitchen table talking. Galen said, "Man, I have never had so much fun!"

Gary laughed and also said, "It sure was. Can you imagine doing that for a living like Warden Bonney?"

"It sure would be fun wouldn't it. You know what I'd like now?"

"What?"

"A drink."

"There's no wine, but dad always kept a bottle of whiskey here."

"I have never had any. How about you?"

"Nope, let's have some."

He found the bottle and said, "The only mix is water."

"Well."

He didn't mix it as strong as he had watched his dad mix it. Galen was eating a piece of cold pizza.

When they took their first sip, "Wow, that burns all the way down."

Gary started eating cold pizza also. They finished their pizza slice before their whiskey. That, they slowly sipped.

Gary said, "You know something, Galen, this whiskey is making me feel relaxed."

"Yeah, I can feel it too. Boy, I'm tired. It tastes awful. Why do people drink it?" Galen said.

"Let's finish our drink and go to bed. It's almost 2:30 now," Gary said. He put two more sticks of wood on the fire and the two went to bed.

* * *

The boys had intended to go partridge hunting after an early breakfast while it was still cool. But neither of them woke until 11 o'clock. They cleaned up and started frying bacon and eggs for breakfast.

By the time Warden Bonney arrived, they had eaten and were writing their statements of the previous night.

While Warden Bonney read their statements, Galen fixed him a cup of coffee. "These are good reports. And they are just like you told me last night.

"How old are you two?"

"Seventeen," they both replied.

"Why aren't you in school?"

"We got excused from classes at noon yesterday until Monday morning."

Bonney finished his coffee and as he walked to the door he stopped and said, "I still think you two should think about becoming game wardens—'course you'd have to wait until you're twenty-one to apply."

"We'll think about it, Mr. Bonney," Gary said.

"You two did a nice piece of work, I'll be in touch."

"Mr. Bonney what about the antlers? Can we have 'em?" Gary asked.

"Yes," and he wrote out a permit giving them the right to possess the rack.

"Are you feeling okay, Galen?"

"Mostly. My stomach is a little queasy."

"Mine too. Do you suppose it's because of that whiskey drink we had?" Gary said.

"That's probably it."

* * *

Later that afternoon they went partridge hunting along the Tomah Stream down to the beaver dam and then out to the dirt road. They came out down below where the moose had been shot. At first, they didn't see the rack. Then Galen spotted a pile of brush and found the rack under the pile. "Looks like Denny tried to hide these."

"Yeah, they were probably coming back for them. We'll have to bring an axe down and cut them away from the skull.

"Galen, there's a partridge on a stump behind you."

Galen fired and that one dropped and another one that was on the ground behind the stump took off. "That makes three. Let's go get the axe, Gary."

They took care of the partridges before hiking back for the antlers. "We'll have partridge for supper and deer steak with eggs in the morning," Gary said.

Before they reached the area of the moose remains, a flock of ravens flew up into the nearby trees squawking, watching as they cut the antlers free. "This is a bigger set than I thought," Galen said.

When the rack was free, they each grabbed an antler and walked back to camp. "We should put these up on the camp," Galen said.

"Okay. They'd be out of place at either of our folks' house."

"We'll put these up tomorrow. Let's fix supper."

They each ate a breast and had one left for the next day. After everything was cleaned up, they sat in the living room and went to bed early. At 10 o'clock they were awakened by a chorus of coyotes fighting over the moose remains. "I hope those coyotes don't come around here," Galen said.

"It's probably a family and the young pups are fighting over it." By midnight the coyotes were still making quite a noisy racket. Just before 1 a.m. the coyotes were quiet. They probably had eaten their fill and left. The boys were able to go to sleep then.

After an early breakfast the next morning, the boys hunted the same route as the previous day and only shot one bird. As they were approaching the moose remains, a huge, lone bear stood up and looked at the boys. He stood his ground watching the boys. "What do we do now, Gary?" Galen whispered. "All we have is birdshot."

"We make a wide detour through the trees on our left," he whispered back.

The bear stood his ground watching the boys detour, never offering an aggressive move. Then he went back to eating.

Back at camp, Galen said, "I don't know if I'll ever feel comfort alone in the woods. I had fun what we did with Denny and Ben, but I don't think I could ever be a game warden."

"I think I could. Watching those two I found it really exciting and then watching how Mr. Bonney toyed with them. But my father is counting on me to be part of the company. I've had my fill of making cabinets. When I finish the trade school I told my dad I wanted to build spec houses for the company. He agreed. If it wasn't for that, I think I would."

Then Gary added, "If'n I did, I'd want to be just like Mr. Bonney. Have you ever tried to drive without headlights at night, Galen?"

"Of course not."

"Me neither, but did you notice how relaxed Bonney was? As calm as if he'd been driving down Rt. 1 in daylight."

"I know; that bothered me at first. I wonder if all game wardens drive without headlights?"

"Probably most of them do. You keep talking, Galen, and you'll talk me into becoming a game warden."

"Seeing that bear, Gary, was unnerving for me. I was glad you were there with me."

In the afternoon they hiked the railroad across the Forest City Road and followed that about a mile where they came to an old clearing. Probably when the railroad was built, there was a cluster of camps for the crews. All that was there now were several apple trees on the border of the old clearing.

In past years, they had always had good luck with shooting their limits of partridges here.

As they were leaving the tracks up ahead there was a cow and calf moose crossing to the north side. Crossing through the middle of the old clearing they saw a fox chasing a rabbit. That ole rabbit was taking jumps of fifteen feet at a time.

"He'll never catch the rabbit," Galen said.

They stopped to watch. The rabbit was beginning to circle through some thick ground hemlock and lost the fox. The fox sat down on its haunches and barked four times and waited and then twice more, and four pups ran right past them to the mother fox. Then she regurgitated a bunch of mice and the fox pups began fighting amongst themselves who was going to eat the most.

The two moved on towards the apple trees. There were five of them on the ground. They each shot one and reloaded. They each were using a single shot, .28 gauge, Stevens shotgun. The other three partridges flew up and perched in the same apple tree. Galen started to bring his shotgun up for another shot and Gary pushed the barrel down and said, "Wait, Galen."

"But, Gary, we can shoot all three. They're just sitting there."

"Take a good look, Galen."

Galen did, squinting his eyes against the sun. "Uh oh, they're too dark for an ordinary partridge. And they have a red dot on the side of their head."

"Yeah, we just shot two spruce partridges."

"Are we in trouble, Gary?"

"We might be if anyone—Warden Bonney—was to find it."

"What do we do?"

"It was an accident, but we leave them right there. It won't be long and the foxes will find 'em."

As they started following the edge of the clearing northwest Galen said, "Boy, am I glad Ben and Denny didn't see us shoot them."

"Yeah, me too."

A little further and the ground dropped off about five feet and there was a yellow birch tree with nine partridges budding. Galen started at the left hand edge of the flock and Gary at the right hand edge and they fired and reloaded and started working towards the center of the flock. They each shot three birds before the others flew off. "That was pretty good shooting," Gary said as they picked up the six partridges.

From there they continued following the edge of the clearing back to the tracks. When they approached the road they both unloaded their shotguns and no sooner and Warden Bonney pulled up and stopped on the shoulder of the road. "That's pretty good partridge hunting. I know you boys wouldn't be out here without licenses so I won't bother to ask for them.

"Are your shotguns loaded?"

"No," they both said and they broke them down so he could see.

"That's good. You know it is illegal to hunt from the railroad now."

"We didn't know. But we'll keep it in mind."

Galen told him about the bear they had seen on the moose remains. "Could you tell if it had an orange ear tag?"

"I hadn't thought about it before but now that you mention it," Galen said, "I do remember he had an orange tag in his right ear. What does that mean?"

"He's a cantankerous male bear. And the orange tag means that if he becomes a nuisance bear or aggressive, he is to be shot on the spot. I removed him once from Orient and two months later from behind the general store in Brookton.

"It's good you didn't try to push him. He won't leave the remains now until he has had all he wants. He's probably trying to bulk up for winter. I estimate his weight close to six hundred pounds."

"How did you decide that?" Gary asked.

"I've done some research measuring across the paw pad on the front feet. I've found that a bear will weight a hundred pounds per inch.

"If I were you, I would not keep any food outside. That would only be inviting trouble.

"You two be careful. I'll keep you informed what Wilber and Bagley decide to do."

They went back to camp and warmed up the last of the pizza. "This is still pretty good," Galen said.

Later in the afternoon, they went back up along the railroad to the same clearing. The spruce birds were back under the same apple tree and the two dead ones were gone. They walked on by and when they came to the yellow birch tree there was another flock of partridges budding.

They each shot only one. That would make them each their daily limit. "You know, Galen, if it had not been for Ben and Denny shooting that moose, and if we had not gotten acquainted with Warden Bonney, I wouldn't have thought twice about shooting as many of this flock as we could."

Galen laughed and said, "Let's go back to camp and fry up one partridge breast and some deer steak. This way we'll have four birds each to take home."

A strong wind started blowing about the time when they went to bed. In the morning, most of the tree leaves had blown off. The wind was still blowing, but not as strong.

After eating a hearty breakfast, they packed up and cleaned the camp. It was time to go home. As they were closing and locking the door, Galen said, "I don't know when I have had so much fun. And I certainly have a new respect for any man wearing the game warden's uniform."

"Just imagine, Galen, the stories Warden Bonney must have. Hell, he could write a book," Gary said.

They talked about Ben Wilbur and Dennis Bagley and Game Warden Lloyd Bonney all the way home.

* * *

They stopped at Galen's house first and as they were dividing up the partridge breasts and deer meat, Galen's mom and dad, Suki and Ashton Merrill, came out to greet them. "Did you boys have a good time?" Ashton asked.

"We sure did, Dad. Wait until I tell you about it. We have some deer steak also."

"Did you shoot a deer, son? I didn't think it was deer season yet," his mother said.

"It isn't, Mother. That's part of the story. And no, we didn't shoot it."

Ashton was watching as Gary was grinning and knew there was more to the story.

"I'll see you in school tomorrow, Galen. Don't forget to tell your Mom and Dad about the bear."

"What's this about a bear?" Suki asked.

"Come inside, Mom, and I'll tell you all about our trip."

When Liz saw the deer meat in the cooler, she naturally thought the boys had shot an early deer, too. Then over a cup of coffee, Gary told his mom and dad all about their trip. Except for the two spruce partridges.

"Dad, Galen and I both had never been so excited in our lives as we were when we were watching those two men butchering the moose. And then watching Warden Lloyd Bonney toying with the two. I certainly have a newfound respect for game wardens. I wonder why we have never seen Warden Bonney before?" Gary said.

"Well, after what you have just told us, there's a good chance he has seen us. Perhaps he simply held back watching us and we never saw him. He probably knows every camp in his patrol and whether the occupants are poachers or not."

"He asked us if we would want to become game wardens."

"What did you say, son?" Charles asked.

"I told him I would think about it. But I still plan on going

51

to college next year."

The next day in school, everyone wanted to hear all about them helping to catch two night hunters. Even the teachers.

There was a letter from April in the morning mail, and one also for Galen. For a few days, all he could think about was April. The night hunting caper, moose and bear were forgotten.

Chapter 4

That evening Galen wrote April a long letter telling her all about his and Gary's hunting trip.

Business had increased so much at the cabinet shop, Charles and Gary didn't go deer hunting at the camp. Both Gary and his dad, and any worker that wanted to, worked on Saturdays and Sundays.

"It's too bad, Charles, you and Gary couldn't take the time to go deer hunting at the camp," Liz said.

"I know; we have just been so busy."

"You'll work yourself into an early grave, Charles." She didn't dare ask him about his smoking. She knew he would often have his pipe in his mouth without any tobacco. She wanted to laugh then, thinking his pipe was more of a habit than needing to smoke, but she didn't laugh. It would only upset him.

* * *

In December, both Gary and Galen sent their applications to the admission office at C.M.V.T.I. and M.I.T. They should hear back before March if they were accepted or not.

April was also making plans. Once she was settled at the army hospital in Yomitan, Japan, she was soon asked if she would like to specialize in any particular field of interest and she would. Plastic and reconstructive surgery. In December she also started studying to be a nurse practitioner.

She had given up the idea of becoming a doctor. It

required too many years of study and internship. Where as a nurse practitioner she would be on a level of medicine between nursing and a doctor and she had really become interested with plastic and reconstructive surgery. She would be able to help many people. Her mother had written her and said she thought she had made a good decision.

In early December, both Gary and Galen received a letter from Warden Bonney.

"Galen, you have a letter from a Game Warden Lloyd Bonney. Is he the game warden in Forest City you told us about?" Suki asked.

Galen read it to himself first. Then his mother asked, "Well, what does he say?"

"The two poachers, Ben Wilbur and Dennis Bagley, are requesting a jury trial in superior court. The two men knew Warden Bonney had been at his residence at the time of the act and they have lawyered up questioning everything Warden Bonney did. He says that so far, he has been able to keep our names out of it, but we will be subpoenaed to testify. This might be a delay tactic to buy time for them to come up with the money for the fines. But regardless, Gary and I will have to be in court. But the trial may not happen until spring. But he will give us a telephone call as soon as there is a court docket."

"I don't know about this, son. I hope your father is home when this comes to trial so he can go up with you."

"If he isn't home, Mother, Gary and I will be just fine."

Charles and Liz were both proud of the two boys testifying against two poachers and particularly after how they had been responsible for Wilbur and Bagley's apprehension. And they had no problem with the boys traveling to Houlton to testify.

* * *

Between April's nursing duties and her studies for practitioner, she wasn't having much free time to see a lot of Japan, outside the Tori Army Base. She wasn't complaining, but at the same time she felt as if there was some force, some entity, that was pushing her.

April's friend she had met on the bus, Debbie Carpenter, who had also gone to Japan with April, was not able to cope with military life or disciplines and she was sent home with a medical discharge. This weighed heavy on April. They had become good friends.

After two days, she was so busy with her work duties and studying, she soon forgot about Debbie.

* * *

In the middle of February, the area was inundated with two heavy wet snowstorms only a day apart. One night after Charles and crews had the house and shop cleared of snow and snowbanks were pushed back, Charles said, "Sweetheart, what do you think about selling the cabinetmaking business?"

"What brought this on?"

"Well, after clearing the snow after these two storms, I was tired. I don't have the energy that I used to have and I get winded easy. I began thinking maybe it's time to stop and sell the factory."

"What about Gary?"

"He has already said he is not interested in the cabinetmaking business. He wants to build houses."

"How much is the business worth, if you do sell?" she asked.

"I would have to have someone appraise it. The only drawback—we'd have to sell the house and land. Everything.

"Buy some land and build a new one."

"Do you have some land in mind?"

"I would like somewhere on the river and no neighbors."

"I don't want to be too far out of town, Charles."

"What would you say if we built a house on the back knoll in the field. We can see the river from there. It's quiet and it is far enough from the shop so we wouldn't be bothered with the shop noise and you'd still be close to town."

"I think that would be a better idea."

"Okay, how about a Katahdin Log Home made with pine logs."

"And hardwood maple flooring and a fireplace."

"Then it is settled. As soon as the ground dries, we'll start."

* * *

Liz wrote a letter to April the next day telling her about their decision to build a new and smaller log house and selling the business.

When Gary arrived home for the weekend, Charles and Liz told him what they had decided. And much to their surprise he said, "I think that is a grand idea, Mom and Dad. You have worked your whole life, Dad, building up the company. You have earned a rest."

"And you, Mom, how long have you worked in the hospital?"

"Twenty-five years, all told. And I have been recently thinking about retiring."

"Well, it seems as you both are totally in agreement. I hope you'll allow me to build your house."

"Certainly."

"But what about you, Gary? I always thought that when Charles was ready to retire you'd take over?" Liz said.

"Dad knows I want to build houses. So whatever is best for you two."

That was a load off both of their minds. Particularly his mother. "I only hope you don't sell the camp."

* * *

The next week both Gary and Galen received their acceptance to their college. Gary was only a little more excited than Galen.

Galen could have managed very well without a degree in

either advanced computer sciences or electronics, but he had always had a lifelong dream and these two degrees and the knowledge he would gain would only be a steppingstone to his real ambition.

* * *

Much to her surprise, April telephoned her Mom after she read her letter about selling the business and building a new smaller house. "Mom, you and Dad owe it to yourselves to stop working so much. And don't worry about Gary and me. We'll be okay."

As soon as the field was clear of snow, Charles and Liz walked to the top of the knoll to look around. "I'd forgotten how nice it is up here, Charles. This is where I want the house. I don't think we need to look anywhere else. Besides, we can see some of the Kennebec River."

"I agree, sweetheart. This will be a good place to retire."

"Have you said anything to your men that you'll be selling the company?"

"No, I wanted to wait to be sure I was making the right decision. I will tomorrow."

That evening Warden Bonney telephoned both Gary and Galen and advised each a deputy sheriff would be serving a subpoena to appear in the Aroostook County Superior Court in Houlton on March 20th. "That's in two days, son. Maybe you should call Galen and get it squared away between you."

That evening both boys were served a subpoena. Gary called Galen, "Galen said his dad is home and he would like to drive us to Houlton."

"Certainly, that would be good."

The next morning both Gary and Galen had a meeting with the principal and he was very understanding, "... and maybe on Monday you can tell the entire high school all about the case. I know I would be very interested to hear it."

Charles and Liz watched Gary to see if he was nervous

about having to testify. The same as Ashton and Suki were watching Galen. And much to their surprise the boys were actually excited about testifying.

Both boys were wearing a tie and sports coat. And Mr. Merrill was wearing a dark blue suit.

The subpoena said court would start at 10 a.m. on Friday morning so they had to leave Skowhegan by 6 a.m. That would give them enough time to stop at Pittsfield for a cup of coffee and donuts.

Back on I-95 again, Ashton said, "You boys seem unusually calm, considering you'll have to testify in court today." He had expected the boys to go over and over what each would say. But no, they only talked about what college life would be like.

Gary was enjoying the ride in Ashton's Cadillac Escalade car. "This sure is a nice vehicle, Mr. Merrill."

"Thank you; I enjoy driving it."

They were north of Newport and suddenly Ashton saw blues in his rearview mirror. He looked at the speedometer and it read 92 miles an hour. "It drives and handles so nice sometimes I'm not aware how fast we are traveling.."

He pulled over and stopped and lowered his window. "Your license, registration and insurance card please."

While Ashton was getting the documents, the officer asked, "Why are you in such a hurry this morning. I tagged you at 92mph." Ashton handed the trooper the documents and said, "These two boys, my son, Galen, and his friend, Gary Newman, have been subpoenaed to testify in superior court in Houlton this morning." Then Ashton handed the trooper his C.I.A. identification.

Galen knew his father was trying to use his C.I.A credentials to worm his way out of a ticket. The trooper went back to his own vehicle and after a few minutes he came back and said, "Why are the boys having to testify in superior court, Mr. Merrill?"

"They witnessed some illegal hunting in Forest City and notified Warden Lloyd Bonney."

"Warden Bonney, yeah, he's a hell of a game warden. Slow it down, Mr. Merrill, and have a good day."

Galen knew his father could worm his way out of a ticket. But he didn't say anything. But Ashton did slow down, until he was beyond Old Town, then the speed was 75 mph and he kept it at 80 mph.

They passed a sign that said Houlton 120 miles. "I have never been north of Bangor and this looks like pretty desolate country. There's nothing but trees," Ashton said.

They pulled into the scenic turnout north of Medway for a pee break. "There are no restrooms here. People just go up in the bushes." There were several well-used foot paths.

Back at the car, Ashton said, "This is a beautiful view. Is that Mt. Katahdin in the background?"

"Yes," Galen said, "and that body of water is Salmon Stream Lake."

Back in the car and cruise control set at 80 mph they arrived at the courthouse twenty minutes early. Warden Bonney met them at the front entrance.

"Good to see you again, Gary and Galen. I know Mr. Newman, so you must be Galen's father," and Bonney shook his hand.

"The D.A. wants to see both of you before court. Follow me." Ashton followed in behind the boys.

"You're just in time," D.A. Wells said.

"Franklin, this is Gary Newman and Galen Merrill and this is Galen's father Ashton Merrill," Bonney said.

"Have either of you ever been in court before?"

"No, Sir," they both said.

"There is nothing to be afraid of. All you have to do is tell the truth, and don't ramble on when you answer my questions or the defense attorney's."

"I'm surprised they hired an attorney and went for a jury trial," Bonney said.

"I think when most of the information you had came from the boys that made them seek an attorney. And I'm surprised their attorney requested a jury trial."

"Who is the defense attorney?" Bonney asked.

"Harold Filbuster from the Filbuster and Filbuster firm in Bangor. He's good and terribly expensive.

"Boys, when you speak look at the jurors. They are the ones you'll be talking to. Speak up and be clear. It's almost time, so we'd better go in."

Franklin Wells led the group and had them sit in the first seats behind the prosecutor's table.

Ben and Denny were sitting at the other table with a smartly dressed man. Harold Filbuster.

"All rise for the Honorable Judge Winston Archibald," the bailiff said, and everyone stood. When they were seated, the jurors came in and took their seats.

"Are both councils ready?"

"Yes, Your Honor," they both said.

The judge then read the charges. "Mr. Ben Wilbur and Dennis Bagley, you both have been charged with night hunting. To wit, a bull moose. Possession of moose meat in closed season. Possession of deer meat in closed season and littering. How do you plead?"

Attorney Filbuster stood and said, "My clients plead not guilty, Your Honor."

"Prosecutor, call your first witness."

"My first witness, I call Game Warden Lloyd Bonney." He was sworn in and took his seat and D.A. Wells asked, "Would you tell the court your name and what you do for work?"

"My name is Lloyd Bonney and I am a Maine Game Warden."

"How long have you been a game warden, Mr. Bonney?"

"Twenty-two years."

"On October 15th, last fall did you have an occasion to visit Mr. Wilbur and Mr. Bagley at their home of residence in Codyville?"

"Yes, I did. I was home on a regular day off with my wife when at 10:30 p.m. I received information of a moose being shot off the Hay Road in Forest City not far from Tomah Stream."

"What did you do then, Warden Bonney?"

"As I said earlier, I was on a day off and I put my uniform on and left to drive to a house trailer in Codyville."

"How did you know to go to this residence?"

"Part of the information I was given was a white Ford pickup and the license plate number 7731HJ. I was familiar with this vehicle and I know the owner and where he lived."

"Who was the owner?"

"Ben Wilbur."

Attorney Filbuster stood and said, "Your Honor, I must object to any information Warden Bonney might have had as only hearsay. And I would like it stricken from the record."

D.A. Wells stood and said, "Your Honor, Warden Bonney has only told the court about the information he was given. That led him to drive to Wilbur and Bagley's residence. If the court would prefer, I can put on the two young men who gave the information to Warden Bonney.

"I was about finished for the time being with Warden Bonney. But I will recall him later as events progress."

"Does the defense have any questions of this witness?"

"Not if you'll reply to my objection."

"Call your next witness, Mr. Prosecutor."

"The state calls Mr. Gary Newman." Gary walked up trying not to show how nervous he was. He was sworn in and he sat down. "Would you tell the court your name and where you live?"

"My name is Gary Newman and I live in Skowhegan, Maine."

"How old are you, Mr. Newman?"

"Seventeen."

"On or around October 15th were you and your friend at a camp in Forest City?"

"Yes, we were."

"Who owns this camp?"

"My mom and dad. Charles and Liz Newman."

"What time did you arrive at your camp on the 15th?"

"About 8 o'clock in the evening."

"What did you do after you arrived?"

"I started a fire in the fireplace and my friend Galen Merrill started the gas cookstove to warm up some pizza we had bought in Lincoln. We had only started to eat the pizza when we heard a high powered rifle shot not far from the camp."

"What did you do then?"

"Galen and I just sat there looking at each other and maybe five minutes later there was a small caliber shot. Only one."

"Then what?"

"I said that sounds like illegal hunting and on our property. I'm not sure now who suggested we go see, but we each pulled on dark colored sweatshirts and Galen took a flashlight and I took a pair of binoculars and we walked right along out the driveway and then a little slower down the road. When we could see the pickup backed square across the road, we could see a small light behind the pickup and two men talking. The two men stopped and finished a beer they were drinking and they each threw the empty can into the bushes and the one called Ben got two more out of a cooler inside the pickup."

"Ben was trying to get Dennis to work faster. He was afraid the game warden would catch 'em."

"I object, Your Honor. Did the witness hear Mr. Wilbur say this or is he assuming that's what he meant?"

"Good point. Can you clarify that answer young fella?"

"Dennis told Ben to stop his complaining and then he said,

'Didn't we see Bonney's pickup at his house?'

"Dennis also said he wasn't worried about Bonney, that he's an old man now. And Ben replied, 'But he got us two years ago.' Then Dennis said, 'Yeah, but tonight we know where he is.'"

"Is that what you wanted to hear Mr. Filbuster?"

Filbuster sat down without answering.

"You can continue now, Mr. Newman."

"Galen and I sneaked up to the front of the pickup so we could get the license plate number."

"Did you write it down?"

"No need, my friend Galen has a marvelous ability to remember things."

"Then what?"

"They were quiet and I assumed they were working cutting up the moose. Then some time later I could hear something like someone chopping wood with an axe."

"Did you later discover what this was?"

"Yes, but not until we saw the legs had been cut off so they would fit in trash bags."

"Then what did you do?"

"After they left, Galen and I hurried back to camp and we agreed we should go tell Warden Bonney."

"That's all for this witness, Your Honor."

"Any questions from the defense?"

"Not at this time, but I reserve the right to recall him later."

"Call your next witness, Mr. Prosecutor. You may step down Mr. Newman."

"The state calls Galen Merrill." He was sworn in and he sat down.

"Would you tell the court your name and where you live."

"My name is Galen Merrill and I live in Skowhegan, Maine."

"And how old are you Mr. Merrill?"

"Seventeen."

"Was this your first trip to the Newman family camp in Forest City?"

"No, I have come up with the family several times. "

"You heard Mr. Newman when he made the remark that you have a marvelous memory. Is this so?"

"I do not have a photographic memory, but I remember most of what I see and hear."

"So did you remember the license plate number or did Mr. Newman?"

"I think we both did."

"You heard Mr. Newman testifying. Did he make any mistakes or is there anything you can add?"

"Well, a couple of things. Before they loaded the moose legs into the pickup, they both finished a second can of beer and they both threw the empties into the bushes."

"Do you know what kind of beer?"

"Yes, I never thought of it before until Gary was testifying, but when Ben opened the door of the pickup and took two cans out of the cooler, the dome light came on and I could see they were both Budweiser cans.

"They put the four legs in separate plastic trash bags and Dennis said, 'We'll put the backstraps in another trash bag and we eat those tonight.'

"There are two more things that we did that Gary didn't mention."

"And what was that?"

"When we left the camp, we closed the gate across the driveway in case whoever was in there couldn't drive into the camp to see if anyone was in.

"While they were cutting off the legs, Ben was complaining about being caught and Dennis said he wasn't worried about that old man. Ben said, 'Yeah, but he got us two years ago and we had to do ten days in jail."

"That's all for this witness."

"Does the defense have any questions?"

"Yes, Your Honor. Mr. Merrill, you said you are seventeen years old. Why were you and your friend not in school?"

"We were excused by the principal."

"You mean he just randomly decided to let you skip school?"

"I'm not sure what you mean by *randomly let us skip school*. We asked if we could leave Thursday at noon and return on Monday. He said we could."

"Is this your last year in high school?"

"Yes."

"Did you and your friend get together sometime after the two drove off and concoct this story?"

"No."

"You both said you are seventeen. Would you have us believe that two kids were out doing what a game warden does? Were you scared?"

"Scared? Hell no! Excuse me, Your Honor. Heck no. I have never had so much fun."

"You would have the court believe you think it is fun to put two hard working men in jail?"

"Doing what Gary and I did was fun. It was exciting. In the dark of night watching two men breaking the law and not one of them with the least suspicion we were there watching them. Yes, I was excited."

"Do you hunt, Mr. Merrill?"

"We were up in October partridge hunting."

"Have you ever shot a deer?"

"No."

"Moose?"

"No."

"Have you ever violated a fish and game law?"

"Yes." As soon as he answered he realized he had been

baited into a trap. He looked at Warden Bonney, his father and Gary. Gary shrugged his shoulders and nodded his head. The judge saw the nod.

"Well, Mr. Merrill, maybe you aren't so squeaky clean. What law did you violate?"

"Two days later while Gary and I were partridge hunting we each shot a spruce partridge by mistake."

"So you and your friend Gary are poachers also and you want this court to believe you?"

Galen didn't answer. But he wasn't ashamed for admitting it.

"That's all for this witness, Your Honor."

"Any redirect Mr. Prosecutor?"

"A couple of questions to clarify a couple of points."

"Go ahead."

"Mr. Merrill you said the principal excused you and Mr. Newman so you could go hunting. Is this something he does often?"

"No."

"Why did he allow you two to skip class to go hunting?"

"He let us go because I maintain a 4.0 point score and Gary maintains a 3.8 score."

"Fair enough. Did you know that you were shooting spruce partridges?"

"We didn't know until we walked over to them. "

"What did you do with them?"

"There was a mother fox with pups and we left them there for them."

"No further questions, Your Honor."

"Defense?"

"No recross."

"I'd like to recall Warden Bonney at this time."

"Well, I think we'll break for lunch and we'll start again at 1 o'clock."

"Mr. Bonney, you must know of a nice restaurant closeby?" Ashton asked.

"Yes, the Elm Tree. Follow me."

As they followed Bonney to the restaurant, Galen said, "Do you think Mr. Bonney will charge us Gary for shooting a spruce partridge?"

"I don't know."

"What's wrong with shooting a spruce partridge?" Ashton asked.

"It is against the law to shoot one, because they are so tame you can almost walk up to 'em. And besides they aren't very good eating."

They found an empty table. "Rebecca."

"Hi, Mr. Bonney."

"A pot of coffee please."

"How much coffee do you drink each day, Mr. Bonney?" she asked.

"A pot."

"The beef stew and biscuits are very good."

Rebecca came back with a pot of coffee and four cups. "I think we'll all have the beef stew and biscuits. My treat."

"Thank you, Mr. Bonney."

"You going to charge us, Mr. Bonney, for shooting spruce partridges?" Galen asked.

Bonney thought about it before he answered. Then he said, "Let's say you two were game wardens and you came upon two teenagers who had just shot two spruce partridges. What would you do?"

Ashton was beginning to like this man, Warden Bonney.

"Think about it, the circumstances. While you're thinking, I'll tell your dad a story. One day seven years ago I was waiting for a fisherman to come back. He was in a canoe on Tomha Stream and when I found his pickup I sat there leaning against a tree with my legs out straight. Just enjoying the day while I waited. Eventually I saw this spruce partridge walking towards me. I didn't move a muscle and he kept coming. He got up on my legs and stood there for a moment looking me over. Then he got down and walked off. I don't know what it is with spruce partridges, but sometimes you can walk right up to 'em and so many have—too many have been shot, and if they weren't protected, hunters would shoot every one."

Ashton asked, "Well, boys, I'd like to hear your answer."

"I think Galen and I would agree, that under the same set of circumstances we wouldn't."

"When we pulled the trigger, they were sitting in the shade under an apple tree and we had no way of knowing."

"So now you two know a little, a very little, what it might be like to be a game warden."

"I know one thing, Mr. Bonney, we both have talked about this. That after seeing you in action that night at their trailer we have a new respect for you and game wardens."

Their stew and biscuits came and there was no more talk about poaching.

Lunch over they went back to the courthouse. Ben and Denny were already there. While they were waiting Ben asked Denny, "Do you see how that kid's dad looks at us. There's something about him that tells me no one wants to cross him. He looks like a fancy dude, maybe a school teacher. But that look he gives us makes my skin crawl."

The judge entered the courtroom and everyone stood and then the jurors came in.

"Mr. Prosecutor, your next witness."

"I'll recall Warden Bonney."

"Mr. Bonney, now that we have the information that led you to go to Codyville, maybe we can continue.

"I understand you already knew who owned the white Ford pickup and you were familiar with the plate number and you drove to their residence in Codyville. Take it from there."

"When I walked by their pickup, I could see the four trash bags in back. I knocked on the door and Mr. Bagley opened it and invited me in. The boys were with me and I introduced them as friends staying with my wife, Mary, and me. I didn't want them going after the boys afterwards if they knew the boys were alone at the camp.

"I told the two everything Gary and Galen had told me, as if it had been me there watching them butcher the moose.

"I also told Mr. Bagley that I was going to take the meat from the two earlier deer they had shot. When Mr. Bagley didn't respond immediately to this, I told him he could either give me the deer now or if I had to I'd get a search warrant. And with a warrant I'd go through their house trailer with a fine-tooth comb. Ben went into a back room and came out with about fifty pounds of wrapped and frozen meat. I confiscated the rifle they used to shoot the moose, a .30-06, and asked Mr. Newman to put it behind the seat in my pickup.

"Bagley and Wilbur were frying the backstraps in a large frypan and asked if they could keep that and eat it. I said yes.

"I then wrote out summons for night hunting, possession of moose meat, illegal possession of deer meat and littering. Then we transferred the four moose legs to my pickup and the deer meat and I and the two boys left and returned to my home in Forest City."

"No further questions, Your Honor."

"Defense council any questions?"

"Yes, Your Honor."

"Mr. Warden, as I understand you, you were on a regular day off when all this took place is that correct?"

"Yes it is."

"So, you called yourself out. Did you get approval from a supervisor?"

"No, I did not."

"Would that actually be standard operating procedure

instead of calling yourself out?"

"According to the S.O.P. yes. But these were exigent circumstances."

"How could not requesting approval be exigent?"

"The illegal act of night hunting and killing moose was, as we say, still hot. It was timely. I was the only district game warden in the area within fifty miles. When the boys described the pickup and gave me the plate number, I knew who the two men were. And as I said, the crime was still hot and I knew where they lived. If another game warden had to be called in, all of the information I already had would be cold and there's nothing to say what the two intended to do with that much moose meat. And I didn't want to some time later have to chase after them all over the country."

"So you admit, you violated your own, as you say S.O.P.?"

"That is correct."

"The two boys, Gary Newman and Galen Merrill, were at the time juveniles, why did you find it necessary to take them with you to Mr. Wilbur and Mr. Bagley's residence? Were you thinking straight? Or were you only showing off?"

"I took them with me because I had no personal knowledge of what had expired near their camp. I only had their word of what happened. And I wanted them to make a positive identification of Wilbur and Bagley."

"If the shooting of a moose at night is such a horrendous crime, why didn't you arrest them and take them to jail instead of calmly writing summons?"

"An arrest is to ensure someone's appearance in court. Not to make the process any more difficult than necessary.

"I have had both of the defendants in court before and they never failed to appear. I knew they would make the appearance. If for whatever reason they did fail to appear, I know where they live and work."

"I have no more questions for Mr. Bonney, Your Honor."

"Any redirect, Mr. Prosecutor?"

"No, Your Honor."

"Does the defense intend to call witnesses?"

"May I have a moment to confer with my clients?"

"Make it short."

In a quiet voice, Mr. Filbuster said, "You two didn't quite tell me the entire story. If I put either one of you on the stand, it'll only convict you. I don't see there is much more we can do."

"Your Honor, after conferring with my clients, we will not be calling any witnesses."

"Does the prosecution rest?"

"Yes, Your Honor."

"You may begin your summation to the jury."

"I'll not take up too much of your time and rehash everything you have heard here today. I'll only say Mr. Newman and Mr. Merrill were very responsible young men. They reported to Game Warden Lloyd Bonney what they had seen and the conversations they had overheard. They reported the crime to the only person who could do anything about the crime. And being a responsible game warden that Mr. Bonney is, he called himself out before the hot case went cold. Thank you."

"Is the defense prepared to address the jury, Mr. Filbuster?"

"We are, Your Honor. Most of the evidence of this case was told by two juvenile boys who instead of being in school were on a hunting trip. A lot of this case rests on the testimony of these two boys who themselves admitted in court they violated the law the very next day when they shot spruce partridges. No one saw who shot the moose at night. Maybe just by chance my clients happened to stumble upon a dead moose that someone else had shot. As I said, much of the case rests on the reliability of law breakers themselves."

"The jurors are excused." Everyone stood and then Judge Archibald returned to his chambers.

"Now what, Mr. Bonney?" Gary asked.

71

"We wait. I don't think it will take long. This case was pretty cut and dry. The only thing the defense had to work with was my calling myself out without first obtaining permission and the reliability of Gary and Galen."

"I really don't understand why they requested a jury trial," Ashton said.

"Sometimes they'll request a superior court trial while they try to come up with the fine money. But their attorney, Filbuster, had to know any jury would not have any sympathy for poachers in a case like this."

"Maybe the two didn't tell Filbuster the whole story," Ashton said.

"That probably was the case."

"How big is Forest City where you live, Mr. Bonney?" Ashton asked.

"It is an unorganized township. I don't believe there are eighty people living there. I live close to the border crossing and that is actually the only built up portion of the township."

"Then as I understand, you don't have backup from other law enforcement agencies?"

"I work alone most of the time."

"Doesn't it bother you when you approach a vehicle at night and you suspect them of night hunting or some other crime?"

"Not really. I *am* being a little more cautious now. That comes with age."

"Yeah, but you must have come up against some real bad-asses."

"A few. I arrested two known mafia figures one night. I've come across drug deals and mental people with a gun wanting to shoot someone."

"I'm amazed. I never in my life thought about game wardens enforcing the law in the woods."

"Well, we have one thing going for us. The people we

encounter are usually afraid of the dark and they know we live and work in the dark and feel very comfortable."

"What about your family, though?"

"Mary and I had a son and daughter early in our marriage and it was rough on her and my son and daughter. I was away from home a lot. The kids have moved on and Mary has gotten used to me being gone."

"Amazing and I don't think I would want your job, Mr. Bonney."

The bailiff walked over and said, "The jury has a decision, if you would return to the courtroom."

"That was quick," Galen said.

Everyone was seated and Judge Archibald asked, "Madam Foreman, have you come to a decision?"

"Yes, Your Honor."

"What is the jury's decision?"

"We the jury find the defendants Ben Wilbur and Dennis Bagley guilty on all charges."

"Thank you and you are excused. The defendants will rise." They stood and Judge Archibald continued, "You have been found guilty on all charges by a jury of your peers. I have in front of me a certified copy of your past history. Two years ago you both were found guilty of illegal possession of deer meat, two years prior to that you two were found guilty of night hunting. Prior to that, you both have a few minor violations which I will not even consider. It would appear you still have not learned your lesson. Before I sentence you, do you have anything to add, Warden Bonney?"

"I was the officer in charge on all of the earlier charges, Your Honor, so I am quite acquainted with both defendants. With all the encounters I have had with them, they have never given me any trouble. They are devious and sneaky and will go to extremes not to get caught. But once caught they give up without a struggle. Game over. I also know them both to be hard workers."

"What would you recommend for a fine?"

"I would overlook the littering and each of the other three charges has a mandatory fine and sentence."

"Is that all Warden Bonney?"

"There is something else I'd like to caution them about."

"Go ahead."

"I would strongly suggest that you stay away from the Hay Road and the Newman camp. If anything should happen to the camp, I know where you live and I know where you work."

"Very good point, Warden Bonney. And I would suggest you two take his caution literally. Warden Bonney has also spoken well for you. But the final decision comes down to me. Do either of you have anything to say in your behalf?"

"There's not much I can say, Your Honor," Denny said, "As Warden Bonney said, *Game over.*"

"Each of the three charges carries a mandatory fine of a thousand dollars each. And each case there is a minimum three day sentence in jail. I'm going to sentence you each to thirty days. I could have given you each a year. If I ever see either of you in my courtroom again, I will use the maximum sentencing allowed, a year in jail. Are you two currently working?"

"The contractor we work for has shut down for spring mud season."

"Do you have the fine money with you today?"

"No, but we could have it here Monday morning if you would release us until then."

"I'll take your word you'll be at the clerk's office Monday morning by 10 a.m. If you are not, I'll send Warden Bonney to bring you back. Is that clear?"

"Yes, Your Honor, it is. And thank you."

"Case closed," and Judge Archibald hit the bench with his gavel.

Ben and Denny were leaving the courtroom Ben could be heard by everyone, "So, Denny, we don't have to worry about that old man, yah!"

Before leaving the courtroom Judge Archibald said, "Young Gary and Galen."

"Yes, Sir."

"You both did a very good job testifying and sneaking around watching those two. Maybe someday you'll become game wardens."

"You know before leaving town I think we should return to the restaurant before we hit the road. Mr. Bonney, will you join us?"

When Bonney only ordered coffee and a slice of apple pie with a thick piece of cheese, the others changed their orders for apple pie and cheese. The waitress brought a pot of coffee to their table.

"You surprised me, Mr. Bonney. I half expected you to verbally blister those two. But instead you kinda spoke well of them."

"They aren't bad boys. They just like to push the envelope and see if they can outsmart me. When they work, they work seven days a week and when they aren't working they play as hard. A thousand dollar fine for shooting a moose at night or possessing illegal meat is a hell of a fine when you stop and think about it."

"Do you think this will stop them from poaching?" Ashton asked.

"They'll behave themselves for a couple of years, but they won't stop. But I don't think they'll do any more illegal hunting around Forest City."

"What did you do with all of that meat?" Ashton asked.

"There are a lot of poor people in Forest City who can't afford to hunt for deer or moose and can't afford to buy meat. So I gave it to as many people as I could."

"Look," Gary said, "they're coming in here."

"Do you suppose they're looking for trouble, Mr. Bonney?"

"I don't think so. This is a pretty popular restaurant."

Before taking a seat, Ben and Denny walked up to their table and Denny said, "No hard feelings, Mr. Bonney?"

Ben added, "We know you were only doing your job."

"No hard feelings, boys. Are you going to be able to come up with that much money?"

"Oh yeah, no problem."

Ben said, "Boys, you won't have to worry about your camp."

They turned to leave and Bonney said, "Aren't you going to eat?"

"Nah, I saw your pickup parked here and I just wanted to come in and say we hold no hard feelings," Denny said.

"Thank you."

"Well if that don't beat all. They get a month jail and a $3000.00 fine and they stop to say they hold no hard feelings. It's too bad more of the world wasn't like what I've seen of people here."

Galen had never heard his father do so much talking.

"How far out of our way would it be if we went back through Forest City? I'd like to see it," Ashton asked.

"Maybe an hour out of your way."

"I'd like to see this part of the state."

From the Elm Tree Restaurant they followed Warden Bonney through Houlton to Rt. 1. Once they left Hodgon there wasn't much but old abandoned farms and woods. There was the occasional house. For Ashton, the drive was like taking a step back in time. He could see by some of the buildings that at some time people were pretty prosperous. But there was no industry now and he wondered what people do for work out here. He saw several old and rusting skidders in beside old rundown houses. It was no wonder why people left.

In Orient, Rt. 1 topped out on some high ground and there was a million dollar view of Grand Lake.

They drove through Danforth, a small country village. But

he did see a high school building.

They continued following Rt. 1 to Brookton where they turned onto the Forest City Road. At the mouth of the Hay Road Bonney honked his horn and waved. "Take this right, Mr. Merrill," Gary said.

He stopped at the gate and which was never locked and he opened it.

"I have an idea, Mr. Merrill. If we drive home tonight, it will be close to midnight before we get home. Or we could stay here and drive home in the morning."

"It would make more sense to stay the night."

"I'll call your mother and let her know we'll be staying here tonight."

"Cell phones don't work out here, Mr. Merrill," Gary said.

"I think my car phone will work, Gary."

Gary watched him punch in a seven digit number and then Ashton said, "This is agent 799 requesting Code 1, line 2. Then he punched in his home telephone number. He stood back while he was talking with his wife. When he finished, he repeated the process and said, "Come here Gary," and he gave the phone to him and got out of the car so Gary could get in and able to reach the car phone.

"All you have to do now, Gary, is punch in your home telephone number."

"Hello," Charles said.

"Dad, this is Gary."

"How'd it go in court?"

"They both were found guilty on all charges. I'll fill you in when I get home tomorrow."

"Where are you calling from now?"

"We are at camp and plan to spend the night here and drive home in the morning."

"How can you call from camp when there isn't any cell service?"

"I'll explain when I get home, Dad."

"This is a nice location," Ashton said, and something tells me we should have eaten more at the restaurant."

"Galen will make some pan bread, I'll warm up a can of Dinty Moore beef stew and you can make some coffee. There's only instant."

"How do you make pan bread, son?" Ashton asked.

"Mix in a little water with Bisquick for a dough and then flatten it like a pancake and fry it."

"Where did you learn to make pan bread, son?"

"Here."

"This beef stew is really quite good. I would never have imagined. And this is the first time I have had pan bread."

After they had eaten, Ashton asked, "How far away was the moose shot?"

"Not far. We have time to walk down before it is too dark."

Beyond the driveway the Hay Road was still too soft for vehicle traffic. "We were here, Dad, when we first saw their light and pickup."

They walked around the corner and a huge bear stood up on his hindlegs. "Damn, he's back, Gary."

"Just walk backwards slowly. He is more interested in whatever is left than he is with us. But I don't want to push it."

As they were backing up Galen said, "Hey, Gary—he has an orange tag in his ear."

They turned around and kept walking. "What does the orange tag mean?" Ashton asked.

"He is an aggressive nuisance bear and the orange tag means he will be shot if he causes any more problems," Gary said.

They didn't stop until they were back inside the camp. "You boys have encountered that bear before?"

"Yes, last year. He was feeding on the moose remains and when he saw us, he stood up. We only had single shot shotguns with 7 ½ birdshot."

"And you two enjoy coming up here? Amazing," he said.

To top off the bear, at midnight, a coyote started yowling not far from camp. Ashton woke up lying on his back listening. In his career, he had often times been in a tight position but never had he felt so uncomfortable as when they saw the bear and then to top that off his son told him what the orange tag meant. He was proud of his son how he had managed to grow and become a young man without him being around as much as a dad should. *Yes,* he was proud.

Chapter 5

When Gary arrived home his mom and dad wanted to hear all about the trial. "I wish we could have been there," Charles said.

Ashton was like a young boy telling his wife, Suki, all about the last two days. He was more excited about the trial and everything he had learned from his son, Galen.

That evening before going to bed, Galen wrote a long letter to April, telling her about the whole trial and staying over at the camp.

April has been in Japan for nearly seven months and every waking hour was dedicated to her work, where she was now in charge of her shift and busy with her practitioner's studies. She was finding the studies more involved than she had first thought, but she was stubbornly determined to succeed. It was almost as if there was some external force driving—or maybe a better term would be guiding—her to stay on course.

* * *

As soon as the field was dry, Charles hired a contractor to dig a hole for the foundation, put in a septic system and driveway. Then he and Liz took two days off from work and drove to the Katahdin Log Home headquarters in Oakfield. They had drawn up their own plans and after a half of a day talking with Mr. Gordon they had ordered a complete package of dry pine logs to be delivered the last week in May.

Once the package was delivered, he would let Gary and crew build the house. In the meantime, he was busy talking with prospective buyers for the company. He had turned down two offers that he figured were ridiculously low.

When the entire package arrived from the Katahdin Log Home Company, Charles and Gary separated everything into separate piles. The foundation was in and decked over, and the septic system and drilled well.

Gary and Galen graduated from high school and Galen was busy every day with his computer business. His new security program was still selling and each month he was receiving huge checks from different credit card companies.

He had by now sold enough of his security programs to more than pay for his four year expenses at M.I.T. His father and mother were both extremely proud of him.

In August a possible buyer for the company from Portland approached Charles with an offer he couldn't refuse.

The prospective buyer currently had a smaller company that he wanted to expand. Charles had one stipulation, that the new owner would not lay off any of the workers and bring new crews in. This didn't seem to be a problem.

They had agreed to purchase and the closing would be September 15th.

By the first of September, Gary and crew had almost completed the new log house for his mom and dad. "Mom, I have noticed how more relaxed Dad is now. I think selling the business was the right thing to do. At first I wasn't sure."

"I'll tell you something, Gary, if you promise not to repeat it," Liz said.

"Go ahead, Mom."

"We have been financially well off even before the sale. He hung on this long, hoping you would want to take it over. He knows you want to build houses and not cabinets and he is okay with that. He's worked hard and now we'll be able to spend more time together. I'm happy he found a buyer."

The day came when Gary and Galen had to say goodbye. They had been more brothers than best friends ever since kindergarten. "For the life of me, Galen, I don't understand why you think you have to spend four years at M.I.T. You already know more about computers than your professors. Hell, Galen, you already have your own computer company. I wish you well though and I will miss your friendship."

"There's more that I want to understand about computers, Gary. I have me an idea that has been sort of rotating around in my mind. And if I'm to do anything with this idea—well I need to know more than I do about computers and programs."

"Can you give me an idea about what you are thinking?"

"Not entirely, but I'll tell you this: I know you, as well as anyone who has a computer, plays card games. I've played a few thousand games and I started noticing the computer would cheat. While playing poker I'd bet on a spade flush and when the betting was over I'd notice the computer change my three of spades to a three of clubs and I'd lose. Another time I had a clubs flush and when the betting was over the computer would change one club to a spade.

"There were other games when I knew when the computer would cheat, I knew what the next card the computer would play. This got to me. So one day I hacked into one of the card playing programs to see if I could find if the program had been purposely programmed to cheat. I went through everything and I couldn't find anything. So I checked other card playing programs and I wasn't able to find that the program or any program had been programmed to cheat.

"So I started thinking whether computers could actually think, given enough data. And this is what I want to discover."

"There's more that you aren't saying isn't there?"

"Yes, because I'm not sure yet what I will do when I have my answer."

"I can respect that. Only someday I hope you'll tell me the rest of the story," Gary said.

"I'll miss our hunting trips to Tomah Stream. If you ever hear anything about Ben and Denny, write me a letter and tell me."

"What will you do with your computer company while you're at M.I.T.?"

"I'll come home often and my mother said she would help out keeping the account straight."

* * *

Galen left for college two days before Gary. For the first time in a long time, Liz and Charles were alone. But they were so busy moving and cleaning the old house and preparing to close on the sale of the business they had little time to miss their children.

April had spent a year now in the army and eleven months in Japan. Two more months of study and she would be a licensed nurse practitioner. She had decided to work for a few months in that capacity, then change to plastic and reconstructive surgery.

She was very excited and happy about her work but she really missed her family. And she enjoyed Galen's letters. It was a joyous link to home.

* * *

The closing date for the sale of the cabinet company was only two days away, and Liz watched her husband closely for any signs of sadness or regrets for selling. Instead he remained happy and joyful. He had no regrets.

The new house was complete now right down to the last detail. "Gary did a nice job with the house didn't he, Charles?"

"Yes, and he finished sooner than I thought he would."

The 15th arrived and Charles met with the new buyers and the old farmhouse, the factory and ten acres of land was transferred. Afterwards, Charles sat outside on the patio with a cup of coffee. And wondering if his father and grandfather would have approved of him selling the business and the farmhouse. In all honesty, the business had grown beyond any expectations he might have had when he started the cabinetmaking business.

At the end of that week, Liz would finally be done at the hospital. She had worked there for thirty years. There was a small celebration for her at the hospital on Friday and afterwards Charles took her out for dinner.

Gary came home on weekends and he half expected his folks to be somewhat depressed after they both had retired. But instead they each were happier than he had seen them for a long time.

In October, Charles and Liz went to the Tomah Stream camp for a week. Which stretched into two weeks. They arrived mid-afternoon on Saturday. They unpacked and put things away and Charles cleaned the ashes from the fireplace and started a fire and then he mixed a drink for them both and they went outside to enjoy the last of the sunshine. "I thought there would be more whiskey in the bottle than there was, Liz."

"It's nice out here, Charles. Smell the softwoods. That's sweeter than perfume," she said.

They went to bed early and slept well, and after breakfast while Liz was taking care of the kitchen, Charles was busy splitting firewood and filling the wood box by the fireplace and then he started picking up all of the dead branches around the camp. Liz came out to help him.

Just as they were finishing Warden Bonney pulled into the yard. "You're just in time for a cup of coffee. Come on in."

"Coffee is almost done. It'll only be a minute," Liz said.

"What brings you out here, Mr. Bonney?" Charles asked.

"Please, call me Lloyd. Since the Wilbur and Bagley cases, I have been keeping an eye on this camp. When I saw the gate open, I thought I'd better check it out."

"Thank you."

"Did the boys come up with you?"

"No, they are both in college."

"I never had the chance to tell you what a nice job they did with the Wilbur and Bagley case. I couldn't have done a better job myself; and they both testified in court like they were old hands doing it. I know they both are in college, but they both would make good game wardens."

"What about Wilbur and Bagley? They still in the area?"

"Yes, they usually take the summer off to fish and poach, but after spending a month in jail, they both decided they didn't want to do that again, so this summer they both got a job driving dump trucks and will go back in the woods in November. I come out here often and seldom see any tire tracks, even in the mud.

"And I think word went around the county about them having to spend a month in jail because I'm not getting any complaints and I'm not hearing any suspicious shots."

"Well, I guess that's a good thing," Liz said.

Bonney finished his coffee and stood up and asked, "How long are you folks up for?"

"We're both retired now, so at least a week. Maybe longer," Charles said.

"Did Gary tell you about the bear with the orange tag in his ear that they saw eating on the moose remains?"

"Yes, he did."

"In June, he became a problem again and climbed in the open window of a car parked in the dooryard. The woman had been grocery shopping and although the groceries were all in the house, the bear could still smell the scent of food in the car and climbed in. He did about $10,000.00 damage before climbing out. I caught up with the bear two days later and shot it."

"How big was he?"

"I estimated between six and seven hundred pounds. Thank you for the coffee."

"Stop in anytime you're in this way, Lloyd," Liz said.

After lunch, Charles put the chainsaw in the back of his pickup and they went for a ride to the end of the road where G&P had had a woodyard three winters ago. He was looking as much for some salvage hardwood he could cut up for firewood. Almost at the end there was a white maple tree down across the road.

As he worked up the tree Liz threw the wood into the pickup body, leaving the heavier pieces for him. Then they threw all the branches off to the side and out of the way. They drove down to the end to turn around. "They did a good job of cleaning up," Liz said.

"Yeah, and I'm surprised."

Back at camp while Charles was splitting the pieces, Liz piled the wood in the back of the woodshed to dry out for next year.

Neither one was much for getting up early in the morning to go partridge hunting. Even after waking they would lay in bed relaxing and talking. Then after lunch they would go for strolls. Sometimes down the road to the end and sometimes up the railroad tracks to the same old clearing where the boys shot a lot of partridges.

They only shot enough partridges to have for two suppers. They were at camp to relax and enjoy each other. After two weeks and their food running low they decided it was time to go home.

On their way home Liz said, "April has been in Japan a year now. I wonder how much longer she'll be stationed there?"

"Well, she is still studying plastic and reconstructive surgery. She'll stay until she finishes. I would think."

"I miss her, Charles."

"So do I."

* * *

April was getting homesick, too. But she couldn't do anything until after the end of the year. Then with her training she would be reassigned to a base or hospital that had a greater need for her expertise.

She had been so involved with her studying to become a nurse practitioner, working and studying plastic reconstruction, that she had actually seen very little of Japan.

Gary was a good craftsman building cabinets for his father and he was a plausible framing and finish carpenter. His studies started right at the beginning with more book material than actual hands-on. But even though, he was learning some that he didn't know.

And his drafting classes started with mechanical drawing and blueprint reading. Later the class would advance to computer drafting. He was enjoying both classes and he was excelling.

When he had decided to pursue a career in carpentry, he had felt guilty about not wanting to take over the cabinet business from his dad. But now with only a few months study and learning new advancements in the field, the guilt was no longer there. And he was happy his dad had sold the business and his mom had also retired.

Galen had some knowledge with electronics, but now he was being introduced to another whole new world of interest. He stayed up late every night studying. Sometimes to the point where he would wake up in the morning still at his desk.

So far, he found his computer classes rather rudimentary. But he did find the classes informational. It was more like a refresher course of material he already knew. But he didn't let on and he never told anyone he already had his own company.

At Christmastime, Gary and Galen were able to spend a few days at home with their folks. And April—well, April was still in Japan. But the nurses had a Christmas celebration for the patients. And although she would rather have been home with her family, she enjoyed herself at the celebration. And she telephoned home and they all talked with her for a long time.

Chapter 6

One cold windy morning in early January, the temperatures had dropped to -30° and shortly after Charles had driven down to the mailbox to retrieve the morning's *Bangor Daily Newspaper* the wind started to howl and blow drifting snow into the driveway. He put his pickup in the garage and went into the house. "Is the wind getting stronger, Charles?"

"Yes, it's really a gale out there now. I wouldn't want to be lost in the woods on a day like this."

"Remember how the old farmhouse would creak and crack in high wind?"

"Yeah, sometimes the wind would blow so strong I was afraid it would move the house off the stonewalled cellar."

"Remember how the boards would freeze and crack. Sometimes it was as loud as ice freezing on a lake," Liz said.

"Would you like another cup of coffee, Charles?"

"Yes, and regular coffee."

"Nope. You know what Dr. Henderson said, 'One cup of regular coffee a day.' You'll have to be satisfied with decaffeinated."

"Alright, but make it strong."

He sat down at the kitchen bar and began reading the newspaper. "Well I'll be damned!" he exclaimed.

"What's the matter now, Charles?"

"Do you remember Game Warden Lloyd Bonney?"

"Sure I do."

"He skipped one grade and was recently promoted to lieutenant."

"Isn't that a little unusual, to skip one pay grade level?"

"Normally, but someone must have thought he warranted the rank. He'll be a good man."

"I liked him. I would have liked to have met his wife."

"Maybe when we go up next we can."

* * *

April had completed her training with plastic and reconstructive surgery. She was now a nurse practitioner and an assistant to Dr. Ralph Ames in the reconstructive laboratory. She would also assist during surgery when needed. But her primary duty was in the lab making prosthesis components and a silicon base rubber compound for replacing ears, fingers and facial tissue.

In the middle of January, a young soldier stationed in South Korea had been shot by a sniper in the right cheek and ear. He had immediately been taken to a hospital in Seoul, South Korea, and when he was stabilized he was transferred to the Tori Army Base Hospital in Yomitan, Japan.

After three weeks of rehabilitation, Cpt. Dr. Ames said he was ready for reconstruction surgery. Ahead of the first surgery April mixed the silicon, rubber and a stabilizer and poured the compound into a mold. Two days later she removed the new formed ear and cleaned and polished it.

When Dr. Ames had the new ear attached it looked almost exactly like his original ear, comparing it to his personnel file photo. The next surgery to reconstruct the right side of his cheek was more difficult and April mixed the compound again using a softener this time instead of a hardening stabilizer for softer tissue composition.

There was a noticeable difference, but Cpl. Dayton was satisfied. He looked at himself in a mirror frowning at first. But slowly he began to smile. "Almost like new," he said.

"You did good work, Lieutenant," Dr. Ames said. "You have a natural talent for plastic reconstruction."

"Thank you, Captain Ames."

That night as April lay in bed thinking about her life in the army, a nurse practitioner and now a plastic reconstruction technician ... *where am I going? Somehow I feel my whole life has been leading up to this. But this isn't where it stops. I feel like there is something, some invisible force that has been guiding me. But to what?*

She didn't sleep much that night. She couldn't clear her mind of these thoughts enough to relax. But after breakfast the next morning, "Lieutenant Newman," Captain Ames said.

"Yes Captain?"

"You are to report to Major Williams office at once."

"Yes Sir."

"Come in, Lieutenant. I have been talking with Captain Ames and he speaks well of you and your work."

"Thank you, Sir."

"You are rotating state side. You have been reassigned to Fort Benning, Georgia, at the Benning Martin Community Hospital in the plastic reconstructive wing." Major Williams gave her her orders and said, "This is March 25th, you have a thirty day leave coming. So be at Ft. Benning on April 30th.

"Oh, and your plane leaves 1000 hours. So you'd better hurry. And good luck, Lieutenant. You do good work."

"Thank you, Sir."

Before the plane took off, she had time to telephone home and told them she was being reassigned to Ft. Benning, Georgia. But not about her thirty day leave. She wanted to surprise them.

The plane had to refuel in Hawaii and April telephoned Galen about the news and asked if he could come home in April. "Yes, we have spring break. Plus I drive home every other weekend."

"Don't say anything to my family about me coming home. I want to surprise them."

"I can't wait to see you, April."

"Me neither. Got to go."

Galen was so excited about seeing April again, he had a difficult time concentrating on his studies.

* * *

From Hawaii to San Francisco she slept soundly. And from San Francisco to Boston. Before reaching Boston she telephoned Galen and told him her flight would be arriving at 2 p.m. Friday.

He told her he would skip the afternoon computer class and meet her at the airport.

He was at Logan Airport early and waited at her arrival terminal. Others were there waiting, too. At 2 p.m. there was an announcement, "May I have your attention, United Flight 409 from San Francisco is now landing and passengers will be debarking soon."

His excitement and anticipation of seeing April again was making his heart rate increase. Another ten minutes passed before the first passengers began to enter. He saw an army uniform and he knew it was April.

She spotted Galen and began smiling and then she ran to him. They embraced and kissed hungrily, not caring who was watching.

"I have missed you so much, April. You're more beautiful than I remember."

"Oh, how I have dreamed about this day and seeing you again, Galen. Right now, though, I need a restroom. I've been cooped up in that plane for seven hours and every time I went to use the bathroom there was a line waiting. I need to pee really bad, Galen."

They found a restroom only a short distance from the arrival gate. Galen waited happily outside.

After they picked up her three pieces of luggage, they

walked out to his car in the parking lot. With luggage inside, they each got in and before starting the engine, April leaned over and kissed him.

"I have an idea," he said.

"I hope it's the same idea I have."

"We head for home, but there is a Holiday Inn near the Kennebunk exit. There is a fine restaurant there, too. I would enjoy spending the night and then driving home in the morning."

"We haven't left yet. That's exactly what I was thinking, too. I'm hornier than a rabbit in heat."

They both laughed.

"You look real nice in your uniform, sweetheart."

"Thank you, but I'll be glad to wear civilian clothes again." She also heard him say *sweetheart* and she lightly squeezed his thigh.

"How much longer do you have in your enlistment?"

"I'm only halfway through my three year enlistment."

"I'll still have another year in college.

"Where will you go when your leave is over?"

"To the Benning Martin Community Hospital at Fort Benning, Georgia. I'll be in the plastic reconstruction unit."

"Do you like being a nurse?"

"Oh yes. I find a lot of satisfaction helping the sick, and more in particular those who have lost a limb or disfigurement."

Then she told him about Corporal Dayton and how happy he was when he looked at himself in a mirror.

"How is your computer business?"

"When I first put my security program out for sale, I never dreamed I would sell so many programs."

"How many have you sold?"

"The last I checked, it was nearly eight hundred thousand."

"Wow, with money like that why do you still drive this old beater?"

"I would like a new vehicle, but I don't want to put on airs and no one at M.I.T. knows I have my own computer business."

"I guess I can understand that.

"You have changed, Galen."

"How so?"

"You are taller, your shoulders are broader and you have filled out. And excuse this expression, but you used to be the quiet little boy. But you aren't that little boy anymore. I noticed the change had started when we kissed on the riverbank."

"Thank you, sweetheart."

There it was again and she squeezed his thigh again.

"Do you like military life, April?"

"It's been good to and for me, but I haven't seen much beyond my studies and my duties. It's regimented and I have learned a lot about discipline. At the end of my enlistment, I will be leaving the army, though."

"Good."

She squeezed his thigh again and smiled.

An hour after leaving Logan, they pulled into the Holiday Inn in Kennebunk. Galen went to the office and asked for a room for two for one night and registered as husband and wife.

"This is a nice room. I need a shower and clean clothes."

He lay on the bed while she showered. He was falling in love. He always knew he had dear feelings for her, but when he first saw her in the airport and his heart began to beat faster. There was no question then about April or his love for her.

The bathroom door opened and April standing in the light wearing only her underwear looked at Galen and asked, "What are you smiling about?"

"I was thinking of you while you were in the shower and now looking at you wearing only your underwear—well, I kinda forgot what I was thinking about." She smiled.

She lay down on the bed with him and as they kissed she undid his pants and unbuttoned his shirt. "Take these off," she said.

While he took his shirt, pants and underwear off, she took her own off. At first they cuddled and fondled each other and kissing with hunger and passion and need. "I wanted to wait until after we ate, but I can't wait any longer," she said, as she pulled him over on top of her. She didn't have to pull very hard.

She screamed with joy and ecstasy and said, "I never imagined love making would be like this."

"Great isn't it!" They each were lost deep within the joy and passion of the other.

When they each were finally fulfilled they lay exhausted in each others arms. She was resting her head on his chest and she asked, "How did you register?"

Without hesitating he said, "As husband and wife."

"I like that."

"So do I. I love you, April. I suppose I always have."

"And I fell in love with you on the riverbank. And now I'm hungry. And we both are going to need nourishment for later tonight. Come—let's get dressed."

As they were eating their baked haddock special, April said, "I have a year and four months left to my enlistment and at that time you will have another year at M.I.T. I don't want to get married until my enlistment is up.

"At that time, I'll get a job in one of the hospitals in Boston. While you study, I'll work."

"Sweetheart," April said, "I don't understand why you are studying computers with your abilities. I mean when you were twelve you built your own computer. You wrote your own security program and formed a company. How much more do you hope to learn?"

"Let's say I'm fine tuning my computer knowledge. I'm also studying electronics."

"I'm reading between the lines, sweetheart, but I think you have something in mind. Right?"

"Yes. I'll tell you but you must keep it a secret."

"Okay."

"I intend to create an A.I."

"When will this come about?"

"Oh, not until I graduate from college. Right now all I have done is make notes."

"I'm full, are you?"

"Yes."

"Let's go back to our room."

April found a soft music channel on the television and they stripped down to their underwear again and lay on the bed talking. "When you called and told me you were flying into Boston, I thought I'd died and gone to heaven."

"At first I had a difficult time to believe it, too. I had no idea I was being reassigned.

"There is one thing though, Galen."

"What?"

"I would like an engagement ring and I'll wear it with pride."

"If we leave early enough, there is a jewelry store in the Maine Mall. Won't our parents be surprised."

"Mine sure will. They don't even know I'm coming home. I wanted to surprise them."

"They certainly will be."

"Okay, enough talk," she said.

* * *

They had a glorious night of friendship, talking and making love over and over. And what was best, they were truly friends first.

As Galen had said they were up early and walked into the dining room just as it was opening for the day. They both were anxious and ate hurriedly and then back on the road. "We need to get you, us, a new vehicle with a full front seat so I can sit close to you."

It was a short ride to the Maine Mall and the parking lots

were already filling. They found a nice jewelry store. "I don't want a big gaudy diamond."

It didn't take long to find exactly what she wanted with a yellow gold band. "Will there be anything else?"

Galen said, "No." But April said, "Yes, I want a tiger eye ring for my fiancé." She turned to look at Galen and said, "It'll be a year and a half before we can marry. I have your ring to wear and I want you to wear mine." No argument.

"No, on your left hand."

Back on I-95 again Galen said, "I think we'll still be home before lunch."

"You said earlier you wanted to develop an A.I.—artificial intelligence."

"Yes."

"And this probably isn't just a spur of the moment idea."

"No, actually I have been thinking about it for a few years now."

"How did you get started on this?"

"I'm convinced computers are able to perceive and think to a certain extent."

Then he told her about what he had discovered while playing computer card games.

"Creating programs so the A.I. can think or perceive on its own will be easy. I can create an emotional program as well as an auditory program and speech program. I even have the programs worked out in my notes. Building the A.I. will be the most difficult. And, I have started working on 3-D images."

"Are you learning how to do all this from your computer classes at M.I.T.?"

"Some of it, yes."

"Holy cow, here's the Skowhegan exit already."

"We were doing so much talking, I never realized we were this close to home," April said.

"Before we get home and before I forget it, when you are

home for spring break, I think we should get you a new vehicle. You can tell your college friends you borrowed it from your fiancée."

"Okay." No argument.

For a Saturday morning, Rt. 201 was busy.

"Before we get home, what we have been talking about, A.I., I would like to keep it between us for now."

"No problem. I hope I don't give my mom and dad a heart attack showing up like this."

"They'll be surprised I'm sure, but they'll be happy to see you."

At the outskirts of town, April said, "Now I'm beginning to feel at home."

A few minutes later, they drove by Galen's house. His father's car was home.

Gary was home and was raking the front lawn. He recognized Galen's car. Then he recognized his sister. "Mom! Dad!" he hollered as loud as he could.

They both came running out, "What are you hollering about?" his dad asked.

"April! She's with Galen."

"Oh my word," Liz said and she began to cry.

April had the door open before Galen had stopped, and she ran to her family. Galen stood back watching, happy for them all.

"Why didn't you say you were coming home, sweetheart?" Liz asked.

"I wanted to surprise you."

"You sure did," Charles said and chuckled. He was the first to see April's engagement ring. But he didn't say anything. He would wait for April to tell them.

April turned to look at Galen and she said, "Well, come join us, sweetheart." Again Charles smiled. Then Gary noticed.

"Why are you two smiling so?" Liz asked.

"Mom—Mom, Galen and I are engaged."

"Engaged? When did this all happen? Come in and tell us the whole story. I was making a pot of coffee."

"Congratulations, Galen. I couldn't think of a better man for my sister."

"Sit down and tell us the whole story. When did this happen?" Liz asked again.

"Yesterday, Mom. I flew into Boston yesterday and Galen was waiting for me."

April and Galen told the family the whole story and about their plans when April's enlistment was over.

"How long are you home for, sweetheart?" Charles asked.

"I'm on a thirty-day leave. Then I have to report to Ft. Benning, Georgia."

"Sweetheart, I really should go see my folks. They'll be wanting us for dinner probably tomorrow."

"We'll plan on it."

"I expect to have you here for supper tonight," Liz said.

April walked with Galen out to his car. "These are going to be a busy two days," Galen said, as he kissed her goodbye. "Later."

Galen's parents were as surprised as the Newmans. His mother, Suki, had all kinds of concerns and questions. His father, Ashton, smiled and said, "I can see by how excited you are, son, that you are really in love. And I know you well enough to know that you do not do anything without first doing a lot of thinking. And I also think you two are handling this very well. By that I mean you'll still have a year of college when she is discharged from the army.

"I probably haven't said this enough, son, but your mother and I are both very proud of you and you have our support and blessing."

"I'll expect both of you for dinner tomorrow."

Galen and his mother talked a lot about his computer

company, since she was helping to oversee things in his absence.

"I must say, you and April are showing good sense deciding not to get married until her enlistment is up. That shows you both are being very responsible," his dad said.

"I'm so happy for you, son," his mother said.

After lunch, Galen and his mother talked over his computer company business. "Your security program is still selling, son. When you first told us you were programing a security system, I never imagined you would be this successful. In another year you will have sold over a million copies."

"I have to ask, as adept as you are with computers, why are you wasting your time in college?"

"I'm learning more advanced computer technology, and besides, I'm also studying electronics."

"To what end, son?"

"There is so much that I'm learning about electronics that ties in with computers."

"I suppose."

* * *

April and her family were also talking. Everyone wanted to hear all about her experiences in the army and Japan.

April wanted to hear all about Gary's time in college. "I'll finish my first year in seven weeks and then one more."

Listening to his children talk about their experiences, Charles was very happy. He and Liz had done good by them.

Galen arrived an hour early for supper. While April was helping her mother with a pork roast, the three men talked in the living room. Gary and Galen did most of the talking and Charles sat back content and listening.

Everyone complimented Liz and April for a fine supper. "You know I've been away for so long, it really seems strange to sit down at a meal with my family."

After supper it was too cold for a walk, so Galen and April drove down to the river and parked so they could watch the water flowing by. The water level was still high.

They cuddled and did a lot of talking about their future.

That night he had to say goodbye and kiss her at her house and then he drove home.

At the breakfast table in the morning, April asked Gary, "What are your plans, Gary, when you finish college next year?"

"In February I'll post an ad online for custom building houses. If I do well enough, I'd like to build houses on speculation. Building houses on spec, I can use my drafting training and draw up my own plans and blueprints."

"That sounds interesting. Are you seeing anyone?" she asked.

"There's a girl in my drafting class and we go out some."

"What's her name?"

"Marlene Kingsley from Leeds, Maine."

"Anything serious?"

"Nah."

At dinner with Galen and his family, the atmosphere was more subdued. Aston, though, was particularly interested in April's travels and her training. His mother, Suki, tried not to show it, but she was concerned that April was older and she wondered if she might only be using her son, Galen, for her own gratification. However, she tried to remain pleasant.

Galen had to leave to drive back to Boston at 4 o'clock and as he and April were walking out, Suki said, "Be sure to come again, April, before you have to leave for Georgia."

"I will, Suki."

"Will you be home next weekend, sweetheart?" April asked.

"Now that you are here, you bet I'll be back. I love you, April, and I suppose I always have."

"And I love you too, sweetheart. Drive safe."

* * *

Galen and Gary both were back in class and April spent

time with her mother, talking a lot about her work in Japan and what she would be doing in Ft. Benning. They went shopping for a new wardrobe for April, for groceries, and they went for walks.

Charles was happy watching his wife and daughter enjoying each other's company.

Galen was able to come home the following weekend, but the next weekend he had to stay at M.I.T.'s IT lab. But the week following was spring break and he and April spent several glorious days together.

On Tuesday they drove to Bangor car shopping. Not wanting a new vehicle to be too showy, they settled on a new Toyota Rave SUV, cinnamon red. As the saleswoman started filling out the paperwork, Galen said, "We want both our names on the sales forms."

"And your name, sir?"

"Galen Merrill."

"And yours ma'am?"

"April Newman Merrill." Galen never even batted an eye. He understood.

They were allowed only $2,000.00 for the old trade-in. And April insisted she pay half of the price. Again Galen understood and he didn't say anything.

They spent another night together in the Holiday Inn in Kennebunk off I-95 and in the morning he drove her to the airport, where they said a tearful goodbye.

"Well, Liz, the boys are back in college and our daughter is on her way to Ft. Benning, Georgia. Does it make you feel old to see our children off, making a life of their own?"

"Not old, sweetheart, but a bit lonely."

101

Chapter 7

Before Gary's college closed for summer break, friends of Charles and Liz, Phil and Doris Knowlton, visited the Newmans one evening and asked, "Is Gary going to be around this summer, Charles?"

"He'll be home in two days for the summer."

"I would like to ask him to build us a house like yours. Doris and I have already been to Oakfield and the Katahdin Forest Products, and we have ordered the package. The foundation is in and backfilled, and I'd like Gary to take it from there."

"I'll go out on a limb, Phil, and tell you Gary will be happy. And as a guarantee, if for some reason Gary can't, then I'll do it."

"I couldn't ask for more than that. As soon as he gets home, have him come over to see us."

"What about help, Phil? He'll need probably three."

"I already have three young fellas lined up and waiting."

"What are you going to use on the roof, Phil?"

"Green steel roofing."

"That's the only way to go, Phil, in this country. I always wanted to steel roof the old farmhouse, but I never got around to it. It sure is nice."

* * *

Two days later when Gary arrived home for the summer, he was so ecstatic, he drove over to the Knowlton's without eating lunch first.

Phil took him to the lot so he could see for himself. The Katahdin log home package was there. "Have you talked with an electrician yet, Mr. Knowlton?"

"Yes, Dave in Oakfield suggested I contact one as soon as I could. So I called the same electrician you and your dad used when you built his house, Sanderson Electric. I didn't realize the electrician would have to bore holes through the logs for wiring and outlets boxes as the walls went up. Jim Sanderson said he wouldn't have any problems. Apparently he has wired a few log homes."

Gary and Mr. Knowlton went over the shipping list to make sure everything had arrived. "Everything is here, Mr. Knowlton. I'll be here at 6 o'clock Monday morning."

"Please, call me Phil."

Back at home, his father asked, "What do you think? Can you have it done before college starts?"

"That shouldn't be a problem. With one year of drafting and reading blueprints, these plans make more sense to me now."

Gary arrived at the site at 5:30 a.m. A half hour early. He wanted to make sure the three men didn't have to wait for him. The three arrived in separate vehicles right on time. Gary introduced himself. He was acquainted with the three, Don, Fred and Ralph. Of the three, Don had had two years as a carpenter's helper. The other two were just strong boys looking for a summer job.

Before doing any building, Gary first wanted to see how square the foundation was. There was an "L" where there would be two bedrooms and a bathroom and an entryway leading from the garage to the kitchen. When they were finished checking, everything was within a half inch square. "That's pretty damn good," Gary said. "I guess we can build to it."

The garage floor had been poured and power-troweled smooth; that would come later.

By the end of the day, at 5 o'clock, they had the deck

down, squared and leveled and plywooded. "That was a good days work, guys. See you in the morning."

Phil Knowlton had not showed up all day. He stayed away purposely so not to distract them.

The next morning, they set up a long table for the radial arm saw for cutting the logs to length. The electrician, Sanderson, also showed up.

As the logs were nailed down, he bore holes that he would need for running the electric wiring.

By the end of Wednesday, the crew had the walls and gable ends up.

At supper that evening Charles said, "Your mother and I are going to camp tomorrow morning and we'll be back Sunday afternoon."

"Are you going to do any fishing?"

"We plan to, weather permitting."

"Will you be okay, son, getting your own meals?" Liz asked.

"I'll be okay. I'll probably eat at the diner."

Liz made a potato salad dish and a ham casserole.

The notches were already cut in the gable logs for the long purlins. By the end of Friday, the roof was closed in with tongue and groove roofing boards.

Gary went to breakfast at the diner early Saturday morning. There was a new waitress, a pretty, friendly seventeen-year-old girl, Allison Jacobs. Then he drove up to the jobsite to inspect it. Mr. Knowlton was there.

"It's looking good, Gary, and you're moving along faster than I thought you would. When will you be ready for the roofer?"

"Anytime after Tuesday. We still have the insulation to put down and plywood on top of that.

"Did you want us to stain it or are you getting someone else?"

"I hadn't thought of that, so you and your crew might as well."

"And the interior?"

"Might as well do that also."

"We'll do the inside first while the roofers are on the roof."

Mr. Knowlton was satisfied and Gary went home to clean the house and wash out his work clothes.

* * *

Galen came home at the end of the school year and took care of business at his computer business and then he flew to Ft. Benning, Georgia, to spend a three-day weekend with April.

"How do you like working here compared to Japan?"

"The Tori Army Base was cleaner and newer, but here I can at least understand everyone."

"Are you kept busy?"

"Surprisingly busy, and that surprises me."

To save money, April lived on base but this weekend Galen had rented a nice motel room and once her shift was over, she didn't have to stay on base. Because she was of emergency services, she did have to remain reachable by her cell phone.

"What are you doing with your time this summer?"

"For a few months I have been working on 3-D schematics of an A.I."

"Not to change the subject, but I've been thinking once I graduate I would like us to move to the Falmouth area."

"Why Falmouth?"

"Well, if we get—or when we get—the A.I. built, I have an idea we'll be doing some travel and being closer to a jetport will be more convenient, and Falmouth would give our A.I. better exposure."

* * *

After lunch, Gary spread out the Knowlton's house blueprints to review what his next step would be, after the roof was complete and the interior and exterior had been stained.

That evening after the kitchen was cleaned, he decided to go for a walk out back. The family had been seeing a few deer. And these walks he found were a good time for thinking. There was a slight breeze and the air was cool, so he pulled on a green windbreaker. He took his binoculars too.

He hadn't walked but a short distance and two deer loped off. He watched them with the binoculars until they disappeared in the trees. He walked up where the deer had disappeared in the trees and all he could see was branches moving.

There was a hundred yard strip of woods and then it opened to another smaller field and someone else's property.

Much to his surprise, both deer suddenly blew and took off in a god-awful hurry. His heart practically jumped into his throat. He started following the deer and he had only gone a short distance when there was one shotgun shot.

Again, his heart almost jumped into his throat. This smaller field was down hill in sort of a small pocket. He suspected who it might be and he just had to see. So he started moving quietly towards the field and following where the two deer had run. He wished Galen was here with him.

He noticed how quiet it was. It was fading twilight, but there were no birds calling or flying around and no squirrels. It was pretty eerie. He started to move more to the left so he wouldn't come out at the bottom of the field. The only entrance was a dirt road at the top of the field that went back to the paved road.

He was close to the field now and right out in the center of the small field there was a single person bending over a dead deer. He looked through his binoculars. And it was who he figured it might be. John Jacob Joyce, locally known as "J.J." or "Three jerks."

J.J. didn't have a good reputation. He only worked when it suited him and seldom took a bath. He only stood about 5'6" but was as strong as two men. He had shoulder length brown hair and a full brown beard. He was wearing baggy pants and a black and green checkered wool jacket. He also was suspected of growing illegal marijuana on land belonging to another. Although he was never convicted of this. And his only vehicle was an old brown Toyota pickup.

Gary looked for the pickup and saw it still at the top of the field sitting on the dirt road.

J.J. stood up and wiped his hands on the front of his jacket and started walking up to his pickup. He drove down below the deer and stopped and shut the motor off. After he threw the deer in back he again wiped his hand on his jacket and got back in his pickup and drove out of the field.

Gary started running towards home. Once he was in his own field he ran faster. Once at the house he only knew one game warden to call.

"Hello."

"Hello, Mrs. Bonney?"

"Yes."

"Mrs. Bonney, this is Gary Newman. I don't know if you remember me or not. But I need to speak with Mr. Bonney."

"He isn't here, Gary. He had to go to Augusta today. I'll give you his cell number and you can try it."

"Thank you, Mrs. Bonney. I will."

He called that number. "Hello."

"Mr. Bonney. This is Gary Newman."

"Hello, Gary. How did you get this number?"

"Your wife gave it to me."

"Okay, what can I do for you? Do you have another poaching case for me?"

"Yeah, I do. I don't suppose you're anywhere near Skowhegan?"

"Yes, I'm on Rt. 2 just driving across the bridge in downtown Skowhegan."

"You're only five minutes away." And Gary gave him directions.

He was there in four minutes. Gary went out to meet him. "You playing game warden again?"

"Well, I just happened to be there."

"Where?"

"I went for a walk in the field out back here." And he told Warden Bonney the whole story.

"What time was the shot?"

"8:40, and I think it was a shotgun and not a rifle. He is known to hunt with a .16 gauge single shot."

"Tell me about it."

Gary did. "Does he live with anyone?"

"There were times when he'd have a woman. But I couldn't tell you about now."

"Does he live far from here?"

"Actually only about four miles up the road."

"Let's go." Warden Lieutenant Bonney was driving a car now and not a pickup.

"How come you called me?"

"I didn't know who else to call. And how come you happened to be in Skowhegan?"

"My in-laws live in Norridgewock and I had supper with them."

"J.J. lives on a dirt road. No neighbors and his place can't be seen from the road. His place isn't much."

"Is he a fighter?"

"I have never known him to be. But he is strong for his size. Okay, slow down. The road is right by that telephone pole."

Bonney turned his lights off after leaving the paved road. "Wow, this isn't much."

"That's his pickup. He just threw the deer in back."

"If the deer isn't there, there will be plenty of blood and hair," Bonney said.

Bonney parked his car and turned it off and they both got out and shut their doors without making a sound. Bonney walked up to the door and knocked. "Who's there?"

"J.J., it's Lloyd Bonney."

"Come in."

Bonney opened the door and J.J. was sitting at his table eating a bowl of cereal. When J.J. saw the uniform he choked on a mouthful of cereal and he spit it up. "What in hell do you want, Warden?"

"My name is Warden Lieutenant Lloyd Bonney, and this evening you shot a deer at 8:40 p.m. with a shotgun."

"Do you see any deer here? If'n I had me some fresh deer meat, do you think I'd be eating cereal?"

Bonney had seen the black and green jacket hanging up in the entryway.

"J.J. do you have any marijuana here?"

"What's it to you?"

"Well, J.J., it's like this, I have enough information for a search warrant and a warrant gives me the right to search anywhere deer meat could be hidden. I'll search your home with a fine tooth comb.

"Now, J.J., I want that deer and your shotgun and I believe they both are still in your pickup. And I don't need a warrant to search that. Let's go outside, J.J., and look."

J.J. was mad as hell but he also knew he was going to jail and whoever this Bonney was—well he had impressed J.J. enough so he wasn't about to start any trouble.

J.J. pushed his chair back under the table and he turned an outside light on, "J.J., this is the jacket you had on and wiped your bloody hands on it."

There in the back of his pickup was the little deer and it was obvious it had been shot with a shotgun. "Gary, put the deer in my trunk. I'm going to get his shotgun," J.J. didn't say anything, but he was madder than hell.

"John Jacob Joyce, you are under arrest for the illegal possession of a deer killed in closed season."

J.J. was wondering how in hell Bonney knew his full name.

"Gary, go in and turn his lights off and lock his door."

"There ain't no lock."

* * *

J.J. was taken to jail there in Skowhegan, and being inside the jail and watching the booking process was quite enlightening for Gary.

Bonney drove Gary back home. "Lloyd, you might as well spend the night. I'm the only one home."

"Where are your mom and dad?"

"At camp, and my sister is a lieutenant in the army and now is at Ft. Benning, Georgia."

"I'll take you up on that. I've been on the road since three o'clock this morning.

"Do you want this deer?

"Yes, we can hang it up in the garage."

By the time they had it hanging and cleaned up, it was midnight. "Would you like a drink, Lloyd?"

"Yes, that would be a good way to end the day."

Gary mixed one for himself also, but not as strong.

"How old are you now, Gary?"

"Twenty."

"Oh, you still have time, if you ever decide to be a game warden.

"Tell me, you never did say why you were out back here tonight."

"As I said, my sister is in Georgia and my folks are at camp. I just wanted to go for a walk. I jumped two deer and they ran away and then I heard the shot."

"You'll have to write it up and send me the report. He will be arraigned on Wednesday. There's no game warden here currently. Eben Finch retired. So I'll have to be here for the arraignment. My guess will be he transfers it to superior court to give him time to come up with the fine. He'll have to stay in jail now unless he can find someone to make bail. How does he support himself?"

"I've only known him to have an occasional odd job."

"He didn't like what I said about maybe finding marijuana if I had to get a search warrant. That led me to think maybe he sells drugs. Have you ever known him to sell drugs or marijuana?"

"Not for sure, but I couldn't help but wonder if he did."

"It's too bad a sheriff couldn't have a drug sniffing dog go through his place. I bet he would come up with something."

Gary noticed Lloyd had finished his drink and he asked, "Would you like another drink, Lloyd?"

"Yes, that would be good." He fixed another weak one for himself also.

"Why didn't you go to camp with your folks?"

"I'm building a house for a client and I have to have it finished before I go back to college."

"What are you studying?"

"Carpentry and drafting."

"Two good fields.

"You have time, a few years, to be a carpenter and if you decide you want something different you still could consider a career as a game warden."

"I'll think about it."

"I'd better call my wife and let her know I won't be home tonight."

"That went over better than I thought it would. She just didn't like being woken at one in the morning."

"Strange woman," Gary said.

"She has always been an exceptional wife.

"What is Galen doing?"

"He's doing a four course at M.I.T., and he and my sister are engaged."

"What's he studying?"

"Advanced computer technology and electronics."

"Why, he must be a whiz kid or something."

"He's a computer genius."

"He still would make a good game warden. You both would.

"Write up your report as soon as you get up in the morning and I'll take it with me. Then I'll treat you to breakfast at the diner I saw last night."

When Gary woke up in the morning, Bonney had already left and he left a note on the table.

Thank you for another fine job, Gary. Send your report to this email address first thing Monday morning: lt.bonney@maine.gov.

Gary dressed and shaved and before going to the diner. He washed the two glasses and put his dad's whiskey bottle back. It was still early and he was the only patron there. Allison was happy to see him. "Are you alone, Gary?"

"Just me, Allison."

"No, I mean are you home alone?"

"I have been. Mom and Dad are coming home today."

"Where have they been?"

"We have a camp in Forest City."

"I would have come up and cooked for you."

"Maybe next time, Allison. I'll have the breakfast special."

Other people were beginning to come in now. He smiled to himself thinking about Allison. He wasn't sure if she was just being kind, offering to come up and cook for him, or it was an invitation for sex.

He hung around the diner as long as he could drinking coffee and watching Allison. Whenever she looked at him she would smile. Finally he couldn't drink anymore coffee and she needed his table.

He went home and sat down at the kitchen table writing his report. It didn't take him long and after proofing it, he emailed it to Lt. Bonney.

At lunchtime he thought about going back to the diner. But he decided that would be too obvious and he didn't want to be a nuisance. So he warmed up a can of chicken noodle soup. While the soup was warming his folks drove in.

"I wasn't expecting you this early."

"We left right after breakfast," his mom said.

"I'll heat up another can of soup. It'll only be a minute."

As the soup was warming, Gary said, "I had company here last night," and he left it there.

His dad was smiling and his mom went to the bathroom. But when she saw April's bed all messed up she came back out and said, "Okay, who did you have here? April's bed is all messed up." It was easy to see she wasn't happy.

"Oh shucks, I forgot to make her bed. Lieutenant Bonney stayed over," he said.

His mother stormed off for the bathroom. "I'd better wait to explain until Mom comes back."

Charles chuckled and said, "That might be a good idea."

Before coming back, Liz made up April's bed. "Well, why was Bonney here?" she asked.

"Do you know John Jacob Joyce? He's often called J.J."

"Yeah, he's a little weasel."

"Well last night just before dark I went for a walk out back. I heard a shot in the next field that is downhill and I saw J.J. dressing a deer and then he threw it in his pickup and left.

"I called Bonney at home. He wasn't there but his wife gave me his cell number. I called, he answered and he was on his way back from Augusta and he was then in Skowhegan. He came up and I told him what I had seen and we went up to J.J.'s and the deer was still in the back of his pickup. He arrested him and took him to jail.

"Did you know Eben Finch retired?"

"No, it must have been recent."

"What time did Bonney leave?"

"Before I was awake. He left me this note.

"He started me thinking again about being a game warden."

"How do you feel about it?" his dad asked.

"I think it would be fun, but I want to build houses."

"Well after a few years if you decide to change, you can," his mom said.

"That's what he said, too."

Later that afternoon Gary called Galen and told him about J.J. He was in Georgia with April. "I wish I had been there, too."

"Say hello to Sis for me."

Chapter 8

Lt. Bonney was in court at 9:20 a.m. Wednesday morning. He was a half hour early and he waited with Deputy Sheriff Bill Williams.

"Deputy, have you ever suspected J.J. of running drugs?" Bonney asked.

"Oh yeah, but we have never been able to get enough on him to get him in court."

"He'll have to come up with a thousand dollars on this charge or spend the time in jail until the fine is paid. Where is he going to come up with it?"

"I don't know. I'm not aware of any close friends that he could get it from."

"Maybe, Deputy, this would be a good time to stake out his residence. It could be he has the money hidden there. And his grubby appearance may only be to keep you folks from thinking he is selling."

"Good point. I think I'll go talk with Sheriff Butler."

"If he should plead guilty today and ask the court for a few days to come up with the fine then I would bet he has a bundle stashed at his place somewhere. If the court gives him three days in jail which is mandatory, then he has already served that."

"I'd better go and talk with the sheriff now. Good talking with you, Lieutenant."

J.J.'s case was last and the deputy returned in time to be present for most of it.

"How do you plead, Mr. Joyce?"

"I have no choice but to plead guilty."

"I fine you $1000.00 and three days in jail. And I see you have been in jail for three days waiting for arraignment, so time served."

"Your Honor, may I have two days to get the fine. I have no money with me."

"Do you have the money?"

"I can get it, Your Honor."

"Okay, I'll give you until 3 p.m. on Friday to have the money here. If not, I'll issue a bench warrant."

"Thank you."

Bonney and the deputy stayed behind waiting for J.J. to leave the building. "You were right on, Lieutenant."

"I wish you were up there now," Bonney said.

"Deputy Henshaw, a drug agent for B.I.D.E., is already there."

"Good work, Deputy. Let me know how this comes down. Here's my card."

"You did a good job, Lieutenant."

"This was young Gary Newman's case."

"Is he a new warden?"

"No, he's a carpenter. I must get back to the office."

* * *

The roofers arrived early Wednesday morning and Gary was surprised how fast they worked. He had two men spraying the interior walls and ceiling with a clear varnish finish, while he and Ralph started work on the garage.

On his way back to the office, Bonney stopped to tell Gary what happened in court.

"How is he going to come up with that much money?" Gary asked.

"He must have a stash hidden somewhere. Keep that to yourself."

"No problem."

By noon on Friday, the roofers had the roof done. "When the garage is ready give us a call, Mr. Knowlton," the roofer said.

By the close of Friday the four walls of the garage were up. Come Monday, Don and Fred stained the exterior with a clear preservative.

* * *

"That was Gary, sweetheart. He caught J.J. shooting a deer in that small field beyond your property. Bonney was already in Skowhegan and he went up and the two went up to see J.J. and arrested him and took him to jail."

"He'd make a good game warden, I think," April said.

Galen returned home the next day and April, back to the base hospital. Here she was doing more hands on work with plastic reconstruction. She was becoming quite adept with her work and often the doctors would ask for her assistance.

One evening after Galen had closed his business for the day, he drove up to see Gary. He wanted to hear all about the J.J. case. After Gary told him the whole story Galen said, "I always thought there was something peculiar about him. And he always smelled so bad. I would have liked to have been with you."

"Lieutenant Bonney asked about you and said to say hello."

* * *

The first thing J.J. did when he arrived home was to fry up a mess of bacon and eggs. He'd had enough of jailhouse food.

Officer Henshaw had a nice perch off J.J.'s property where he had set up a spotting scope and camera with a telescopic lens. He had no more gotten set up and J.J. returned from court.

An hour later J.J. came outside. Henshaw took photos. J.J. walked to the left across an old pasture and stopped about two hundred feet from his shack. Henshaw took more photos. Then J.J. lifted a sheet of plywood that was on the ground. More photos. Henshaw watched as J.J. retrieved money from a white plastic five-gallon bucket with a lid. Then he replaced the lid and bucket and laid the plywood back on the ground.

Thinking he was safe enough, J.J. counted out $1000.00 while he was standing beside his pickup. More photos. Then he went inside briefly and came back out and got in his pickup and left.

Henshaw waited five minutes then he beat-footed it up to the plywood. The piece of plywood was about one hundred and fifty feet beyond J.J.'s property line.

J.J. had no constitutional right to privacy here so Henshaw flipped the piece of plywood back after more photos. And more photos of the plastic buckets in the ground. He removed all three and laid the plywood back and beat-footed back to his vehicle and down to the sheriff's office.

Inside Sheriff Butler's office; closed doors Henshaw opened the buckets. The white bucket was full of money. The green bucket contained about twenty pounds of illegal marijuana and the red bucket contained an assortment of schedule x drugs.

Henshaw had to explain to Butler why the search and seizure was legal. And Sheriff Butler didn't have any problems with it. "How soon can you prepare a request for a warrant of arrest, Paul?

"We should arrest him before he discovers this is missing."

"It's 1p.m. now, I can have it ready and signed by 2:30 p.m."

* * *

After paying his fine he went grocery shopping before going home. He had no idea what was about to fall down around him.

Henshaw was dropped off and he went back to his hidey hole perch to wait for J.J. to return. When he did, Henshaw radioed his back up and they arrived just as J.J. was putting the groceries away.

Sheriff Butler said, "John Jacob Joyce, we have a warrant for your arrest for trafficking of narcotics!"

J.J. was dumbfounded. But he didn't resist.

"Tomorrow, with a search warrant, we will return and search your premises."

Henshaw put handcuffs on him and he said, "All this because I shot a frigging deer."

Henshaw replied, "Lesson learned. Let's go."

After J.J. was booked and again locked in a cell, Deputy Williams telephoned Lt. Bonney.

That night at home Charles said, "I saw two sheriff vehicles go by this afternoon and they had J.J. inside again."

The B.I.D.E. officers were two hours searching J.J.'s home and property. They found a .9mm colt handgun with the serial numbers ground off and it looked as if an arc welder electrodes had been attached to the gun to remove impressions of the serial number that would lie deep within the metal. They found an AR-15 rifle that had been changed to full automatic and four new Winchester rifles; two .30-30's and two .38-55's. And in his bed mattress, they found an accounting book of his narcotic dealings and the name, address and telephone number of the person that had supplied him with the firearms. From Lawrence, Massachusetts.

The next day the B.I.D.E. officers inventoried the seized narcotics, money and the firearms. The firearms were found to have been stolen four years ago. There was $40,000.00 and an estimated street value of narcotics worth over $150,000.00.

The names in J.J.'s ledger were later contacted and interviewed and three of them were also arrested for trafficking narcotics and another for a violation of the Lacy Act— transporting illegal firearms across state lines and the illegal trafficking of stolen firearms.

Sheriff Butler had a conference with his deputies and the B.I.D.E. officers. "This case has put quite a feather in our cap.

Henshaw, has a court date been set yet?"

"The arraignment will be July 15th," Henshaw replied.

"Have you been able to get any information from Mr. Joyce?"

"All he has said is, he wanted to speak to a lawyer."

"I guess that is not too surprising, considering what he is facing."

"That was some good work, men."

Deputy Bill Williams said, "All because a young man decided to go for a walk one evening."

News of the arrests and investigation soon was seen in every newspaper in the state.

All while this case was being played out, the plumber and electrician had finished their work. The garage was complete and all that remained now was the cabinets. With the house almost finished Mr. Knowlton let the other three men go.

Before leaving they talked with Gary about working for him the next summer after he finished college. That made Gary feel good.

Charles was mowing the lawn after supper and Liz said, "Gary, I need to ask a favor of you."

"Yes, Mom."

"Your father doesn't know what to do with himself. He can only mow the lawn so much. He needs something to do. Would you ask him to help you with the cabinets?"

"I'd be happy to. I'll go out and ask him for help."

"Thank you, Gary."

Charles was just putting the lawnmower away. "Dad, let's sit on the patio and talk."

Liz brought a cold beer for each. "Dad, would you help me with the cabinets and countertops?"

"Are you in a bind?"

"The other three guys are all done and I would feel better if I had you helping."

"Sure, I'll help. What style cabinets do the Knowltons want?"

"She wanted to go with a fancy design with white finish and gold trim but Phil talked her into wood finish. He convinced her her cabinets would look out of place in a log house. So I suggested birch plywood. They went to Home Depot and looked at a sheet of birch plywood and loved it."

"When do you want to start?"

"Tomorrow morning. And Mom instead of you making breakfast, I'll treat at the diner."

"Can you afford it, Gary? You sill have a year of college, son."

"No problem. I've made good money this summer."

While Charles was taking a shower, Liz said to Gary, "Your father is happier already."

"I should have asked him to help sooner. Next summer I'll remember."

"Thank you, son."

* * *

They were at the diner five minutes early before it opened. And they were the only ones for a while. They all had French toast and bacon.

"Allison, my mom, Liz, and my dad, Charles."

"Are you folks going back up to your camp soon?"

Gary grinned.

"Not for a while," Charles said.

"Are you having her up at the house when we're gone?"

"Only Leiutenant Bonney, Mom." Charles was smiling.

Allison came back in a few minutes with their breakfast and asked Gary, "When do you go back to college, Gary?"

"Not until the first week in September."

"Maybe before then we could go out to dinner?"

"That sounds good. How about next Saturday?"

"Oh boy, I can't wait," she said.

"I'll be in touch before Saturday."

Charles was smiling again and thinking how times had changed.

Liz thought Allison was being more than a little forward and she wasn't smiling. But she didn't say anything.

After breakfast, Gary and his dad went to work and Liz went after the mail. There was a letter from April.

They worked on the wall cabinets first, so they could get in close to their work. "This is the first time I have worked for wages since I was a boy," Charles said.

"Does it make you feel young again?"

"No, but it seems good to be working."

At the end of that first day back at work Charles said, "Before I eat supper, I need a good hot shower. My muscles are all knotted up. I guess I'm not as fit as I thought."

"Your muscles needed to be used, Charles, that's all. They'll loosen up."

The end of the next day was better. And by the end of the third day he came home in a jolly mood and still felt fine.

The Knowltons stopped by on Friday, not so much to inspect their work, but to show his wife, Doris, her new kitchen.

"These cabinets are so beautiful. I would never have imagined they would look so nice. It is more than I anticipated. Thank you, Gary," she said.

"Thank you, but the praise should go to my dad. I can do a fine job with cabinets—but Dad is an artist.

"I think when I start building houses for a living, I'll hire Dad to do all the cabinets. He is a real artist when it comes to cabinets and finish work."

Praises like this from his son really made Charles feel good.

"Everything looks done, Gary," Mr. Knowlton said.

"Almost, we still have to secure the counter and bar tops and then I want to walk around and check everything. We'll be done and our equipment will be out of here by noon on Monday."

On their drive home, Charles said, "I liked what you said about me doing your cabinet work on the houses you build. But I'm not interested in doing any framing."

"When I first started the house, I wasn't sure if it would be finished by the time I'd have to leave for college. Now I have two weeks."

"What are you going to do?" his mom asked.

"Oh, I don't know. Maybe spend some time with Allison up at camp."

"Gary!" That's all Liz could say. While Charles only grinned. "Don't encourage him, Charles."

"I didn't say a word."

* * *

Gary treated his mom and dad to breakfast Saturday at the diner. Allison came right over and asked, "Are we still on for tonight?"

"I'll pick you up at 6 o'clock."

Later Gary thought about stopping to see Galen, but this was for both of them their last weekend before college resumed and he figured Galen would be with April at Ft. Benning.

Gary and Allison had a nice dinner at the Somerset Deluxe Lounge. As they were finishing their meal a live band arrived and they stayed for the dance. As they were dancing, Gary was thinking how nice it was to hold her in his arms; she was as light as a feather dancing.

* * *

Instead of waiting for Monday to secure counter and bar tops, Gary and his dad drove over after breakfast and they were done by lunch.

When April and Galen said goodbye, they each understood he would not be able to travel to Ft. Benning as often.

This year Galen rented a furnished apartment so he could

study without distractions from a roommate. He also wanted the privacy because he was working on a new security program he was hoping to sell to the United States Government.

He started with the basics of his original program, the Tomah Security, with new additions he figured the government should have and which no other security program was offering. He had gotten the idea talking with his father one weekend about the possibility of a terrorist group being able to completely shut down the government's computer system.

In October while Galen was home one weekend, his parents had a talk with him.

"Son, your mother and I will be moving to Arlington, Virginia. I have been promoted to Deputy Director of Communications for the C.I.A."

Galen interrupted him and asked, "Will you still be agent 799?"

His mother looked surprised to think he knew about his dad. Ashton replied, "I am no longer an agent, but a Deputy Director.

"Until we make the move, your mother is going to retire as bank manager and we will find someone to move into the house and keep it maintained.

"I have already talked with someone, son. A Ms. Arlene Gilbert. She's forty, single and as long as she wants it, it'll be rent free. All she has to do is pay for heat and electricity. And she also understands that when you come home, you will be staying here."

"How long have you been thinking about moving?"

"I accepted the promotion ten days ago. I'm on vacation leave until we move."

"I don't suppose you can tell us now what you have been doing as Agent 799? I mean now that you're inside now."

"I can't, son. Once anyone goes to work for the company, you can never reveal your duties to anyone."

"Okay, you said you'll live in Arlington. So I'm to assume you already have a residence?"

"Yes, when your mother came to Washington two months ago we found a house."

"When your father retires, son, we'll come back to Skowhegan. We both like living here. But now you are more or less on your own and I don't want us to live so far apart."

"I guess I can understand that."

"Just so you'll know ahead of time, when April's enlistment is up next year, we are going to be married, here in Skowhegan. I already have an apartment in Boston and we'll live there until I finish college. And April said she wants to get a job at Boston General Hospital."

"You and April are really serious about getting married, aren't you?" his mother said.

"Yes, Mom, we are."

"Well, if you ever need anything you know you can count on us, son," she said.

"There is something you can help me with, Dad."

"What is it?"

"I have developed a new updated version of my Tomah Security program. I call it Tomah 2. And I have designed it especially for the government. And I don't know who to talk with or how to approach them. And I am hoping you could help me there."

"How is it different from other systems?"

"I can't tell you that until I have a meeting with the department heads who would be interested. I can tell you this much, it is foolproof."

"There is nothing I can do now. But when we get in Washington, I'll make some inquiries. The company does have an I.T. team as I am sure most or every department would have. But I'll look into it when we get to Washington."

"Have you perfected it?"

"Yes, and for the last month I have run several tests and each one has responded 100% effective."

"The only problem might be where you are my son. I know most departments frown on nepotism. I might talk with our I.T. Deputy Director and see if he will set up a meeting."

"Thank you, Dad."

"We don't know how you do it, son. We have talked about this before. You are taking two difficult major studies, you have your own computer company and now you have written an advanced computer security program. Where did you ever find time to fall in love?" his mother asked.

* * *

Gary was in his last year at C.M.V.T.I. and it was part of the carpentry second year curriculum to build a modular home. And this year the 28x52 foot home was for Warden Service, for one of the wilderness districts.

Because of Gary's natural carpentry abilities, he was voted by the other students to be their foreman. The proceeds from the sale of the house would go to funding the next year's project.

Gary returned home most weekends, and sometimes he and Allison would get together.

In October, Charles and Liz decided to spend a week at camp. They bird hunted, rode around the area some and did a lot of relaxing. "You know, Liz, I'm looking forward to working some next year with Gary when he graduates from C.M.V.T.I. I don't know if I want to work every day, but maybe once in a while.

Chapter 9

Galen had his now updated Tomah 2 security program perfected and he locked it in a safety deposit box where he banked in Boston. Now he was spending every minute beyond his studies, making 3-D schematics of his A.I. He started with the skeletal form and after a hundred attempts, he finally had the one he wanted and he saved it.

He had decided on, for the time being, two main computers. One would be in the head and function as the brain and the other one in the chest which would control all the functions of the body. The brain would send digital signals to the chest computer and that computer would send signals to all parts of the body.

These schematics were easy to insert within the skeletal form and he wouldn't worry about building and programming the two computers until much later. For now all he wanted to do was to have his ideas in 3-D form.

On the last day of his exam finals before winter break in February, Galen received an email from the Director of Science and Technology requesting him to come to Washington, D.C. to discuss his new security program to a panel of agency directors.

As soon as he was out of class, he telephoned first his dad, who was out of the office, then he called his mother and advised her, "Mom, I have to come to D.C. and I will be leaving Boston as soon as possible. I will call and let you know when my flight lands at Dulles Airport."

He made flight reservations with JetBlue airlines for first

class. That way he would be served an evening meal. He didn't have time to eat now. It was now 3 p.m. and his flight was scheduled to depart at 7 p.m. He had time if he didn't get hung up in traffic.

Before leaving his apartment he telephoned his mother and advised her when his flight would be in Dulles.

He hurriedly packed his suitcase and packed also two laptop computers and his Tomah 2 program, which he had retrieved from the safety deposit box two days earlier.

He guessed he had everything. He would call April once he was in the air.

* * *

Once he checked in his suitcase—he chose to carry on his briefcase—the passengers were being boarded. He settled down in first class and a stewardess immediately took his dinner order. He chose the Salisbury steak dinner.

He had not prepared any kind of a presentation. So after dinner, he leaned his seat back thinking about what to say. He was soon asleep. And what seemed like only moments later the stewardess was waking him. "You'll have to upright your seat, sir. We will be landing shortly."

As he was bringing his seat back to the upright position, he had flash images of a dream he had had. He could see himself inside his Tomah 2 Security Program. Not so much as a visitor, but instead as if he had actually become part of the program.

He was thinking he had never had an experience like this before. "How odd."

His father was waiting for him. After retrieving his suitcase, he followed him to his vehicle and home.

"Are you prepared, son, for tomorrow?"

"I think so."

"You'll be meeting with top officials from several departments. They may try to intimidate you with how much they know and because of your age. The only advice I can offer is remember the courage it took when you and Gary caught and convicted the two moose hunters and later when you faced down the angry bear that was feeding on the moose remains. If you have this same kind of courage tomorrow, you'll do just fine."

On the drive to his new home, Ashton actually sounded as if he was honestly proud of his son. And he gave him the only encouragement he knew how.

His mother, Suki, was just happy to see her son.

"What time is the meeting tomorrow, Dad?"

"10 o'clock tomorrow morning. Very little gets started before 10 a.m. in Washington."

* * *

Galen slept well that night, much to his own surprise. After showering and shaving he went downstairs for breakfast. He wasn't feeling at all nervous.

He was dressed in a dark blue suit, white shirt with a lighter blue tie with thin vertical red stripes; a powerhouse suit and tie. Ashton smiled. He was seeing another side of his son.

Galen had a light breakfast with one cup of coffee.

"Are you ready, son?"

"Let's go." He kissed and hugged his mother.

"Good luck, son."

"Where is the meeting going to be held, Dad?"

"In a conference room in the capital building."

"You know your way around Washington don't you, Dad?"

"Yes, son."

"Okay, a moment of truth, Dad. I've known for some time you work for C.I.A. and more than an insurance actuarial. So what do you do?"

There was a long moment of silence. "Anyone who works for the company is forbidden to reveal to anyone what their duties are. I'll tell you this much, there have been times when I have done work in foreign countries.

"When I requested to come home, I was promoted to

Communications Deputy Director. Does that help you?"

"Yes, Dad, it does."

They were a few minutes early.

"The one person who will probably be most skeptical will be the Director of National Cyber Agency, Lawrence Hoffer. He sometimes acts like he knows more than the next person."

"One suggestion: if any of them try to unsettle you, don't lose your temper. Keep your cool and move on."

At 10 o'clock the only person who was not there was Lawrence Hoffer. "Gentlemen, shall we get started? The meeting is scheduled to commence at 10 o'clock. If you'll be seated please," Galen said.

Ashton was there to represent the company and he sat with the other directors. Just then the door opened and Mr. Hoffer entered. "What, you starting without me?"

Karl Shiftwood from Homeland Security said, "We were scheduled to start at 10 o'clock. Not ten minutes after." Hoffer sat down without commenting.

"You haven't missed too much, Mr. Hoffer, but I'll start over for your benefit." Ashton had all he could do not to laugh. Boy was he proud of his son.

"To get the preliminaries out of the way, I'll tell you a little about myself.

"My name is Galen Merrill and I recently turned twenty-one years old and I am in my second year at M.I.T. When I was twelve, I built my own computer. When I was fourteen, I created the Tomah Security Program. At fifteen I had the program patented and I also formed my company. Since then I have sold over a million copies of that program.

"Today I have the Tomah 2 Program which I hope to sell to the United States Government.

"I have no idea what security program you are using today, but I have done my research and I know there are numerous attempts everyday from Russia, China, North Korea and the

Islamic nations, to list only a few, to hack into the government computers. I also believe there probably is a small percent of these attempts that are successful. And that's not to say how many countries or hackers have tried to download a virus into your computers.

"It has also come to my attention that the government periodically has to change antivirus software to keep up with changing times.

"With any security program available today not one of you are sure no one will be able to hack into your files. That is impossible with my Tomah 2 Program.

"Are there any questions?" Galen asked.

"Yes," Hoffer said. "I would like to see how this program is written."

"I bet you would and I'll show you, but not until I have a contract."

"What are you looking for with a contract?" Howard Selman, Chief Procurement Director asked.

"An outright purchase of the program."

"What are you asking for your program?" Selman asked.

"We'll get to that later. Right now I'd like to show you what this program can do." He opened his briefcase and removed the two laptops. One black and one green.

He handed Mr. Hoffer the green laptop and said, "My company is the Merrill Computer Service. Try to hack into my company files. I give you this laptop to use because—well, you'll understand.

"Now, Mr. Hoffer, you can send your hack through as many I.P. addresses as you like."

Ashton was really impressed now and he was beginning to understand that he actually knew very little about his son. He watched Hoffer with a lot of interest. Hoffer was sweating.

After a few minutes Hoffer said, "I'm going through an I.P. address in China, to Russia to France." Then he pressed send and instantly the laptop he was using exploded in flames. But not so intently to harm the user.

"Holy shit!" Hoffer said. "What in hell just happened?"

Everyone was standing looking at the burnt laptop and young Galen.

"What happened?" his dad asked.

"Anyone trying to send a virus or attempting to hack into a computer system that has Tomah 2 installed ... this will happen as soon as the hacker hits the send button.

"The system sent a very high frequency signal back to the original computer that will destroy that computer.

"I have destroyed many laptops and desktop computers testing my program.

"Will any of the government's security programs do that? And the kicker is no hacker will be able to download the program to see how it is written."

Howard Selman from procurement said, "I think you have shown us what we have wanted for a long time. What are you wanting to sell this program?"

"There are some twenty million federal employees. Many of these employees will have more than one government computer. My Tomah Security Program sells for $40.00, with no yearly renewal. That comes to $800,000,000.00. My Tomah 2 I'll sell to the U.S. government for ten million dollars."

Mr. Selman from procurement said, "I think your program is what we have needed for a long time. I can't give you an answer today. We'll need some time to talk among our agencies."

"You have two days. Then I return to Maine."

Ashton was more surprised, shocked than anyone at the meeting. He never imagined his son to be so aggressive.

"If we come to a decision before then, how do we get in touch with you?" Selman asked.

Galen gave them his cell number.

On the way home Galen asked, "What do you think, Dad?

Will they buy it?"

"You certainly demonstrated how effective it is and yes, there are hackers every day attempting to create havoc or download files. And the government's security system has to be changed frequently.

"Yes, they are certainly interested. But I have no idea what the yearly cost is now. Ten million sounds like a lot of money, but as you explained the number of federal employees and computers they will have to take all this into consideration.

"When I drop you off at home, I'll have to report to my superior and I'll tell him I'm all in favor of Tomah 2 Program and the cost is inconsequential.

"Don't be surprised, son, if some day two men in black suits approach you at M.I.T. and try to recruit you to work for the company. My suggestion would be to say no."

* * *

That night while Ashton and Suki were preparing for bed, Ashton said, "It's too bad you couldn't have been at the meeting, Suki, to see our son in action. A young man had the committee, everyone of them, mesmerized. One individual tried to heckle him but very subtly Galen put him in his place. He was in control the entire time. He has developed a security program that none of them had ever considered before.

"And what's more, when Howard Selman from procurement said they would have to have time to consider purchasing his program, our son said, 'You have two days.'"

"He actually said that to a room full of Directors?"

"He sure did. And you know the sad part of the whole thing, I have realized because of my position with the company I understand now how much I have missed out on with the family. Until this morning I don't think I knew my son at all."

While his parents were talking, Galen was telling April all about his meeting. "Do you think they will buy the program and at your price?"

"My dad thinks so, after they have had time to consider everything. He also said after he had a chance to think about the proposal, he thought my price was low."

"I really miss you, sweetheart," April said.

"Me too. I can't get away right now, but during the spring break I'm going to try to come down for a few days."

"Oh, I hope so."

* * *

At 11 o'clock Saturday morning Galen received a text from Howard Selman.

"That was Mr. Selman, he wants to see us at 2 o'clock."

"You'd better answer him."

At 2 o'clock Galen and Ashton were back at the capital building. Not everyone was there; Lawrence Hoffer, National Cyber Director, Howard Selman from Procurement, Karl Shirtwood from Homeland Security and Ashton representing the company.

Mr. Selman said, "You gave a short and precise overview of Tomah 2 and your demonstration. I think it was your demonstration that convinced those who were skeptical. But after talking with everyone, Ashton, included, it is unanimous now. We want, we need, your program and will meet your price of ten million dollars.

"How would you like that?"

"You can electronically send it to this account." And Galen gave Selman his account number.

"As soon as the deposit is confirmed, I'll give you the program and show you how to view the contents."

"This probably will take maybe ten minutes."

"I'll wait."

Fifteen minutes later Galen had his confirmation and he gave the CD to Mr. Hoffer and showed him how to open it. "I want you all to understand. I have sold you the program, but I still hold the patent."

"We have a few papers for you to sign, Mr. Merrill."

On the way home, Galen said, "I think you were right. I sold too low. At ten million they were in a hurry to buy it. But I feel good about the sale."

"What will you work on now, son?"

"What makes you think there is something else?"

"With a mind like yours, you'll always have to have a project to work on. You're a brilliant young man. I only wish I had noticed sooner."

"There is something that I'm working on, but it'll take another few years to complete. And no, I'm not going to say what it is. I'll say this, however, when I'm ready the company will be the first people I contact."

Ashton knew his son well enough not to ask any more what he was working on.

* * *

Galen returned home to Skowhegan the following day. During the drive up from Boston, instead of thinking about the sale of his Tomah 2 Program or the A.I. he wanted to build, April was all he could think about. In two months he would fly down during spring break and he would have a few days of ecstasy.

He drove from Logan Airport non-stop to Skowhegan and before stopping at his parents house, he decided to visit the Newmans. For most of his life they had actually been his surrogate family.

The snowbanks through Skowhegan were so high it was like driving through tunnels. There had been snow in Boston but it always soon melts. In Washington, D.C., there was even green grass.

Galen had been so busy with selling his program and thinking of April he had forgotten how cold Maine could be.

When Liz asked him to stay with them while he was home, he accepted without hesitation. The next day he did have to excuse himself for a few hours while he checked into his company. His accountant Rita Howard had the books up to date. "How is the Tomah program selling, Rita?"

"The sales slowed during January, but they are beginning to pick up again."

"I don't know what I'd do without you, Rita."

While Galen was home for a few days, Gary wrote up an advertisement for his carpentry business and Galen helped him to put it on the internet along with a photo of his parents home and one of the Knowlton's home.

On Saturday, Galen returned to his apartment in Boston and Sunday Gary returned to his dormitory at C.M.V.T.I.

By the end of March, Gary had two requests to build Katahdin Forest Company log homes. During spring break he talked with both parties. They both were located in Skowhegan. James and Helen Whitley wanted their house to start the first of June and Gary sat down with them and worked up a contract and a list of materials. Mr. Whitley would have a contractor have the foundation in and ready to build on by the end of May.

Two days later he talked with Ronald and Suzanne Waldo about their log house and Gary agreed to start work on it by August 20th. And each party wanted his dad to build the cabinets.

"Your foot is in the door, son."

* * *

Galen flew into Atlanta, Georgia, Friday night and hopped a shuttle flight to Ft. Benning. April had arranged to take a few days off while he was there.

Saturday morning after love making and breakfast, he told her how much he had sold the Tomah 2 program for. She found this interesting, but she was more excited to have Galen there with her. "I only have a few more months in the Army then we can get married."

* * *

April contacted the Boston General Hospital after Galen

returned to Boston and a week later she had her reply. She was to start work September 20th with Dr. Theodore Hamilton in the plastic and reconstructive surgery department.

Her life was falling into place. She was so excited she called Galen and then her mother and told them the good news.

Gary rehired the same three men that worked with him the previous year and gave each of them a little raise in hourly pay. "I hope things will work out so we can keep working through the winter."

At supper one evening, Liz said, "I'll be so glad when April finishes her enlistment. And living in Boston, she'll be close enough so we can visit some."

"Would you do me a favor, Dad?"

"Sure, what do you need?"

"I haven't the time, but would you inquire if J.J.'s property could be bought?"

"That would make a nice lot. Are you interested to build a spec house or your own house?"

"Mine."

"Why can't you go on living here, son?" his mother asked.

"Well, I could. But there would have to be an understanding," Gary said.

"And what is that?"

"I haven't met anyone I would want to marry yet. But I do enjoy being with a girl on occasion. And I think we'd both feel better about that if I had my own place."

"Understood."

"Has J.J.'s case come to court yet?" Gary asked.

"Not yet and we have been watching the newspaper," Charles said.

The next day after breakfast, Charles went to the bank to inquire about J.J.'s property. "We recently reprocessed that property. Are you interested in purchasing it, Mr. Newman?"

"I'm not but my son is. How big is the lot?"

"There is ten acres. The property is a mess and as is now, it isn't worth much."

"How much did J.J. still owe on the property?"

"Seven thousand dollars. It probably would cost close to that to clean it up."

"What if I write you a check right now for seventy-five hundred. That would cover your cost."

"Done."

Charles had the new deed made out to Gary. At supper that evening, "Son," Charles said, "your mother and I would like to give you this."

"You bought J.J.'s property?"

"Yes, the bank had recently foreclosed and reprocessed it. They were more than happy to sell it."

"How much, seventy-five hundred? That isn't as much as I thought it would be."

"It is a good buy. But as Bob Hinkley said, 'It'll cost that much to clean it up.'"

"I have enough in my account to pay you, Dad."

"Not necessary. Your mother and I talked this over and we want to give it to you. It's a good feeling to know you'll be close. Call it a graduation gift."

"I don't know what to say, except thank you." And he hugged them both.

Saturday morning Gary contacted a local excavator about removing J.J.'s old shack and vehicle and all the trash lying around. Then to clear out all the brush and haul it off and level an area to build on.

He moved the house site a hundred feet down from J.J.'s shack. The soil was fine gravel. There was an old dug well, but Gary decided to have a new one dug.

He stayed up the next few nights until midnight drawing plans for his house. The soil was good gravel with good drainage. He decided to pour a slab and build from that, to keep costs down.

He drew plans for a log house twenty-six feet by forty feet, with a loft bedroom over the kitchen end of the house with a living room cathedral ceiling.

Chapter 10

The base commander called April into his office one morning after breakfast. "Sit down, Lieutenant Newman. Dr. Strongly and Dr. Alfred have spoken very well for you. Your enlistment will be up soon and I'd like to ask if you had any thoughts about reenlisting. There would be a three thousand dollar bonus. When someone is as good as you are we try to hold onto them.

"I'm sorry, Major David. As soon as my enlistment is up, I'm getting married and moving to Boston."

"I had to try. You have another thirty-day leave coming so you could officially leave on August 1st."

"Thank you for the offer, Major, but my mind is made up."

* * *

Gary decided they should be far enough along on the Whitley house by August 1st to let two men start on his house. He wanted to have it closed in before winter and then work on it during the winter.

He and his dad formed the slab foundation for concrete and had a plumber run the necessary pipes for water and sewage. And a concrete company to run the concrete and power trowel the slab smooth. It had to be a smooth finish. This would be his floor and not a wooden deck. Of course carpets and inlaid would cover when he was finished.

Katahdin Forest Products delivered the complete package

August 1st.

His men were working better than he thought they would and with the previous summer's experience with building the Knowlton's house, this one went along even smoother. So the house was completed two weeks ahead of schedule and they started on Waldo's house.

On the 20th he had to let his crew have a free rein as he had to attend his sister's wedding.

Ashton had taken a two week vacation and he and Suki returned to their home to Skowhegan for their son's wedding. By now Suki had no doubts about April's love for their son, and she welcomed her to the family with a hug and kiss on the cheek.

Gary and Galen were able to spend a little time together as old friends do. Gary took him up to his lot and showed him the progress of his house. "Will you have it finished for winter?"

"Probably not, and that'll be okay, too. But before winter is over I'll have it done."

Then on another note. "We all heard about you selling the government a new computer security program. That was quite an accomplishment, Galen. Not only the new program but being able to stand in front of the department heads and tell them they couldn't not afford to buy it."

"Thank you, Gary. You have always been my best friend ... next to April." They laughed.

Liz had two weeks to spend with her daughter before the wedding. She knew both April and Galen shared a lot of love between them and what was even more important they had been very good friends for most of their lives. Even so, she still cried at the wedding. Charles held her and smiled, but his eyes were watery.

Galen and April had talked about taking a honeymoon trip to Europe. It wasn't like they couldn't afford it. But for now they settled for a trip to Halifax, Nova Scotia, and attended Halifax's annual seashore festival.

In eleven days he would be back in class at M.I.T. and April wanted time to familiarize herself with Boston.

* * *

Gary hadn't seen Allison since early spring. Her family was still around but she had left without a word. A new girl had taken her place at the diner, Larene Rioux. A pretty French girl originally from Fort Kent. Her father had been laid off at the paper mill in Madawaska and had found work at the Madison paper mill. She and Gary hit it off right away.

Monday morning after the wedding, Gary stopped at the diner for breakfast. He was early and Larene sat across the table from him while the grill warmed up. He was early and the only patron so far. "What are you doing after work this evening, Larene?"

"Oh probably just sit home and watch the boob tube."

"Would you like to come up tonight? My folks have gone to camp at Forest City for the week. "

"I was wondering how long it would take you to ask me. Of course, I'll come up. I'll pick up a pizza and you can pick me up here."

Gary had a difficult time keeping his mind on what he was doing that day. The diner didn't close until 8 p.m. but Larene's shift ended at 4 o'clock. She had enough time to go home and change her clothes and pick up a pizza to go.

Gary was at the diner at 5:30 and she was ready. She had her own car and she followed him home.

"Before we eat, I need to shower; I'm all dried on sweat and sawdust."

"I'll join you. I can still smell the diner."

They weren't long getting rid of their clothes. They washed each other, with a little playing along the way. "If we don't stop, the pizza is going to be cold," he said.

"I just as soon eat cold pizza." And they played a little longer.

* * *

Needless to say, neither one had too much sleep and they were up early and she reported for work on time and Gary had breakfast at the diner.

He felt refreshed and rejuvenated and his crew had a difficult time to keep up with him.

Once the walls and roof were on the Waldo house, he sent Don and Ralph to start on the walls on his house. The material had all been delivered.

He had gotten very busy trying to build two houses at the same time and it wasn't until the end of the week when he stopped at the diner for breakfast. "Where have you been?" she asked the obvious question.

"I've just been so busy."

"I thought maybe you found another girl. When are your folks coming back?"

"Late tomorrow morning."

Larene wasn't happy, but she did understand.

The Waldos were surprised how fast Gary and crew were building their house. "This will be done before cold weather, I can see now, Gary," Mr. Waldo said.

The interior studded walls were up and sheet rocked and the Waldos wanted handmade cabinets. So Gary hired his dad and had Fred work with him. While the cabinets were being made, he went up to his lot and helped Don and Ralph with the gable ends.

The following week, Gary accepted another job that was also in Skowhegan. This was going to be a two story house with two by six studded exterior walls. It was going to be a winter project. And the whole structure would require more time. But the owners, Henry and Harriet James, were not in any particular hurry, as long as it would be completed by May 1st of next year. This was working out real well for Gary and crew.

The James foundation would not be ready to build on

until November 1st, which would give the crew time enough in between finishing Waldo's house and starting this one, to finish Gary's house on the hill.

With the Waldo house completed with flooring and cabinets, Gary and crew now could concentrate on his house. By the time they had to stop and start the James house, his house on the knoll was done except for the cabinets and finish. And instead of hiring his dad, he kept that open to keep his crew busy.

"But, son, aren't you going to be busy enough with the James house? When will you find time to work on your own house?" his dad asked.

"I guess I didn't think of that. Do you want a job, Dad?"

"You bet."

* * *

Galen still made it back to Skowhegan every other weekend to check on his business and once in a while April was able to come with him. They missed Thanksgiving but were able to make it for three days over Christmas.

"How is it, Gary, you haven't found yourself a good woman yet?" April asked.

"Well there were a couple, but after we went to bed, they soon disappeared. Last summer I met a really nice girl, Larene Rioux, and I thought we had something and then I heard she moved away.

"I have really been too busy to do too much looking."

"When will your house be ready to move in?"

"Before long. There isn't much more that needs doing. The only bad part of that is I'll have to start doing my own cooking, laundry and housekeeping."

"It'll be good for you."

"It's not like I have a lot of extra time."

When he was alone with Galen they would spend most of their time talking about the trips to Tomah. "I cherish those trips, Gary, as much as anything in my life while we were growing up.

144

"And—if not for you jumping in after me, I wouldn't be here now."

Gary laughed and said, "It sure was a cold hike back to camp."

"You know, Gary, I never said anything to my folks about that."

"Why not?"

"I was afraid they wouldn't let me go to camp anymore.

"Not to change the subject, but how is your carpentry business doing?"

"We built three homes since I graduated plus the shell to my house."

"Well, you're doing good then. Have you ever given any more thought about becoming a game warden?"

"I'd be lying if I said no. There are times when I do wonder what it would be like."

Galen laughed then and said, "If you ever do then maybe I could go with you sometimes and catch poachers."

"That was fun, wasn't it," Gary said.

"You keep talking like that and I'll quit M.I.T. and become a warden."

* * *

After Christmas, April returned to work at the Boston General, Galen was back in class and Gary and his crew were finishing his house on the hill.

Two days later Gary contracted a job to remodel an old 1880 barn. The owner a New York based developer wanted to eventually turn it into a hotel and a high class restaurant.

For now the owner, Vinson O'Malley from Manhattan, wanted the original rock foundation repaired with the walls straight and no bulging rocks and eventually with a poured concrete floor power troweled to a glassy finish. Of course the entire barn had to be jacked up with cribbing to support the weight while they worked on it.

145

The exterior shingles were in remarkably good condition. The good barn boards were removed with great care to be used later in the lobby and dining areas. The exterior walls were recovered with plywood.

O'Malley didn't want anything plastic used visibly, so Gary used wooden framed windows and solid wood doors. The steel roof was in pretty good condition so O'Malley wanted the roof scraped clean and painted green. For the siding, O'Malley wanted a combination of slate siding with clapboards.

All this work took the crew until the middle of April. "When I get ready to finish the interior, Gary, I'll call you. You and your men have done an excellent job."

On stormy days when he couldn't work on the outside of the 1880 barn, Gary and crew finished the interior of his house, down to painting and papering the walls.

Now he needed furniture.

He had purposely made the garage big enough for a workshop, with the suggestion from his dad.

By May 1st he had the house furnished and a refrigerator full of food.

Shortly after moving into his home he met an attractive hairdresser, Millie Lambreau. He was grocery shopping Sunday morning and met her in the parking lot. Her paper grocery bag had ripped and the contents were all over the ground. He stopped and asked, "Would you like some help with those?"

"I could sure use some, yes."

He had to crawl under his pickup to retrieve a few items and with his arms loaded he stood behind her as she was bending over emptying her load. When she stood up she backed into him and he dropped his items in order to catch her from falling. "Wow, are you okay?"

"I am now. I'm glad those were cans and not glass jars." They both laughed then.

"My name is Gary Newman."

"Hi, Gary, I'm Millie Lambreau."

"Do you live her in town?" he asked.

"Yes, I have an apartment over a garage on the Waterworks Road. And you?"

"I just moved into a house I built this winter about two miles out on Malbons Mills Road."

"You married Gary?"

"No, and you?"

"No."

"Are you attached or anything?"

"No boyfriend and no husband."

"Would you come up for supper tonight? I'll fix steak and salad."

"I'd love to." And he gave her driving directions.

"What time?"

"6 o'clock."

"That sounds good, I'll be there."

She arrived at exactly 6 o'clock "This is nice, Gary. I love the log walls and everything smells so good. I brought a bottle of wine. I hope that is okay."

"I like wine."

While he fried the steaks Millie made the tossed salad. "You don't have any salad dressing, so I'll make some with mayonnaise, vinegar and ketchup."

"I never thought about that. But it sounds good. How do you like your meat?"

"Medium rare."

"What happened with that goofball who used to live in an old shack here?"

"He was in superior court last week for narcotic trafficking, possession of stolen firearms and firearms trafficking. He was sentenced to twenty years. The D.A. dismissed two smaller charges."

Then she wanted to know about that and he ended up

telling her the whole story.

He tried the salad and her dressing first. "This dressing is very good. I'll have to remember the ingredients."

"This steak is done just like how I like it."

They talked all through supper and when they had finished Millie helped him to clean up then they sat in the living room talking and sipping wine.

"I like your house, Gary. I can feel good vibes."

They sipped more wine and a strong wind started to blow; followed by a downpour of rain. "Rain on the roof is like music," she said.

"You aren't going to make me go out in that downpour and wind, are you?"

"I was hoping you'd stay the night."

"That's what I wanted to hear."

After an enjoyable aerobic exercise of love making they both succumbed to a restful sleep.

Gary was awake before Millie, as he had to be at work at 7 o'clock and she started her day at 10 o'clock. Begrudgingly she got up and dressed and all she wanted for breakfast was a cup of coffee.

Gary was unusually happy and energetic all that day. They were finishing the 1880 Barn, as far as Mr. O'Malley wanted to go now. He liked Gary and his crew, they were doing an excellent job. The price was right, the crew was clean and they were always happy. So O'Malley said, "I'll wait on the interior, Gary, until December. I'm in no hurry and this way you'll have inside work for the winter."

"Thank you, Mr. O'Malley, that'll work out nice."

With the 1880 Barn finished for now, Gary and crew started on another two story studded house. There was another Katahdin Log Home to start, but not for another two months.

Millie only had every other Saturday off from work and this only gave Gary and Millie Sunday to see each other every other week. He was really beginning to like having her at home, if only for a single night at a time.

Gary's mother, Liz, finally came to terms with herself about her son having a woman stay with him on weekends.

"He's a man, Liz, and he needs female companionship." She finally acquiesced.

After a month of this one weekend Gary said, "Millie, it would make more sense if you would move in here with me. You wouldn't have to be paying rent and we could be with each other more than one day on weekends. Besides, I kinda like you."

She snuggled up close and said, "I kinda like you too. It took you long enough to ask me," she said good-heartedly.

"One understanding though, Gary; this doesn't mean we are going to get married." She kissed him and then said, "Maybe someday but not now."

* * *

Galen finished his third year at M.I.T. Now he was traveling back and forth from Boston to Skowhegan to keep tabs on his computer business. April had every weekend off, so he would spend three days in Skowhegan and each weekend with April.

The staff at the hospital liked April and the plastic and reconstructive surgery department were impressed with her abilities.

Most of the time while in Skowhegan he would work on his plans for an A.I. and again the couple of days he was back in their apartment. But the weekends were always for April.

"When will you start building your A.I.?"

"Not until after I graduate next year and then after we have found something suitable in Falmouth to live and with a sterilized clinic. I already have most of the plans drawn on the computer in 3-D. In all honesty this idea is turning out to be more involved than I first thought. But things are beginning to come together."

"I wish there was something I could do to help you."

"Oh there will be when we start building it. I want you in charge of creating the fleshy body."

She heard the WE. So, she was going to be part of this creation.

* * *

April had three days off at Christmas and she and Galen stayed with her folks. And they finally got to meet Millie Lambreau.

Charles and Liz were happy to have their family together again. And Millie took Gary to her folks home in Bangor to meet her family.

Gary and his crew had started the interior work at the 1880 Barn. The barn boards were installed in the lobby and dining room and most of the rest of the interior was sheetrock and some were paneled sheetrock sheets.

Mr. O'Malley would stop in each week only for a few minutes. He was a man who knew what he wanted and he seldom made changes. And he was always happy how things were progressing.

One night after April and Galen had returned to Boston, Charles and Liz laid awake for a while talking. "You know, sweetheart, I'm happy how April and Gary have turned out. If I were to die tonight, I don't think I'd have any regrets," Charles said.

"I know what you are saying. They are young adults now and responsible for their own life. And I think they are pointed in the right direction," Liz said

"What about Millie living with Gary?"

"I guess I'm old fashioned," she said, "It took me awhile— but I like Millie."

* * *

That winter was exceptionally cold. January was more like the arctic and Gary's crew were glad they had inside work all winter at the 1880 Barn. He had to leave twice and left Don in charge while he talked with two more clients who each wanted a Katahdin Log home built and finished by October. One was fairly simple. An L design like his folks house and the other was two stories. And both houses would have asphalt shingles.

There was a lot of finish work required in the 1880 Barn and Gary hired his dad to help out. "I was just waiting for you to ask, son."

During his spring break, Galen and April spent some time in and around Falmouth looking for a house to purchase that would also be big enough so the two could concentrate on their A.I.'s. He had originally wanted to build a separate building, but that would be too time consuming.

"Any idea, Galen, how much it'll cost to build an A.I.?"

"The most expensive unit will be the titanium skeleton."

"Why does it have to be titanium?" she asked.

"For strength versus its own weight. There'll be very little wear and it'll last forever. I have located a company that makes human skeletons and they had done titanium with special orders. And they can also have it totally assembled."

"Would the skull be titanium also?"

"Yes."

"And the teeth?"

"They will be inserted and made from a translucent ceramic. The same as denture crowns."

"So next question, do we have enough money for a house and the A.I.?"

"As of yesterday morning, we have $11.8 million."

They looked at several properties before April had to return for work. Galen drove back to Falmouth to continue looking.

Before returning home Sunday morning he checked out one last property off the Falmouth Foreside Road. The house was empty and locked. He walked around looking in the windows. He liked what he was seeing. He wrote down all the information and called April on his cell. She was just leaving for work. "Sweetheart, I think I found the house." He told her all about it.

"You sound excited. I'm leaving for work now. Talk with you later."

There was also easy access to I-295 and only a short distance from Portland. When April was home from work, he was still excited.

"Here's the realtor's name and phone number. Can you call tomorrow and find out the particulars and how much?"

"You know property in Falmouth and that close to the ocean is going to be expensive," she said.

"The realtor should be able to send you streaming photos of the property inside and out. I'll rely on your judgment; if this appears to be what we need then make a bid and if it is accepted send a deposit electronically."

April spent her lunchbreak negotiating with the broker about the house. It looked ideal for their needs and the asking price was $1.3 million. April offered $900,000 and prepared for an immediate closing.

Ten minutes after making her offer she received a reply that the owner had accepted. April electronically sent $10,000 and she and her husband would be at the realtor's office at 10 o'clock Saturday morning.

Before leaving Skowhegan, $900,000 for a house would have seemed excessively high to April, but now with her travel from Japan, Georgia and Boston, and now Falmouth, that seemed reasonable.

That evening she showed Galen the streamed photos of the house and when she told him the asking price and how much she had offered, "and it was accepted only ten minutes later. I sent $10,000 for a deposit and said we would be at the realtors 10 o'clock Saturday morning."

At first Galen didn't say anything and she was beginning to think she had made a mistake. Then slowly he began to smile and he said, "You're something you know that."

He hugged her and kissed her and said, "I love you, April Merrill."

"I had no idea my offer would be accepted so quick. It was $400,000 less. I offered that only as a starting point."

"You did good," and he laughed.

* * *

Saturday at 10 o'clock they were sitting in the realtor's office. "Do you want to see the property before you sign any papers, Mr. Merrill?"

"I trust my wife's judgement."

A half hour later and all papers signed the realtor, Mr. Jones, referred them to a local insurance broker. At 12 noon they unlocked the door to their new home.

Part of the house had been built over a two car garage. The house was sixty years old and in real good shape.

"These two bedrooms over the garage, we can combine these two rooms and have space enough for the A.I. project. If we find we need more room later, we can remodel another room."

"I have a better idea. The basement is clean and dry, couldn't we section off half of it for our laboratory and put in a better door instead of that metal bulkhead?"

"You know, that might be best."

They had seen what they came to see and there was no since in hanging around the house so they drove to Skowhegan to see her folks and tell them about the new house. Liz had a difficult time thinking her daughter had become such a shrewd negotiator.

Gary and Millie joined them for supper. "When will you be moving to Falmouth?" Gary asked.

"As soon as I graduate and April has worked off her notice to leave.

"How is your carpentry business?"

"Good actually. I now have three full time employees and I hire dad some for finish work and cabinets."

"Any more thoughts about being a game warden?"

"Not really. I have been too busy with the business to think about anything else."

"You can say that again," Millie said. No one commented and Gary pretended he didn't hear her.

Sunday morning, Galen and April drove up to see Gary's new house. "You sure have a nice spot here, Gary."

They all had a cup of coffee and then they returned to April's folks for lunch and then back to Boston. As they were saying goodbye, Liz said, "At least in Falmouth, sweetheart, you'll be closer to home. We both are so proud of both of you."

"Maybe, Mom, when we start shopping for furniture, you and Dad can come down for a couple of days."

"We'll work on."

* * *

For the last two years, Galen had been buying electronic equipment that he knew he would have to have for the A.I. and on weekends they began moving the equipment and some of their personal items to their new house.

His days at M.I.T. were numbered now and most of his spare time he was studying for the final exams. He knew both courses by heart, but failure was not an option for him.

The final day came and all grades were posted on the bulletin board in the main hallway. Graduation ceremonies would be in two days. April called his folks and they would be there. She called her folks and they would be there also.

"Son, I hope you'll drive. I won't feel comfortable driving with so many vehicles on the road and in a big city."

"No problem, Dad. I'll drive and Millie will be my navigator."

They planned to spend one night in a Holiday Inn on the outskirts of Boston and then drive to the college in the morning.

April would meet them at the community hall.

Galen's folks were already there and Ashton said, "If you folks will follow Suki and me, we have reserved seating."

It was a long ceremony, but it was a nice day for an outside activity. Before the ceremony was underway, Ashton said, "Glad you could make it, Gary, you and Galen were always best friends."

"Yes, Mr. Merrill. I'd like you to meet my friend Millie Lambreau."

"How do you do, Ms. Lambreau. And this is my wife, Suki."

"How do you like living in Arlington Mr. Merrill?"

"The only good thing about it I don't have to do so much traveling."

The ceremonies were beginning.

Chapter 11

After the ceremonies, Ashton and Suki treated everyone. "If you'll follow us, I have made reservations for all of us at the Mistral Restaurant on Columbus Avenue."

The traffic was heavy but it was apparent Ashton knew where he was going as he maneuvered around crowded streets.

"Oh my, this is really classy," April said, "and look at all of the white linen with the green shrubbery and a yellow rose on each table. This is beautiful, Mr. Ashton."

"I couldn't think of a finer place to treat everyone. It is French/European cuisine."

"Good evening, folks. I will be your waitress and my name is Rachel. Would anyone like a drink before ordering?"

Ashton spoke up. "Yes, how about a very good chardonnay."

"A very good choice, sir."

There were eight people and Rachel brought back two bottles. She poured each glass and had to open the second bottle.

Ashton stood and said, "I'd like to make this toast to our son, Galen."

"Everyone said, "Hear, hear."

Liz stood up and said, "I'd like to make a toast to both Galen and April. May your futures and lives be as fulfilling as ours has been."

Again, everyone said, "Hear, hear."

"This is some better than your dad's whiskey, Gary," Galen said.

Everyone stopped to look at Gary and then Galen. "I thought some of the whiskey was missing," Charles said.

"When was this, Gary?" Liz asked.

"The night we caught Wilbur and Bagley. After we got back to camp after the two were summoned, we were pretty excited and we had a little whiskey to help calm us down so we could sleep."

Nothing more was said.

"When are the two of you moving to Falmouth?" Suki asked.

"I have four more days left to work. Then the next day we leave Boston," April said.

"What about you folks, Charles?" Ashton asked.

"We'll stay at the Holiday Inn where we stayed last night. And you and Suki?"

"We have a 10 o'clock flight back to D.C."

When they were saying their goodbyes, Gary said, "We have come a long way, brother and I'm glad it was you who married my sister." They shook hands then and Galen said, "I still owe you."

"No you don't, bro, just take care of my sister."

"You can count on it."

Charles and Liz knew what the boys were talking about, but Galen had never told his folks how close he had come to drowning.

* * *

The Newmans returned home and Gary went to work on Saturday to make up for the two days he was off. Don had volunteered to come to work, too.

Millie had to work Saturday morning but she was off in the afternoon and she was tired of hanging around the house waiting for Gary, so she drove over to the mall to hang out with some friends.

The exterior walls of the house were up as was the roof—

but only plywood. So Gary and Don worked on the garage and the entryway between the garage and the house.

Sunday morning after breakfast, a Donald Jalbert called and said, "Mr. Newman, this is Don Jalbert and I'd like to talk with you about building my house."

Gary agreed to meet him at his site on Rt. 201 a short distance from town. Millie went back to the shopping mall with friends.

The lot was cleared and the excavator would start digging the foundation hole the next day. It was to be a single story house twenty eight feet by forty two with three bedrooms and two by six studded exterior walls.

"When is the foundation going to be poured, Mr. Jalbert?"

"Jones Concrete said he would start on it by June 20th."

"That will work out good, Mr. Jalbert. We are finishing out one house now and will start another log house probably on Wednesday. You let me know when the foundation is in and back filled."

He had another two story log home to start in early August. And with his crew he had no doubts he would be able to get them all done before October. If he had to he would hire a couple of teenage laborers.

When he returned home, Millie was not there, so he went to visit his folks. He had lunch with them all while telling them about Mr. Jalbert's house.

"Did you ever imagine, son, you would be this busy?" his mom asked.

"Actually no, that's why I was planning on building spec houses."

They did a lot of talking about April and Galen. Then Liz asked, "What is Millie doing today?"

"I'm not sure exactly. She doesn't like it when I have to go and look at a new job on weekends and leave her home. She likes to hang out at the mall with friends."

That's all that was said about Millie.

* * *

Gary asked his dad to work with Ralph finishing the cabinets and finish work, while he, Don and Fred started the next project. Liz spent three days with April furnishing the new house and getting everything arranged, while Galen worked with a contractor to remodel half of the basement into their A.I. laboratory. Everything had to be sanitized and the walls painted with an organic based paint. Because of the fumes from the compounds and chemicals April would be using, there also had to be good ventilation. The floor was left with concrete, but it was polished and an organic finish was used to seal it.

Two weeks later the laboratory was finished. Liz stayed for three days helping April. During those three days April and her mom had time to walk around the neighborhood and down on the sandy beach.

"You have come a long way in such a short time, April. You have accomplished more already in your life than I, or many women, would ever dream of accomplishing."

After Liz left to drive home, Galen said, "Your mother is real nice."

"When do we start building the A.I.?"

"Just as soon as the laboratory is done. You understand this isn't going to be something we can build overnight. It'll take us time, especially with the first one."

"You said earlier you knew where to order the chemicals you'll need; maybe you should start getting what you'll need."

Galen already had most of the electronics that he would need and he started making the two computers for the A.I. There would be a small one situated where the brain would normally be and he called this computer the brain.

The other computer would be in the chest area. In his spare time during the last year he had been working on this computer, programming it.

"What about the nerves, Galen? Will the A.I. be able to feel?"

"Yes I have spools of very fine titanium wire that we'll run throughout the body to both computers. They will serve as tiny neurons which will transmit impulses to each computer. They'll have to be imbedded in the silicon tissue."

"I understand and I can do my part but it's the electronics where I get lost."

"I'll try to explain as we move along."

* * *

It took some time before April had all of the chemicals and compounds she would need. And finally after four months, they actually began to build the A.I.

Before Galen could do much more, he had to build a computer office in part of the empty basement space for a place for his assistant Rita Howard to work. She had agreed to move down from Skowhegan.

While he was doing this April was mixing compounds to get the correct texture for different parts of the body. Some parts had to be firmer than others, she was only mixing samples and when she had the correct texture for each, she wrote the formula down.

The sale of his Tomah program had slowed but Rita was still selling a few each day. More than enough to pay her salary.

It wasn't until December before he could earnestly start work on the A.I.

* * *

Before finishing his third house for the year, besides finishing the 1880 Barn, he contracted for two more houses. The foundations were both in and back filled and he took Fred and one laborer with him to put the decks on both. Both Mr. Reeds and Mr. Philbrook were not in any particular hurry, as long as they were finished by April. This gave him and the crew inside work for most of the winter. Once the shells were put up. Gary and crew were so busy, Charles and one laborer were doing all of the cabinet and countertop work and some of the finish. Charles was happy to think Gary needed him. He came home after work always whistling and Liz would smile, happy that he was so happy.

Gary's work and his work ethics were so good, he and his company were now building more houses than any other carpentry crew in the area.

"If this keeps up, Dad, I'll have to hire a couple more good carpenters."

"Nothing wrong with that, son."

Gary and crew stayed busy all through the winter months and he already had two more Katahdin Log Homes contracted to build and near the end of April he said, "Don, I have to leave for a few hours to look at another job. You have the crew, Don, any problem?"

"No, Boss, none. Go ahead and line up more work for us."

"Where is this one, Boss?" Fred asked.

"Madison Avenue—actually in Madison halfway up Rowell Hill," he said.

"Is it another Katahdin Home?" Don asked.

"Yes, but as I understand the front will be flagstone siding. I should be back by 1 o'clock."

As he drove by the Towne Motel on the left side of Madison Avenue, he thought for sure he had seen Millie's red Toyota car parked just beyond the office. He only had a glimpse of the car. It could have been one like hers.

He continued on and Mr. O'Dell was there waiting. "Good morning, Mr. O'Dell."

They shook hands and O'Dell said, "Please call me Doug."

He unfolded the blueprints on his car hood. "This is going to be a larger house than I thought. When will you have the foundation in and backfilled?"

"It is scheduled to be done by June 1st. The package is scheduled to be delivered from Oakfield on June 5th. I hope that will work for you, Gary?"

"That'll work out good for us, Doug. I can't give you a quote right now. I'll have to take these prints home and study them. Are you going to be here tomorrow morning?"

"I can be. What time?"

"Would 9 o'clock be okay? That'll give me enough time to get my men started."

"That'll work."

On his way by the Towne Motel, he slowed. The red car was not there. The beauty salon where Millie worked was on the right before he made the lefthand turn onto High Street. Her car was there. He couldn't remember now if her car had been there earlier when he went through. He guessed he wouldn't say anything about it. Not yet.

At home that evening, Millie was awful quiet. And Gary had the blueprints to look over and come up with a satisfactory quote. He purposely kept it high. If Doug objected, he could always sharpen his pencil. He worked on the plans until after midnight.

Millie had gone to bed hours earlier without saying a word. When he tried to cuddle up to her backside she pushed him away and said, "Sleep on your own side."

The next morning Millie got up without Gary and fixed breakfast. "I think I picked up another project. I'll have to go and talk with him today and give him my quote."

"You're getting more work all the time," she said.

"It's getting better."

He kissed her goodbye and left. The crew were just arriving. He worked an hour with them and then left to meet with Mr. O'Dell.

"Good morning, Gary. Looks like it is going to be another nice day."

"That it is." He gave O'Dell his quote and Doug looked it over for several minutes before commenting.

"I think I can live with this okay, Gary."

He went back to help with the crew. The red car was not at the motel.

The next morning he excused himself and said, "I have to tend to something, Don. I won't be long."

It was 10 o'clock when he left the jobsite and as he was approaching the motel he saw Millie and a guy kissing and hugging by her open driver's door. He pulled in behind her.

She immediately recognized the pickup and said, "Oh shit."

Gary shut his truck off and got out and stood by the hood of his pickup. He wanted to be mad as hell, but instead he kept his cool and said, "I have suspected for a while now you were seeing someone else. I want your keys to my house, now."

She took 'em off her keyring and tossed them to him. "I'll set everything you have at my house out in front of the garage. She's all yours." And he drove home and began putting her belongings in cardboard boxes and setting them in front of the garage. Then he went back to work.

When he got home that evening her things were all gone.

After eating, he sat outside in the cool evening air. He was already missing Millie, but he wasn't going to put up with any woman who couldn't be faithful. He didn't love her, but he did like her a lot. And she was good in bed.

The next couple of days, Don knew there was something wrong, but he respected Gary enough not to ask. He had heard rumors about Millie seeing other men but he had kept the rumors to himself. After all, as far as he knew that's all they were. Now there was something wrong and he was not getting involved.

* * *

Gary had breakfast with his folks Saturday morning. "Where's Millie? Is she working?" his mother asked.

"I really don't know. Three days ago I caught her with someone else and I told her to take her things and go."

"I never approved of her living with you and not married," his mother said.

"I needed someone to help out around the house and I really liked her. Plus she was good in bed."

"Well, she's gone now and I'm glad of that."

"Now, Liz, you can't run his life. He feels bad enough without you adding to it."

"I'm sorry, son. I'll say no more."

"How's work going son?" Charles asked.

"Good, I picked up another job Tuesday in Madison half-way up Rowell Hill. A Mr. Douglas O'Dell. It's a big house too."

"Are you going to have to hire more help?"

"Probably another laborer or two."

"When will you be ready for some cabinet work?"

"I'm not sure. This house we are currently about to finish, the owner has already bought prebuilt cabinets. But O'Dell wants his handmade."

"I'm taking your mother out to dinner tonight at Lakewood Restaurant and opening night for the theatre. Would you like to join us?"

"No, you go ahead and have a good time. I don't think I'd be much company."

After finishing breakfast Gary went home to wash his clothes.

* * *

Galen and April had been working on the A.I. for nearly six months now, and April had the body done and Galen was finishing the electronics, which was more time consuming than he had thought it would be.

"What do you think now, sweetheart, looking at the full body?"

"I like it. The skin texture is just like ours. No one would be able to tell the difference."

"My mother called earlier and said Gary and Millie broke up."

"What happened?"

"She didn't say. I hope he is okay. He needs a good woman, sweetheart," and she began thinking.

* * *

Gary went down to the diner for supper. Not being too hungry he had a grilled cheese sandwich and a bowl of clam chowder.

Then he went home and walked out back. He began blaming himself. If he hadn't always been so busy with his new carpentry business and had spent more time with Millie, then perhaps she wouldn't have seen other men. He tried to convince himself of that, but in reality he knew sooner or later, she would have strayed.

He turned around and walked back to his house. There was a breeze and the air was cool. Just as he was walking across the yard towards the house, Sheriff Butler drove in.

"Hello, Sheriff, what brings you up this way?"

"Gary, I hate to tell you this, but your mom and dad were in an automobile accident this evening."

"Oh my God! What happened? Are they okay, Sheriff?"

"No, they're not okay, Gary. They both died instantly at the scene."

"What happened?"

"Where were they going, Gary? They were both all dressed up."

"They were going to Lakewood for dinner and then the theatre."

"About halfway up Rowell Hill a pickup truck crossed the center line and hit your folks. The State Police were called in to reconstruct the scene and they determined that the other vehicle, the pickup truck, must have been traveling about 90mph."

"What about that driver?"

"He died also."

"Who was it?"

"Jason Fenmore from Portland.

"I'm really sorry, Gary. This must come as a real shock. I liked both your mom and dad. Is there anything I can do for you?"

"No. Where are their bodies now?"

"In the morgue. All three bodies are there. There will have to be an autopsy done. Once the M.E. is finished, he'll release the bodies to the funeral parlor. The funeral director will get in touch with you when he has the bodies."

"How long will that take?"

"The autopsies will be performed tomorrow. So, you'll probably hear from the funeral director Monday morning."

"Thank you, Sheriff."

"I'm sorry, Gary. This must come as quite a blow."

"It does."

He went inside and sat down at the kitchen bar. He was wondering whether he should call his sister now or wait until morning. Let her and Galen get a good night sleep. But by then reports of the accident would be all over the news. No, he had to do it now.

He punched in her number on his cell phone and she answered on the first ring. "Hello, Gary. I'm surprised you'd call so late."

"Sis, is Galen there with you?"

"Yes, he's sitting beside me. What's up, Gary?"

"Put your phone on speaker."

"Okay—you're scaring me, Gary."

"April, Galen—Mom and Dad were in a fatal car accident this evening."

April started crying. "What happened, Gary?" Galen asked.

"They were on their way to Lakewood for dinner and the theatre. Halfway up Rowell Hill a driver crossed the center line and into the folks."

"Where are the bodies now, Gary?"

"They are at the morgue. The M.E. will do an autopsy tomorrow. Then they will be released to the funeral director and he will call me then. And then we can make plans."

"I don't know what to say, Gary. They were always like family to me. We'll be up tomorrow, Gary."

He could hear his sister crying in the background. "Galen, is April going to be okay?"

"It comes as quite a shock to us both. I'll take care of her, Gary."

"I'll be at Mom and Dad's house tomorrow. I love you guys. Take care," and he hung up.

He just sat on the couch for a long time, feeling so sorry for his sister. It's bad enough to lose a parent, but to lose both at the same time can be devastating.

He was tired and he knew he'd never be able to sleep. And he didn't want to sit in the dark, so with lights on he lay back on the couch, feeling sorry for himself. First he finds his live-in girlfriend with another man and she's gone, and then he loses his mom and dad. *This has been one hell of a week.*

Then he started to laugh and cry at the same time as he said, "Mom—Dad, you were dressed in nice evening attire. First to dinner and the opening of the Lakewood Theatre. You had dressed to attend the greatest play of your lives. I have no idea where you are now, but at least you didn't have to take the trip alone. And you're dressed for the greatest play ever written."

He closed his eyes then and began seeing family events as he and April were growing up. Come 3 o'clock he was able to sleep for a couple of hours.

Galen was as distraught as April, but for her sake he had to remain supportive for his wife. They went to bed eventually and he held her in his arms all night. Eventually she cried herself to sleep and Galen, he managed to sleep a couple of hours like Gary.

Gary woke up about 5:30 and he was hungry. Thinking Galen and April would leave their home early, he decided to wait on breakfast until they were here.

He was still dressed so he went for a walk out back to clear his head. He had built his house almost to the back line and he had not had the time to clear a hiking trail through the bushes. So he drove down to his folks home and walked out back.

He walked straight out to the back line and back again. There was a lot of pent up nervous energy in him and instead of making the hike again and risk missing April and Galen, he went inside and made a pot of coffee.

When it was done, he poured a cup of black coffee and went out on the patio to wait. It was eighty-five miles to Falmouth, an easy hour and a half of driving. They should be here before 9 o'clock. At quarter of he'd start making breakfast for all of them.

By 8:45 he had ham and scrambled eggs ready to go on the stove. Five minutes later they drove in the yard. He walked out to greet them and April ran into his arms and started crying again. While he was holding her, he shook Galen's hand. "Come in, coffee is hot and I was about to start ham and scrambled eggs."

They sat at the bar counter and Gary poured the coffee. "I'll have some coffee, but I don't know if I could eat anything or not," April said.

"You must try to eat some, sweetheart," Galen said.

"Sis, will you make some toast?" He thought giving her something to do might take her mind off losing her folks.

"On the way up I called my folks and told them about dad and mom and they are flying up today."

"Where's Millie, Gary?"

"She's gone. Last Wednesday I found her at a motel with another man."

"You need you a good woman, Gary, a wife. If you weren't going to marry her, why did you have her move in with you?"

"She was good in bed."

April then realized she had asked a stupid question.

"These eggs are good, Gary," Galen said. "Your cooking has improved since we were kids."

"Have you looked for their will yet?" she asked.

"No, I wanted to wait until you were here. I know pretty much what it says. One day on the job, it was just dad and me and he told me about the will.

"It will be in the safe and the combination is on a file card in his top desk drawer. The executor is Attorney Troy Billings and everything is left to you and me equally. I don't know how much money they had."

"What happens next?" she asked.

"Once the M.E. has finished, he will notify the funeral director at the Howell Funeral Parlor and he will pick the bodies up. We'll have to go talk with him and make plans for the funeral. And we'll have to go see Attorney Billings."

They finished eating and cleaned up, then they found the safe combination and opened it. There was a strong box which was not locked which contained all the important documents they and the executor would need. Plus $10,000.00 in cash. "His emergency funds. He told me once I should keep some ready cash."

"Did you ever know what their net worth was, Gary?"

"No, idea.

"Well, here's a start. This is their savings book and according to this there is $653,149.17."

"I had no idea."

"There's a little over $41,000.00 in the checking. No stocks, no bonds and no life insurance.

"Their will is in here also." She looked at it and said, "It's as you said, Gary."

"All of those documents should be given to the executor," Galen said.

"We'll take the entire strong box and everything in it. Here you hold this box, Gary. I'll see what else is in here."

The three of them spent the rest of the weekend looking over everything Charles and Liz had. And they spent a long time looking at family photos. Once in a while they would be interrupted with a phone call. Friends wanting to express their condolences.

"April, can you write an obituary?"

"I'd like to and I'll get started on it now."

"While you're doing that, I need to see my foreman about me not being around much this week."

"Sweetheart, while you're working on that, I'm going outside."

"Okay."

After spending most of the day together and talking, all three slept better Saturday night. Galen telephoned their assistant, Rita Howard, "Rita, both of my wife's parents were killed in a motor vehicle accident Friday night. We may not be back in Falmouth until next weekend. Can you take care of everything?"

"Of course I can. And tell April I'm so sorry."

"Thanks, Rita."

He called his folks next. "Just checking to see if you were in yet or not."

"We landed in Waterville yesterday. How is April?"

Galen thought about that for a minute. He wasn't aware there was a landing strip that would accommodate a passenger jetliner. Then he thought about who his dad worked for and without question he probably flew a small company jet. And he probably had a rental car waiting for him before he landed.

"Friday night and yesterday were pretty hard on her. She's doing better today."

"Good, why don't you two and Gary and Millie come down for dinner, about 6 o'clock."

"We would like to, Dad. Millie won't be coming. They split."

"See you at 6 o'clock," his father said.

Gary returned a few minutes after Galen's call to his folks.

"Everything okay with your foreman, Gary?"

"Yes, actually I think he likes it when I have to leave. It gives him some responsibility. He's a good carpenter and worker."

"I called my father. They are here now and asked us to supper tonight."

* * *

At the Merrill's home for supper, both Gary and Galen were surprised how compassionate and caring they were. Galen was thinking in that brief moment how much both his mother and father have changed since moving to D.C. He concluded that it might have something to do with his father being home every evening now, not off in some hostile country gathering information.

Their housekeeper/sitter, Arlene Gilbert, even sat down to supper with them. This really surprised Galen. But he understood enough not to say anything.

Gary and Galen both were surprised with the interest Ashton was showing to Gary about his carpentry business. "I understand, Gary, that you are doing very good in the building industry. When I retire, maybe I'll hire you to build us a log house like your folk's house."

"Are you planning on moving back to Skowhegan after you retire?" he asked.

"This is our home; we both were born and raised here."

"I'd be happy to."

After supper, Suki said, "You all are welcome to stay here tonight—but I think you'd prefer Charles and Liz's home."

"Yes we would, Mom, but thank you. As soon as we know when the funeral will be, I'll let you know."

* * *

Monday morning, Gary didn't go to the worksite. He

171

had that much confidence with Don's ability. At 9 o'clock he telephoned Troy Billings and asked if they could come in and talk with him. "Can you be here at 10 o'clock?"

"We'll be there."

"Come in please and sit down. First, I'd like to say how sorry I am about your mom and dad. I liked them both. They were good people."

"Thank you, Mr. Billings, I believe you are our folks' executor."

"Yes, that is correct. It is rather simple, their entire estate is left to you both. But nothing can be done with any of it until the will passes probate, which I do not believe will be a problem.

"I haven't seen you around Skowhegan for a while, Mr. Merrill."

"When I finished college, we moved to Falmouth."

"I should have your address and telephone numbers."

"Certainly," April said. And April handed the strong box to Billings. "We have gone through everything and the only papers or documents we could find are in this box. There is also $10,000.00 in the box."

"I'll give you a receipt for the money. This can not be turned over to you either until after probate.

"I will need your telephone number also, Mr. Newman."

"We noticed a codicil in the will, Mr. Billings, that both bodies are to be cremated. Who do we see about that?" Gary asked.

"The funeral director. Will you be using the Howell Funeral Parlor?"

"Yes," April said.

"He will also see that their obituary gets to the newspaper. Do you have anything written up yet?"

"Yes, I have it with me," April said.

"Okay, your first step should be to talk with a church if that is how you want to go. Get a date set then go to the funeral parlor and talk with Mr. Howell.

"Is there anything else I can help you with?"

"Not at this time."

"I will let you know when the will has cleared probate. Again I'm sorry and I, as well as Skowhegan, will miss them."

They next met with Reverend Hall at the Methodist Church and scheduled the services for 11 o'clock Saturday morning.

From there they had lunch at the diner. Then they stopped at the funeral parlor. Mr. Howell said, "Both bodies have already been released and I'll see to it that they are taken to the crematory in Bangor. The ashes won't be back for the services, but when I have them, Gary, I'll telephone you.

"They both wanted their ashes spread in Mom's flower garden by the house," April said.

Both Gary and Galen said, "That will be a good place."

From Billing's office, they went to the Howell Funeral Parlor. "You won't have to worry about any of the arrangements. My staff and I will take care of everything. Would you have a large photo of the two together?"

"Yes there is one."

"You might bring that a half hour before the service. A catering service will feed everyone next door to the church."

"Let's go home, fellas, I'm drained," April said.

"I'll make some sandwiches and coffee, why don't you two go in the living room," April said.

"Do you like Falmouth, Galen?"

"Yes, but we have been so busy we haven't had time to see much.

"You know, Gary, I quite often think about that night when we caught those poachers. I never felt so alive as I did that night. If it wasn't for my computer business, I think I would enjoy being a game warden."

"I think a lot of that night, too, and I often think what it would be like to be a game warden. There's one problem. Like you, Galen, I really enjoy building houses and the money is good. But I do dream about what it would be like."

They talked for a few minutes about growing up in Skowhegan before April said lunch was ready.

As they were eating, out of the blue, April said, "Gary, you need yourself a good woman, a wife."

"Well if you find one give her my number," and he laughed.

Afterwards they sat in the living room talking. "Gary, do you have any ideas how to divide things? There is $667,149.17 in the bank and safe."

"I think we should own the Tomah camp jointly and I'd really like to have this house. My place is already too small. This house and property should be worth between $150,000.00 and $200,000.00. I'd like $100,000.00 and you can have the rest. How's that?"

"I think that is more than fair."

"What do you think, sweetheart?" she asked Galen.

"I agree, I think that is more than fair."

"Well, that was easy."

"If you two will excuse me for a while I think I should go check on my crew."

"You go ahead, Gary; April and I will take a walk out back."
I'd go for that."

They walked holding hands up across the field. "Mom and Dad used to walk up here often. I'm a little surprised they didn't want their ashes spread here."

"Maybe they thought by having them spread in your mother's flower garden, the house might remain in the family."

"I like how you think, sweetheart."

"I'm worried about Gary."

"How so? He seems okay to me."

"When we leave after the funeral he will be here alone. And between losing Millie and Mom and Dad, everything might come crashing down all at once. All he has is his work."

"And he is too busy working to find a good woman. Unless—?"

She interrupted him there and finished his sentence for him. "Unless we make one for him. We could do that couldn't we? We have the female skeleton. We know how to do it faster now without so many problems."

"I think you're onto something, sweetheart. She would be loyal and never run out on him."

"What about an emotional program, or pleasure? What about sex?"

"I can add an emotional and pleasure program into the computer. Can you make a vagina?"

"That won't be difficult. I'll make a mold and mix up a special silicon compound and mold it to the form."

"Then let's make a woman for Gary."

"We can't say anything to him or he would say, not on your life!"

"I have an idea after we take Frances to D.C. soon, then we can get started on her."

"Then maybe a year from now we can invite Gary to take a vacation with us and introduce him to—how about Nicole for a name?"

"Sounds good to me."

"We could say she is a friend from college visiting us."

"Boy, will he be surprised."

All during the conversation with his wife about a female A.I. for Gary, had for a few minutes, made her stop grieving for her mom and dad. She was happy again. He hugged her and she said, "Let's make love right here, sweetheart. I think it would help to clear my head."

"I'm all for that. It'll clear my head too."

* * *

Gary went to work the next day only until noon. The crew were doing an excellent job. He worked all the next day and

Galen and April spent most of the day with his folks.

April was able to find a large photo of their mom and dad and Saturday morning when they arrived at to the church there were a few people already there. When Galen's folks arrived they sat with Gary, April and Galen in front. The church was filling fast. When the service began people were standing along both sides of the room.

When the reverend had finished everyone went next door to the reception and the Newmans and Merrills stayed behind. Then after a few minutes Ashton and Suki left, leaving the three to say their last goodbyes.

April started crying and Galen hugged her. "I don't know if I can face all those people, Galen," she said.

Eventually the three joined the rest of the mourners and were even able to eat a little. Once April began talking with people she knew, old friends, she was much better.

It was a tiring day and Ashton and Suki asked them to their house for some wine. No one was really hungry.

"We'll be leaving for D.C. in the morning, son," Ashton said.

"Both of us are happy you could make it."

"Yes, thank you so much," April said.

Later back at the Newman house, Galen said, "We should be leaving in the morning also."

"Will you be okay, Gary?" She was more worried about her brother than herself. "I mean, Galen and I have each other and you'll be left alone."

"I'll be okay, Sis. When the ashes arrive, I'll wait to spread them until you are here."

Galen called his dad on his cell. "Hello, Dad, what time are you and Mom leaving in the morning?"

"We leave the house at 10 o'clock why?"

"I need to talk with you before you leave. I'll be there at 9 o'clock."

Later the three sat up for a while talking. Mostly about their childhood and growing up. And Galen was always included in the talks.

Finally, April said, "I need to go to bed. Goodnight, Gary."

"Me too," Galen said.

"I'll see you in the morning." He waited until they had their bedroom door closed and he went outside. He sat on the patio looking at the stars. They were bright tonight.

To keep his mind from thinking of his mom and dad or Millie, he tried to think about work. Just before midnight, he lay down on the couch in the living room without taking his clothes off.

He spent a fitful night. He slept alright, but he kept seeing imagines of Millie and then his folks He was awake at 6 o'clock and he got up and made a pot of coffee, Galen and April would soon be up.

At 9 o'clock Galen knocked on his folk's house side door. "Come in, son."

"Dad, I need to talk to you alone."

"Okay we'll go out on the porch. Your mother is upstairs packing."

"Now what is this all about, son?"

"Dad, April and I have built something that we would like to sell to the C.I.A. And we need your help to set up a meeting for us."

"Can you tell me what you have?"

"I could but I'd rather not."

"Would it have anything to do with A.I.?"

"Yes, but how did you know?"

"I'm your father, son, and I remember how you used to talk when you were a teenager."

"Okay, but will you keep this to yourself?"

"Sure, I'll help. I'll talk with the director and the deputy director in charge of foreign affairs."

"That's all I can ask. You won't be disappointed. There will be three of us to give the presentation."

"Who is the third person?"

"Frances Dubois, an associate."

"I'll get back to you before the end of the week. Are you sure about this?"

"Oh, quite sure."

"I'll see if I can set up a meeting as soon as possible."

"Thanks, Dad. And I'd better get back now. Have a good trip back."

* * *

On their way home, Galen told April what he had talked with his father about. "Will he help us?"

"Yes, and he has known all along we were working on an A.I." And he told her how his father knew.

After April and Galen left, Gary went back to his house on the hill to do some laundry. He had decided to sell this house once his folks' will was through probate and move into the folks' house. But until then he would stay at his house. That is until the house brought back too many memories of Millie.

Not being able to shake those memories, after his laundry was done he went back to the other house and the memories of his mom and dad. This being alone is going to be difficult.

He was missing his sister and Galen already. He moped around all afternoon and then in the evening he went for a walk out back.

For supper all he had was a can of soup. He was hungry but he knew he couldn't eat. He was on the patio until midnight and up early in the morning.

He ate a slice of buttered toast and coffee and then he went to work. And he was having a hard time to keep his thoughts on work. At 10 o'clock, Don said, "Gary, what's the matter man? You're walking around and trying to work but your mind isn't here. Between your woman screwing someone else and your folks dying, it's an awful load to carry. And Gary, you aren't doing yourself or the crew any good here pretending to work. Why don't you take the week off, go up to the Tomah camp for a while and get your head screwed on right. Then come back next week. Me and the boys have got this."

"Maybe you're right, Don. I'm not doing anyone any good here."

"I'll have my cell phone with me. Call if you get in a bind.

"And Don, Thanks."

Chapter 12

Gary made sure his house was locked up and then he packed a few clothes and locked the house and headed north to Tomah Stream.

Being alone on the road wasn't helping his mental state. His thoughts were revolving from Millie to his mom and dad. He turned on the radio to a country western station. That helped for about five minutes.

At 2:30 p.m. he pulled into the IGA parking lot in Lincoln where he bought bread, milk, a variety of canned goods and a half gallon of whiskey.

At 4 o'clock he shut his pickup off at camp. The peaceful surroundings were having a quieting effect on him and he unloaded his pickup. He was hungry so he warmed up a can of Dinty Moore beef stew.

Then he mixed a whiskey and water drink and sat outside in the warm sunshine.

* * *

Galen received a call on his cell phone from his father Monday at noon. "Son, I have the meeting set for you on Friday at 10 a.m. I know it's short notice but the only other date would be in July."

"We'll make it, Dad. We'll be at your house on Thursday. If that's okay, there'll be three of us. Frances Dubois, our associate."

"That'll be fine, son."

"Thanks, Dad."

"We have our meeting sweetheart on Friday."

"How are we going to travel, Frances can't get through the metal detectors?" April asked.

"One of two ways. We can hire a private jet or we could buy a new Cadillac SUV. I'll leave it up to you."

Without hesitation she said, "The new SUV. Let's get a matching red one like my Rav 4."

"At the same time, we can pickup some clothes for Frances."

"How should we dress?"

"This is a business meeting and I'll let you explain about plastic reconstruction. So I'd say an elegant pant suit."

"How much are you going to ask?"

"I thought about $3M. We may have to lower it some. But that's a good starting point."

"I'd say."

"I'm going to try Gary and see how he is doing."

"Do you think he might think that you are checking up on him? What I mean is maybe you should wait until tomorrow. After all, it has only been one day."

"I know, but I feel so bad for him. He has no one to turn to. We have each other."

"I still think you should wait for tomorrow."

"Okay."

"When do we leave?"

"Tomorrow."

"When do we buy the new car?"

"Let's go now."

* * *

Gary finished his drink and mixed another. And he drank that one much faster than he should have. But still he mixed another. He sat down and began sipping. "I thought alcohol was supposed to make you forget your troubles and make you feel better. I don't." He finished that drink, his third.

Now he had to go to the bathroom. He didn't feel like eating, so after the bathroom he went back outside and began walking the gravel road away from camp.

He didn't follow the road very far before he turned around and went back to camp. He was mad as hell at Millie and he was really missing his mom and dad.

The sun was beginning to set and he sat on the couch starring at the floor, wishing he could just go to sleep, and for a few hours at least forget his loneliness. "Maybe another drink will help me to sleep."

He sat at the kitchen table now with another whiskey and water. He closed his eyes trying to block out images of Millie. But that only led to more memories of his folks.

That drink gone he staggered outside to pee. Then he mixed another drink and sat on the couch now. For someone who had never drank much alcohol he had now consumed five drinks and his vision was blurry. His eyes were jumping all over the place. *I think the whiskey is working. I stopped thinking of what's her name and my folks are home and probably sleeping now,* he thought.

"One more drink and I might be able to fall asleep."

This one he drank back at the kitchen table. He chugalugged that drink and stumbled his way to the couch and lay down. That was a mistake even with his eyes closed everything started spinning round and round. Even when he opened his eyes, the spinning was worse.

Then he felt sick and he knew he was going to vomit and he stumbled to the toilet just in time. He retched and retched until his stomach was empty and then he had the dry heaves and those were even worse. He sat on the floor with his head over the toilet bowl.

After awhile the retching stopped and he made it back to the couch and lay down and passed out.

The S&L train went through the Tomah crossing, less than a half mile away and blew its loud air horn. This startled Gary awake and he rolled onto the floor. "Oh man, what time is it?" He looked at his watch. "6:30. Oh man my stomach hurts and so does my head." And he was thirsty. He made it back on the couch. At least things had stopped spinning.

As he lay there moaning, he hoped his crews were getting along okay. No thoughts yet of Millie or his folks. He got up eventually. He had to pee and he was thirsty. But his stomach still ached and he knew he'd never be able to eat anything and keep it down. "I guess this is what's called a hangover."

He drank some water and then fixed a cup of coffee. The hot fluid felt good in his stomach. "How much did I drink last night?" and he looked at the half empty, half gallon bottle of whiskey. He poured what was left down the sink. "I don't want anymore of that."

Mentally he was feeling better, but his stomach and head were still hurting. "I need some fresh air," so he left to walk to the end of the dirt road.

It was a nice day with a little breeze. There were times when he was in the shelter of trees on both side of the road and the blackflies swarmed around him. He walked by where the two poachers had killed the moose, almost ten years ago now and the area was growing up.

Beyond the old kill site, he came to their property line. Well painted with orange paint. The old log landing was growing back to bushes and someone had cut up all the hardwood short ends for firewood.

He found deer and moose tracks in the mud, but no bear tracks. He was thankful for that. He sat on an old stump for a few minutes enjoying the day and fresh air. His headache was gone and his stomach was feeling better.

His cellphone rang. The caller I.D. said April. "Hello, April."

"Hi, Gary. How are you doing?"

"I'm feeling better."

"Are you at work?"

"No, I'm at camp."

"Why on earth are you at camp? I thought you'd be at work."

"I needed to get away and clear my head."

"Is it working?"

"Well I got falling down drunk last night and passed out. I got up this morning with an awful hangover, but somehow it also cleared my head. I'm feeling pretty good about things now. Except for my stomach. It is still a little upset."

"Well, I must say you sound cheerful. But you should dump the whiskey."

"Already have. I'm going to stay another day or two and go home."

"Gary, Galen and I left this morning for D.C. We're driving down. I'll call again when we're back."

"Have a good trip."

"He's sounding pretty chipper for someone suffering with a hangover," Galen said.

Hearing from his sister improved his mental outlook and he started back to camp. When he reached the old kill site, he left the road to look at the ground where the remains had been. There was nothing there now. Not even a piece of hide or bone.

He decided to walk down to the stream and follow that back to camp.

Two hundred feet away from the kill site he found a puddle of black ooze. His first thoughts were someone had changed the oil in a skidder and left it. But there hadn't been any equipment in there for more than eleven years. And besides this was Newman land.

He looked closer and he saw a bubble rise to the surface and pop. He touched it with a finger and it felt like oil. He smelled of it and it had an oily smell. "Well, I'll be to go to hell! This is crude oil."

He stood up and looked for their property lines. He couldn't see it. So he knew he was well within the Newman property.

Instead of hiking through the woods back to camp he ran up the road for several glass Mason jars his mother always kept in one of the base cabinets. He put four pint jars in a bucket and returned to the site.

He filled the four jars and wiped off the drippings with his handkerchief. Back at camp he dipped a piece of kindling in one jar. Just the tip and only a little oil and then he tried to light it with a match. It burned and he grinned.

While he was eating another can of soup, he decided to drive home tonight. He hadn't thought about Millie all day and he had finally accepted the passing of his mom and dad. *I will always have loving memories of you.*

As he drove, he was excited and he wanted to tell April and Galen but he didn't like the idea of putting something this important over the air. Someone might be listening.

* * *

When he showed up at work the next morning, the crew and Don especially were surprised. "We all thought you'd be gone all week. Welcome back. You get everything worked out?"

"Yeah, I had to get drunk and pass out to do it. I'm okay now though.

"I'm impressed how much you guys have done."

As they were working, Don asked, "What are you going to do with your house on the hill?"

"Sell it."

"How much?"

"Are you interested? If you are I'll use you a little better."

"Yes I am, while you were gone I took my wife and kid up to look at it.

"Would you consider $60,000.00? That's all furnished, too"

"In a heartbeat."

"Can you come up with the money?"

"No problem with my wife working, too. On the chance you would sell, I think I have ours already sold."

"Sounds good, Don. You let me know when you want the closing."

* * *

Galen, April and Frances arrived at his folk's house Thursday at noon. Frances had actually helped out with some driving. Ashton didn't get home from the office until 6 o'clock.

"Dad, this is Frances Dubois, my father, Ashton Merrill."

They shook hands and Frances said, "Pleased to meet you, sir."

After dinner, Galen said, "We three have been on the road and we probably should call it a night."

As they were lying in bed, April said, "Do your mom and dad suspect anything with Frances?"

"I don't think so."

At breakfast the three ate sparingly and no coffee. They didn't want to have to go to the bathroom in the middle of the presentation.

"My, you three look like you were some high priced business executives," Suki said.

"In a way, Mom, we are. We have to sell the company on what we have in our briefcases."

Ashton looked at Galen and smiled and said, "I have no worries about you three. Just go at it like you did last time, son."

"Probably it would be better if you follow me," Ashton said.

Frances said, "Thank you for your hospitality, Mrs. Merrill." Then he took her hand and instead of shaking it, he kissed the back of her hand. Suki turned a faint shade of pink.

It wasn't a long drive but the traffic was unusually heavy. But they were there on time.

"Gentlemen, I'd like you to meet my son and his wife, Galen and April, and their associate Frances Dubois. This is the Director of C.I.A., Boyd Wilson and Deputy Director of Foreign Activity and Intelligence, Bruce Rynheart."

All three said at the same time, "Gentlemen."

"As you requested, we have a large digitron screen," Wilson said.

Galen downloaded his disc and said, "Gentlemen we have an actual functioning A.I. that we would like to sell to you. I'll let my wife April do the presentation with an overview of the fleshy body. April."

She brought up a schematic of the skeleton structure and then the silicon forms she used to make the body. "I used a silicon base to make the different body parts. Different places of the body have a different skin texture, so I had to use different compounds to create the correct toughness of, let's say the arm, hands, legs, ears and feet. The entire body is then finished with a special compound that when it adheres to the silicon it will feel just like skin. The skeletal head is also made in this same manner."

She went on to explain how the silicon forms were attached to the skeleton. "And the teeth are actual denture inserts. The mouth is also a composition of silicon and the tongue and throat. The silicon must breathe and it must be kept lubricated. And Mr. Dubois will get to that."

Ashton was proud of his daughter-in-law April. He thought she had given an excellent presentation. She was precise and didn't stumble for words, nor did she keep repeating herself.

"Gentlemen, my name is Frances Dubois, and as Mrs. Merrill said, the silicon compounds and forms have to be lubricated. So our A.I.'s drink and eat. Minerals from the food dissolve in water and Mrs. Merrill purposely made the forms porous so that water moves as a mist consistently along with nutrients, will work or flow throughout the body. The A.I.'s body will tell itself when it is time to eliminate the liquid and excrements. There are filters within the body that filters the water the same as kidneys do. The filters will flush themselves and the impurities are expelled in the excrement."

"Thanks, Mr. Dubois," Galen said as he stood up. "I studied advanced computer technology and electronics and I graduated with master degrees in each. It has always been my life's ambition to build an A.I.

"The skeleton is titanium and all movements are preformed with electrical components. We tried to make the A.I. as life-like as possible.

"There are actually two computers, one in the head which we call the brain and one in the chest. The brain accumulates data, processes it and sends signals to the chest, what it is to do. All this happens as fast as humans can think and respond."

"What form of electrical energy do you use?" Director Wilson asked.

"There is a lithium battery here," and he pointed to it on the screen. "There is also a rectenna in the head."

"I'm not familiar with this rectenna," Deputy Director Rynheart said.

"The atmosphere is filled with electromagnetic waves of energy. There is a special antenna disguised as hair; there are three hairs made of very fine gray titanium. These antenna receive the electromagnetic energy and sends them inside the skull to a convertor which converts the energy to 24 volt A.C.

"Since there is always electromagnetic waves of energy in the atmosphere this power source is always working, recharging the lithium battery.

"This power source is sufficient to power the computers and recharge the battery. When more energy is required such as if the A.I. had to run, fight or lift heavy objects a nuclear chip, battery, will automatically come online."

"What is the active life span of the chip?"

"I was told under these circumstances, ten years."

"There are titanium neurons that attach to all of the body parts and when the computer activates a particular neuron that body part will act much like our own muscles. But it can't do it all so that's when the power chips kick in."

Galen went on to explain the vision, hearing and speech capacity of the A.I. "There is one point I'd like to emphasize, our A.I. has the ability to speak and understand English, Russian and Chinese. If you wanted, let's say Arabic, you would simply insert an Arabic program chip in the chest computer." And he pointed to a hidden opening in the chest area, on the screen.

"I believe while we have been explaining how our A.I. works you have been able to see how useful it would be for the company, particularly in your foreign activities and intelligence department.

"How tall is the A.I. and how much does it weigh?" the director asked.

"Mr. Dubois, you can answer that," and Galen slightly nodded and smiled. Dubois nodded back and smiled. Ashton saw this exchange and he understood and he had all he could do not to burst out laughing.

"Gentlemen, I am five feet and eleven inches tall and I weigh one hundred and sixty-five pounds."

Ashton couldn't hold it back any longer. He burst out laughing. And after a hesitant moment the others did also.

Then they all wanted to touch Dubois and feel the texture of his skin. "You certainly had us baffled, Mr. Merrill. He could pass in any crowd as just another human."

"That's precisely the point, Mr. Director."

"Now, if you'll let me finish, there is a little more. Mr. Dubois is also equipped with his own e-mail capabilities, within the hair are antenna for e-mail and the internet. In any circumstances, he can communicate with his handler and vise-versa, at a moments notice. He can also use the internet for research and information gathering. And this system is also protected with the Tomah 2 security program.

"There is, however, one drawback. Because of his titanium structure, he could never fly commercial and pass through a metal detector or screening. Unless previous arrangements had been made with the airline.

"How long did it take you to build Mr. Dubois?" his father asked.

"Building an A.I. has always been a dream of mine for ten years now. While in college I worked on computer 3D schematics and gathering necessary components. Once we were able to start building, we were a year building and testing. At first there were a few minor problems that had to be overcome, but now Mr. Dubois functions 100%.

"I might add we possess a patent on the A.I." Galen said.

"Okay," Director Wilson said, "I think you have sold us and we all know in our business how useful A.I.'s could be. My next question, Mr. Merrill, how much?"

Without any hesitation Galen said, "Three million dollars."

"We'll need time to think this over," the director said.

"You have until 10 o'clock tomorrow morning. If we do not hear from you by then, we'll assume you are not interested and we'll return home."

Ashton was chuckling to himself. He suspected after Galen sold his Tomah 2 program to the government, that he would have a similar response here. And he did.

"Let's say we agree to this price and if we want another one, how long would it take you?"

"We are currently working on another but for different reasons. And I believe we could have another completed in a year. Now that we have worked the problems out of Mr. Dubois."

"You drive a hard bargain, young Mr. Merrill. Is he related to you, Deputy Director Merrill?" he asked jokingly. "There's no need to waste your time or ours. I'll purchase, Mr. Dubois," Director Wilson said.

Galen gave the director directions to wire transfer the money into their account.

"While we wait for the confirmation, April, would you show the gentlemen where to access the chest computer and how to turn him off and on.

"Would you remove your shirt, Frances?"

They watched as the A.I. removed his knotted tie and unbuttoned his shirt. They were amazed with his dexterity.

"You'll observe I made his chest hair heavy. This was to hide the slight seam made when the opening is closed." She peeled the opening back, exposing the chest computer. "Here are the basic knowledge chips and here are the language chips. You can see there is room for more. Mr. Dubois is capable of adding or removing these chips."

"Okay, Frances you can button your shirt and retie your tie." Again they watched in fascination.

"If you would have a seat, Frances." He sat down in a chair. "The power switch is not visible, but it is under the skin below the left ear, here," and she pressed it and he went lifeless. When pressed again he was reactivated.

"Mr. Galen, have you ever considered working for the company?" the director asked.

"No thank you, Mr. Director," Ashton smiled his relief.

"Mr. Director, I have confirmation. And now I can give you this cd. Just remember we hold the patent rights."

"Certainly, Mr. Merrill. And I believe after we have some time to work with Mr. Dubois we'll be requesting another."

The three directors next witnessed something extraordinary when Galen and April said goodbye to Frances Dubois. They shook hands and Frances hugged each one of them.

* * *

That evening at the Merrill house, Suki said, "You mean Mr. Dubois was an artificial intelligence? Unbelievable. He seemed so nice. I had no idea."

"Neither did I," Ashton said.

"You two—ah the three of you surely gave a remarkable presentation. You don't compromise very well do you, son. You more or less gave the director a figure and if he didn't like it, you were not going to haggle. No one has had any problem with the Tomah 2 program and I think this helped to sell him on your price."

"It's too bad you couldn't have been there, Suki, to watch these two."

April's cell buzzed. "This is my brother, Gary, and I must take this."

"Go right ahead, dear," Suki said.

She put her phone on speaker so all could hear. "Hello, Gary, are you home now?"

"Yes, when are you and Galen coming home?"

"We are leaving tomorrow morning."

"Would it be asking too much to ask you to come to Skowhegan? I have something very important to talk with both of you."

"We can do that, Gary. Is anything wrong?"

"Quite the quandary. I have some good news and I don't want to tell you over the air."

"Okay, we'll see you sometime Sunday."

She hung up and said, "What do you suppose?"

Galen said, "No idea. But he did sound excited."

"We should leave by 6 o'clock tomorrow morning, to get ahead of Saturday traffic in D.C.," Galen said.

"Maybe sometime you and Mom can go with us to our camp in Forest City."

"I would like that, April. I have heard so much about it from Galen over the years," Suki said.

That evening they sat outside in a screened in patio talking. "Sweetheart, did you ever tell Mom and Dad when you were fourteen how close you came to drowning?"

Galen thought he'd have a little fun. "You mean that weekend when the three of us stood naked in front of the fireplace at camp?"

The expression on Ashton and Suki's face was priceless. "Yes, that weekend."

Suki said, "You were only fourteen and you were naked?"

"It was in the winter, Mom, and I would have drowned if not for Gary and April."

The two told them the whole story without leaving out anything. "That was my first taste of whiskey."

"Why didn't you ever say anything about this before?" Suki asked.

"I was afraid you wouldn't let me ever go to Tomah Stream again."

"You mean Gary jumped right in after you?" Ashton asked.

"He never hesitated for a second," April said. And she was so proud of her brother.

"I'll have to thank Gary the next time I see him," Ashton said.

"No, Dad. Gary doesn't handle praise so well," April said.

"We three had never been so cold," Galen said.

Ashton was a stubborn man and he was determined to find a suitable way to thank him.

* * *

The D.C. traffic was light. They had pushed on their trip down. Each of the three taking turns driving. But on the return trip they drove only as far as Boston before spending the night in a motel.

The next morning Galen asked, "Do you want to stop at home before we drive through?"

"Not unless you want to. I have enough clean clothes."

"So do I."

At the Portland exit Galen said, "Do you want to drive. I could use a break."

They arrived in Skowhegan at 10 o'clock and Gary was home. "So how did your meeting go with the company? Did they buy your A.I.?"

"They were very interested and they didn't quibble about the price tag."

"I even gave a presentation also, Gary."

Gary put his arm around his sister and hugged her.

"Now it's my turn," and he handed them a Mason jar of crude oil.

"What's this?" April asked.

"Galen?"

"It looks like oil."

"Unscrew the lid and smell it. Be careful not to spill any."

He carefully removed the lid and they both smelled it. "It smells like oil but different somehow."

"That's because it is crude oil."

"Where did you find it, Gary?" Galen asked.

"I was out walking at camp and I went behind where the moose had been shot. About two hundred, this was bubbling out of the ground."

"There must be tremendous pressures underground to bring the oil to the surface."

"That's what I have been thinking, too.

Gary brought the photos up he had taken of the oil on his cell phone. "Here are some photos I took."

Galen and April looked at the pics and said, "I wonder how long this has been there?"

"Then we should do something soon," April said.

"Exactly. Yesterday and this morning I have done some internet research about oil companies. Irving Oil has a refinery in St. John, New Brunswick. So they would be the most likely to have more interest. Chevron Resources has been doing some prospecting in northern Maine. Getty Oil might be interested, as well as Exxon Mobil.

"All I could find were generalities and no specifics. Can you hack into an oil company and look for answers?"

"It would only take me a few minutes to get in. But I don't want to use your computer, Gary. I would feel more comfortable using my equipment. Thereby, I could bounce around the hack to several oil rich countries."

"What information are you looking for?"

"Companies pay their engineers a high bonus for bringing in a well. We already know there is oil. There was some information about land bonuses and leases. But I couldn't find out any more than that. How much do they pay in royalties and once an agreement has been reached the companies are not required to start drilling and pumping oil immediately. They can hold the rights as long as they want."

"You know what I would prefer, would be to sell the land and camp and the rights to the oil."

"I also tried to find out what it means when the crude oil bubbles to the surface and couldn't find out anything."

"Well I think I can get most of this information, but as I said, it'll have to wait until we are home."

"I wish I could have seen your A.I. I know you have been talking about building one for years."

"I may be wrong but I think Director Wilson will want another," Galen said.

"Are you going back to work tomorrow, Gary?" April asked.

"Yes, I hope I can keep my mind on my work."

* * *

Galen and April left for home Monday morning and Gary went back to work. His crew noticed the change with him and once again Gary was glad to be at work. In his absence, the crew had accomplished a lot.

At lunchbreak, Don said, "My attorney said we could close on your house Friday morning."

"That sounds good to me, Don. You do realize the house comes furnished. All I want is my personal things."

On Wednesday he received a phone call from Attorney Troy Billings that his folks will had cleared probate and he and April were to be in his office Monday morning at 9 o'clock.

That evening Galen called, "Gary I have all the information we'll need to negotiate with the oil companies."

"That's good, Galen. Can you two come up for the weekend? The will has cleared probate and Billings wants us in his office at 9 o'clock Monday morning."

"We'll be up and maybe in the afternoon we can talk with Irving Oil in Bangor. I'll call and make an appointment."

"Don, on Monday you'll have the crew again. I have to be in Attorney Billings office in the morning. My folks will cleared probate and in the afternoon I have an appointment with Irving Oil in Bangor."

"We're alone, Gary. Can I ask you a personal question?"

"Go ahead, Don."

"Since returning from your camp in Forest City you have been a changed man. Now an appointment with Irving Oil? Are you planning on leaving?"

"I can't give you a solid answer, Don. But I'll say this much. If I do the company will be yours. And keep this to yourself until I know more okay."

"Sure, no problem.

"Are you sure, Gary, you want all of your furnishings to go with the sale? I mean they are all new."

"My folk's home is full of furniture. So yes, I'm sure."

"At $60,000.00 that is quite a bargain."

When Gary returned home from work on Thursday the funeral director had left two packages containing Charles and Liz's ashes. For now he placed the urns on the living room mantle.

Friday morning Gary and Don closed on his house and then

they went back to work. Gary had already taken his personal things from the house.

That evening Galen and April arrived. "We have an appointment at 1 o'clock at Irving's. After reading all the information I could find I agree with you, we would be better off with a total sale of the property with all mineral rights. Royalties; bonuses and leases can get very confusing and complicated."

"I agree a hundred percent," Gary said.

April saw the urns and she began to cry silently. "Sunday morning I want to spread their ashes in Mom's flower garden."

"I downloaded the photos of the oil to my computer and printed them on photopaper. It looks better."

All evening they talked about the pros and cons of a lease agreement and in the end it came down to an outright sale of the property and the mineral rights.

After breakfast on Sunday morning without saying a word to one another, Gary, Galen and April changed into good clothes and then carried the urns to the flower garden.

Rather than putting the ashes in a hole or in a pile, the contents of both urns were spread throughout the garden.

"There, it's over," April said, trying to hold back tears. As were Gary and Galen.

Galen said, "Mom and Dad, sometimes you two were more like my true parents than my mother and father. Thank you."

Gary said, "Thank you, Dad and Mom, for all you have ever done for me."

April repeated the Lord's Prayer and then said, "Thank you, Mom and Dad." Then she cried. Galen put his arm around her and the three stood there in silence for a long few moments.

Chapter 13

Monday, Gary, April and Galen were at Billing's office at 9 o'clock. "Your folks will was pretty much straightforward. And I have done what you asked. Both of your names are on the Tomah camp and property and the house is yours, Gary. And here are your checks. The cost of funeral and cremation have both been paid as well as my fee.

"So, unless you have any questions, you are free to go."

Their first stop was at the bank. April had her check electronically wired to her account. "We have time for dinner at the Dysart's Restaurant before we talk with Irving's people," April said, "I'm hungry."

"As a suggestion, eat something before a meeting," Galen said.

As they were eating, Gary said, "Sis, is there anything of Mom or Dad's that you'd like to have?"

"I would like something to remember Mom and Dad by. I'll look around when we get back."

They were at the Irving office ten minutes early. "Good afternoon, we have an appointment with George Tilburn."

"And your name?"

"Newman and Merrill."

"Oh yes, he is expecting you. Down this hall and the office at the end."

"Thank you," Gary said.

"Come in, have a seat. I am George Tilburn."

"Hello, Mr. Tilburn. This is my sister, April Merrill, and this is her husband, Galen, and I am Gary Newman."

"Now, Mr. Newman, what can I do for you?"

"We have recently discovered oil on our property. This is a photo of what was found," and he handed him the color photo.

"This isn't some discarded crank case oil is it?"

"No Sir. It bubbles out of the ground." And Galen handed him the jar of oil. "This is a sample. And I'm sure you must have a laboratory here that can analyze this."

"How long has this oil been bubbling to the surface?"

"That we are not too certain about."

"Did you touch it or smell of it?"

"Yes, the oil was warm and it has a slight sulfur smell."

"Janice, would you come in here please."

"Yes, Mr. Tilburn?"

"Would you take this sample to the lab downstairs and tell Frank I need the results ASAP."

"Yes, Mr. Tilburn."

"Where was this discovered?"

April chimed in here, "We aren't prepared to disclose the location until we have some sort of a deal."

Gary was surprised with her answer.

"Yes, yes, I can understand that. You say you own the land, is that correct?"

"Yes, there's five hundred acres.

"The fact that it is bubbling to the surface is a good indication that it might be worthwhile to explore."

A half hour later Janice was back with the computer results of the sample. "Thank you, Janice. Oh my word, I have never seen a carbon content this high before. And there certainly is the presence of propane, which is making the crude oil come to the surface."

"I can tell you now that we would be very interested.

"I can offer you a sizable bonus for finding the crude oil and we can offer you a standard lease agreement, a Producers Form.

"Let me stop you there, Mr. Tilburn. We are not interested in any lease or royalty contract," Gary said.

Tilburn interrupted him and asked, "Then what do you want?"

Galen said, "We offer this property for sale, no royalties, bonuses or leases."

"Well, I'm not sure about that without knowing more about the location," Tilburn said.

"You have an oil refinery in St. John, New Brunswick, and I believe Irving owns part or has an interest in the railroad that crosses Maine to the refinery. Am I correct, Mr. Tilburn?"

"This is true. Go on."

Galen took over for Gary, "So Irving transports a lot of crude from all over to the refinery. And probably most of the crude oil Irving has to purchase, I—or we—think it would be beneficial to Irving, instead of having to purchase so much crude they could ship their own crude that sits in their backyard, so to speak. Now which would be more economically feasible?"

"That would go without question."

"You see, Mr. Tilburn," it was Gary's turn now, "we understand that these mining rights and leases sometimes don't happen for years to come. And we're not interested in that."

"Okay, let's say we might be interested in purchasing the property, how much are you asking?"

It was April's turn now. "Ten million. And you can start pumping immediately or wait five or ten years."

"You realize you have me over a barrel. You do realize with a producer's form and royalties you might be looking at more than ten million in the long run."

"We have thought of that, Mr. Tilburn," Gary said, "but we would be satisfied right now with a clean sale for ten million."

"How do you propose to do this? I mean I must see the site first."

"If you wire the amount into an escrow account then we will take you to the site tomorrow morning," Galen said.

"I can't believe I'm doing this. But I'll do it. Whose name is on the account?"

Galen said, "The Newman-Merrill Company."

"Janice, will you come in here again please?"

"Yes, Mr. Tilburn?"

"Wire transfer $10M dollars into an escrow account for the Newman-Merrill Company."

"Yes, sir."

"And print out a receipt and statement."

"Yes, Mr. Tilburn."

"How did you happen to find this?"

"I was out exploring and just stumbled onto it."

Ten minutes later Janice was back with the statement and receipt. Tilburn looked at it and then gave it to Galen.

"We will meet you here in the parking lot tomorrow morning at 8 o'clock."

"Galen, I probably should cancel the appointment with Exxon Mobil," Gary said more for effect than anything.

"Good idea."

Tilburn heard.

"Tomorrow morning Mr. Tilburn," April said. "I don't think you'll be disappointed."

Once in their vehicle Galen said, "There isn't any reason to drive back to Skowhegan and back here in the morning is there?"

"No, but I'll have to call my foreman, Don."

"Hello, Don?"

"Gary."

"Can you get along without me tomorrow? This business in Bangor has stretched into tomorrow. I'll see you Wednesday morning."

"Actually I'd prefer to go back to Skowhegan," Gary said,

"Only a suggestion though."

"You know that would make more sense."

* * *

After a big breakfast, Newman and Merrill met George Tilburn in the office parking lot. "Are you ready, Mr. Tilburn?" Galen asked.

"Let's go," he sat in front with Galen and April and Gary in back. "This is a nice vehicle. What do you do for work?"

"My wife and I own a computer company."

"Can you tell me now where we're going?"

"Up to you, Gary."

"We're going to Forest City."

"Which side of the border?"

"What do you mean? Which side of the border?" Galen asked.

"The boundary line splits the town. So half is in Maine and half in New Brunswick."

"I guess we didn't know that. This side of the border."

"And there is a railroad there, that does go to St. John. You three have done your homework."

They stopped briefly in Lincoln for coffee and donuts and they arrived at camp at 10:30 a.m. "Whose camp?"

"It's ours, but it goes with the property."

"This is a beautiful location."

Galen drove right to the site where the moose had been shot. "I didn't know if I would recognize this spot or not," Galen said.

"If you haven't seen where the crude is bubbling up to the surface, how would you recognize this spot?" Tilburn asked.

"You tell him, Gary."

"Nine years ago, Galen and I were up hunting partridges and the first night we heard a rifle shot and ran down here and found two men cutting up a moose. We got in touch with the game warden and before the night was over we went with the game warden and then testified in court against them. This spot has grown up some and it looks a little different."

"Where is the crude?"

"About two hundred feet from the road."

They all got out and Gary led them to the crude. "Right there, Mr. Tilburn. It is twice as big now as last week."

"I have never seen anything like this before," Tilburn said. He touched the oil. "It is a little warm and I can distinctively smell sulfa. However faintly. This is remarkable. Where is the railroad?"

"We turned on to this road about two hundred feet before crossing the tracks."

"Listen," April said. "The train is going through now."

Everyone was silent, listening.

Tilburn said, "With an active site like this, we would have to start setting rigging immediately."

"I'm only guessing, but I'd say this probably will turn out to be a huge deposit of crude oil and if you would go with royalties instead of an outright purchase, overtime you probably would more than double the value."

"Now after seeing this, I'll agree to purchase the property for the 10M dollars. If that is the route you still want to go."

Gary looked at April and then Galen and they both nodded their heads, yes. "I guess that confirms it, Mr. Tilburn. We'll sell."

"Okay, when I get back to my office, I'll inform our company attorney that we want a closing tomorrow morning at 11 o'clock. You bring the deed and as soon as the papers are all signed the escrow account will be yours."

Tilburn started to make a call on his cell phone and Galen said, "You won't to be able to reach any tower here. You'll have to wait until we are on our way to Lincoln."

"We would like to take a few minutes and take some of the personal things from the camp," Gary said.

"Certainly."

They found a box in the shed and they filled it with a picture album, camp log book, a .38-55 rifle and shotgun and two pictures on the walls.

"We had some good times here," April said. "And without a doubt my most memorable will be the time when we three were standing nude in front of the fireplace trying to get warm when Mom and Dad walked in." All three began laughing. And April told Mr. Tilburn the whole story.

"You know," Galen said, "with oil rigs set up here I don't think I want to come up to camp anymore. Everyone ready?"

"Let's go before I start crying," April said.

Before leaving, Tilburn wanted to see the property markers. "All we can show you is the two along the road. The other two are deep in the woods."

"That'll be fine."

Galen crossed the tracks and showed him the east line and then the west line on the west side of the railroad tracks.

"How much road frontage is there?"

"Two thousand feet," Gary said.

"I'll have our surveyor come up and run the lines."

As they were leaving Topsfield, Tilburn was able to call his office and told the company attorney to start the paperwork, "for the closing at 11 o'clock tomorrow morning."

"There, everything is done until tomorrow."

"I don't suppose there is any way I could convince you three to come to work for Irving Oil is there? I have never met three people who in a short period have had so much information coming into a meeting. I'm impressed."

* * *

Galen, April and Gary drove back to Skowhegan and there was just enough time for Gary to check on his crew.

"Everything is looking good, Don. I have to be in Bangor tomorrow morning at 11 o'clock and I don't know if there'll be any time to stop by or not."

204

"Gary, can you tell me what's going on?"

"I'll fill you in tomorrow, Don. If I'm late getting back, I'll drive up and talk with you at your house."

After supper that evening, April started putting together some things she wanted to take home. Most of her mother's clothes she packed away in boxes to be taken later to a Goodwill outlet. She wanted some of her mother's knickknacks and a few photos.

"When I have time, I'll go through Dad's clothes and pack what I don't want for Goodwill, too."

The three of them stayed up long into the night talking. "I feel bad in a way selling the camp and land. I hope Mom and Dad would understand," April said.

"I think the folks would have done the same under the same set of circumstances," Gary said.

"Dad wasn't the kind of person just to let things go. If he knew the crude oil was bubbling out of the ground, who knows what would have happened if left unchecked, he would have done the same thing I think," Galen added. "I am sorry to see the camp go. Maybe we could buy another camp somewhere."

"That's an idea. In my spare time, I'll look for one," Gary said.

At 11 o'clock the next morning, they walked into Mr. Tilburn's office. "Let's go to the conference room. We'll be more comfortable there."

"This is our attorney, Edgar Witherspoon."

"Good morning, did you bring the property deed?" he asked.

Gary gave the deed to the attorney. He excused himself and left the room and then he came right back.

"While Janice is typing a new deed for you to sign, I'll go over what these papers are. I understand by selling your property that all mineral claims go with the sale of the property. Is that correct?"

"Yes."

"Then I'll have to have you Gary and April sign this agreement form."

Janice was back with the new deed. "Now I'll have to have each of you sign this new deed transferring the property to Irving Oil."

Once they had signed, Galen took the deed to read it. "Okay, Mr. Witherspoon, we have lived up to our bargain and now the payment," he said.

"How would you like that?"

Galen said, "Electronically transfer 5M dollars to April's account," and he gave Witherspoon the routing number. And the other 5M to Gary's account," and Gary gave him his routing number. "As soon as we receive confirmation of the transfer, I give you this deed."

Five minutes later both April and Gary's cell buzzed with a text confirming the transfer. Galen handed the deed to Mr. Witherspoon and said, "Thank you, gentlemen."

George Tilburn walked with them out to the parking lot. "I hope you won't later regret the sale of the property."

"I don't think we will, Mr. Tilburn," Gary said, "and thank you."

"You three are remarkable and I like your business ethics," and he shook their hands and left.

* * *

"I'll take the boxes of clothes to the Goodwill store so you won't have to bother with them, April. It's been nice having you two here."

"You take care, Gary. And Gary I have a girlfriend that I worked with at The Boston hospital that is coming up to visit next year sometime. I told her about you and she would like to meet you."

"I'll look forward to meeting her. What's her name?"

"Nicole."

"Nice name."

Gary and Galen looked at each other and shook hands and Galen said, "Maybe now you might consider becoming a game warden."

"I'll think on it. Drive careful and thanks, Galen."

The first thing Gary did after they left was to take the clothes to the Goodwill store. Then he went to see Don at the new house.

"Hello, Gary."

"Don, can the crew get along without you?"

"Hey, Fred, you have it for the rest of the afternoon."

"Let's sit in my pickup, Don. I suppose you'd like to know what I have been doing."

"Oh yeah, to say the least."

"When I went to camp to clear my head, well I got drunk and passed out and the next day I went for a walk trying to get rid of a hangover when I found crude oil bubbling out of the ground. Me, my sister and her husband have been working a deal to sell the property to a petroleum company. And today we closed on the sale. I'd rather not say which company bought it or for how much."

"What about your carpentry business?"

"This is what I'd like to do. You're as good a carpenter as I am. I'd like you to slowly take over the company. In the meantime, I'll work with you how to figure up contracting bids and costs. While you are slowly taking over, I would like to do the cabinet work like my dad did, if that's okay with you."

"So are you looking to sell the business? You have made a good reputation in the housing industry."

"No, I'm not looking to sell, you simply take over."

"You mean it?"

"Yes, what do you say?"

"Yes, of course."

"Good, tomorrow morning I'll be at work for a couple of

hours, then I'll leave to look at another job."

As they were leaving Gary's house, Galen said, "I like how you broached Gary with Nicole. It'll get him thinking and anticipating. And we have to get to work on her."

The next morning at work, Gary asked, "Can the crews take it Don? I'd like you to see this new site also."

"Fred, you have the guys finish shingling the roof today and clean out inside, so we can start the interior walls tomorrow."

"Okay, boss man."

"Fred has turned into a good worker."

Gary drove out the Middle Road in Skowhegan about three miles. The owner was there waiting, "Good morning, Mr. Winslow, this is my foreman, Don Hadley."

"Good morning. I was going to go with a framed house, studded with 2x6, but while you were up north I checked out your log house and I liked it and my wife and I have decided on the log house. We have an appointment with Katahdin Log Homes next week.

"The hole for the foundation will be dug next week and I don't have a date confirmed yet for the foundation."

"We can't give you an estimate now without looking at the blueprints. When you have those then call me or Don. Here are our phone numbers," and he handed Wilson a file card with their home and cell phone numbers.

"We are finishing one project now and will begin another next week and we have a big project for September. But we could work you in between them. The log homes go up pretty easy."

"Okay, Gary, as soon as I have talked with Katahdin Homes, I'll be in touch with one of you."

* * *

Galen and April talked constantly on their drive home in Falmouth. "I think we have Gary anticipating meeting Nicole."

"That was pretty clever mentioning Nicole to him now. He'll have months to think about meeting her. And I can't wait to get working on her. She'll have to have a pleasure and emotional program, but we won't have to install the internet capability."

"How tall should we make her?"

"Isn't the skeleton we have for a 5'7" woman?"

"That's right."

"I'm going to miss the camp, April."

"We have a lot of memories there that's for sure."

"Do you suppose Gary is seriously thinking about becoming a game warden?" she asked.

"I think we both would be, but he has his carpentry business and I have you and my computer business. No, I think he dreams about it, but I don't think he will. Although he certainly would make a good one."

Chapter 14

Gary worked with his foreman, Don Hadley, teaching him how to work up an estimate. He already knew blueprint reading and layout and he was a good finish carpenter, but not quite as good as Gary or Charles.

Don enjoyed the new responsibility and he was becoming an excellent lead man and supervisor.

By the middle of that fall there was enough inside work to see the crew through the winter and Gary was now only doing finish work or cabinet work. And he was always available to help and advise Don.

In his spare time, he was beginning to look for another camp in the wilderness. He had found several ideal camps on small rivers or deadwaters but they were all up north in the county and he figured they were too far away for Galen and April. He was in no hurry.

He spent Thanksgiving with Galen and April, and Galen's folks, Ashton and Suki, also arrived for the weekend. Ashton was interested, and more so surprised, that the three of them had managed to sell the property in lieu of leasing and royalties.

One evening while the three men were sipping brandy in the living room, Ashton said, "The company is quite impressed with Frances Dubois. There was only a short training period at Langley and then he was sent into the field on easy missions at first. But I can tell you this, his ability to speak and understand Russian has proven invaluable and you were correct about his internet abilities. His handler as well as I are both quite impressed.

"I think in the near future the Director will be contacting you for one or two more like Mr. Dubois."

Both Galen and April were hoping no one would ask to see what they were working on now. They even kept the laboratory door locked.

By the end of December, Galen had most of the electronics finished in Nicole and before April could start closing the body, he started running dozens of tests each day until he was satisfied.

"You were correct, sweetheart, when you said Nicole would be easier to build," April said.

"I have an important question."

"Oh, what's that?" April asked.

"If Nicole is to be a companion for Gary, what about sex? Will it seem real?"

"The vagina and canal will have to be made from a durable compound, and I have that, and the texture must also be soft."

"Okay, this might be fine for Gary but will Nicole experience any pleasure?" he asked.

"You have already installed a pleasure program, correct?"

"Yes."

"Okay, I have an idea. I think."

"Well, what have you come up with?"

"To anyone else this might sound bizarre, but I think you'll grasp the idea."

"Well, tell me," he said.

"Don't you dare laugh at me."

"April!"

"Okay, okay, here goes. You know I really get into our love making. We hold off on our love making until I am extremely horny. Then you run neurons to my breast and several places in my pelvic area, to your computer. And while we are enjoying ourselves the computer digitally records my orgasm and climax.

Can you do it?"

At first Galen just looked at her with no facial expression. Then he said, "Sweetheart, you are genius. Of course I can record it. I would never have thought of that. Every time she has sex, the stimulation in these areas, the sex program will run." Then he hugged her and kissed her.

"Wait a minute, lover boy, we go on the wagon now."

"How long?"

"I'll know when the time is right."

* * *

After the turn of the new year, Gary was looking at property for sale on the computer and saw a large parcel for sale in Cornville, that bordered the Wesseransett Stream, just below where Bog Brook flows into the stream.

He was now only doing cabinet work for Don and he wasn't needed until Friday. That gave him three and a half days to look at the property. The land was not far from his home in Skowhegan and it was easy to find. He strapped on his snowshoes and began exploring. It took some time to locate the southern property pin. He had driven too far to the north of it. He snowshoed the east-west line to the stream.

The wood had been harvested a few years ago, but it was in good shape. The lumber contractor had not butchered the land or trees.

He was seeing many moose and deer tracks, and just before he reached the stream he found a four inch hole in the snow. When he snowshoed straddling the hole a partridge came flying out of the snow between his snowshoes. Startling the hell out of him.

He continued on. He wouldn't soon forget that experience. He saw more partridges but they were budding in yellow birch trees.

There was an old camp on the property that set back from the river about two hundred feet. The door was locked but he could look through a window and see all he needed. The floors and sills appeared sound. The asphalt roof needed work. The windows were double pane Andersons. There were two double size beds in the back separated by a blanket. The exterior walls were cedar shingles that had turned gray. There was no porch; only a set of wooden steps up to the kitchen door.

There was also five hundred acres of land, which was mostly second growth forest.

He followed the camp road back to the highway and he found the north line about two hundred feet beyond the camp road.

On his way back to Skowhegan, the more he thought about the land and camp—well, he was beginning to want it. It would be a nice fix-it-up project when he wasn't doing carpentry work for Don.

At home, he went back on the computer to the same site. The realtor was asking fifty thousand for it. The realtor was located in Madison, Williamson Reality. He found the phone number and called.

Mr. Williamson answered, "Mr. Williamson, I was just up looking at the property you have listed in Cornville that borders the Wessrunsett River. I looked the camp over, found the property lines and walked over and through the property. The forest had no immediate value as it has been harvested, and the camp is doable but small. You have it listed for fifty thousand. I can give you, tomorrow morning, twenty thousand dollars."

"Before I can say yes or no, I'll have to contact the owner. I'll get back to you."

"If I don't hear from you within an hour, there is another property that I'm looking at."

"You'll hear from me, Mr. Newman."

Ten minutes later, Williamson called back. "My client will accept your offer of twenty thousand. Can you be here at 11 o'clock?"

"Yes, I'll be there."

After supper he called the Merrills and Galen answered. "Hello, Gary."

"Hi Galen,"

April picked up on another phone, "Hello, Gary."

"Hi, April."

"Hey look, I looked at some property today in Cornville. Five hundred acres on Wessransett River with a sixteen by twenty camp with cedar shingles. He was asking fifty thousand and I offered him twenty thousand and we close tomorrow morning. I want you to understand you two can use it anytime you want."

"As soon as the snow is gone, I'll go in for a couple of days and put a new roof on and build a screened in porch."

"Maybe we can come up and help, if we can."

"That would be great."

* * *

The property closed and the previous owner was a Janet Harold. On Friday he started building cupboards and cabinets for the winter big project. He was happy doing carpentry work again.

But after a week he was done and Edgar Witherspoon and wife marveled with her new kitchen.

Galen and April were so sure about the sexual pleasing program that they continued work on the body of Nicole. The neurons were all run to the breasts and pelvic areas and all he had to do now was load the program as soon as they had April's orgasm and climax responses.

The second week of February one evening she said, "I'm ready, I cannot wait any longer. How long will it take you to attach the neurons to me?"

"Maybe five—six minutes."

"Well get to it. I can't wait any longer."

When they were through April said, "There that should make Nicole smile."

In March, Galen and April received a hand delivered message by a company agent, from Director Wilson. "What do you suppose he wants?"

"I am to wait here for your answer, Mr. and Mrs. Merrill."

"Open it, Galen."

"It says Frances Dubois is working better than he had any right to expect and is requesting two more Duboises to be made. And he gives us a year and a half to complete them."

"Will a year and a half be enough time?"

"Oh, I think so."

"I am to take your written reply back on the message."

Galen wrote on the back eighteen months from May first. And gave the message back to the agent to be delivered to Wilson.

"Now we'd better get busy."

"How much more do you have to do for Nicole?"

"I can't think of anything."

"I like the pixie-like hairstyle. It looks good with her bronze colored hair," Galen said.

"Let's activate her and let her get some experience and accustom to being around people. Maybe tomorrow I'll take her shopping for clothes," April said.

"You know sweetheart, if we are to start work on two more A.I.s in May, then we should invite Gary to go on a vacation with us and to meet Nicole."

"Okay, if you call him tonight, I'll make travel plans and hotel reservations on the Bahama Island."

"Wow I like the sound of that."

Nicole was activated and it was as if she had just woken from a deep sleep. "We have run several tests, Nicole, to make sure there are no problems. Do you know who we are?"

"Of course I do, you are Galen Merrill and your wife, April."

"I have an idea, sweetheart. Let's the three of us eat out

tonight. This will give Nicole some experience," April said.

"Good idea. We'd better get changed."

As they were waiting for their meals, they told Nicole they were going on a vacation to the Bahamas and a friend, April's brother, was coming also, "And we hope you'll like him Nicole. We have a week to prepare you, I'll be working with you every day."

Nicole was enjoying the occasion out for dinner. She ate sparingly and only had one glass of wine. As she ate, she kept looking all around her. Taking in everything. How people walked, talked, treated each other, table manners and the smells intrigued her. This was like her first day of life and she had assimilated so much information.

* * *

The next day April took Nicole clothes shopping and she found this interesting and fun. "How do I buy things, April? I do not have any money."

"Well after our vacation if things go the way we hope, this little problem will solve itself."

"There is something else. My brother Gary will ask sometime what you studied in college and where have you been working."

"What shall I tell him?"

"That you studied business and you have been working as a receptionist in the Boston General Hospital. This also will work itself out before the end of the vacation. Now we need to get you a woman's handbag with all the necessary items any woman would carry."

"How will Gary take to me being an A.I.?"

"Galen and I will break this to him a little at a time. If you simply be who you are, a beautiful friendly woman, I don't think there will be a problem when he learns."

Galen talked with Gary and he was excited about a vacation to the Bahamas. And he was even more excited about meeting April's friend, Nicole.

"Sweetheart, how will we get to the islands? Nicole will never be able to pass through a metal detector."

"A private jet. I already have one that will pick us up at the Portland airport."

"This is going to be a costly vacation isn't it?" she said.

"Yes, but we all can afford it."

* * *

During the week while Galen was ordering more parts for the next two A.I.'s, April worked with Nicole every day. Not just at the house, but around town so she could become somewhat familiar with life and cities.

One day Galen had to take a trip to Portland for electronic parts and two titanium skeletons while April continued working with Nicole. "There will be music at the hotel and dancing. I think I need to teach you how to dance."

While Galen was working in the laboratory, April and Nicole were in the living room. April turned on some slow melodies. "We'll dance what is called a waltz and usually it is the man who leads. Take my left hand with your right hand. Now place your left on top of my right shoulder. That's right. My right arm goes around you and I place my hand, usually in the middle of your back. We'll go slow at first so you'll get the idea. Follow me.

"Okay that is good now put a little rocking motion in your hips like this. Not too much. What you do is try to keep in step with the beat of the music. Like this. That's right, you have the idea.

"Now when two people really like each other there is no space between them like this—" and she held Nicole a little tighter; pulling them both closer together. And she brought her left hand in close to their bodies.

April continued dancing and Nicole was doing an excellent job, moving her feet in step with April's and swaying her hips in tune with the music. "This is very good, Nicole. Now there is another position I will show. And most couples who really like each other will hold their partner in close like this," and she put both of her arms around Nicole as if she was going to hug her. And Nicole followed suit. "Now in this position even though the beat of the music has not changed, the couple usually slow their step and beat. I'll show you. That's right, you still sway your hips, but much slower now. And your head should raise on my shoulder." Nicole did and they danced beautifully.

The music changed and April pulled away and said, "You have that down very nicely.

"There is another lesion I want to teach you. Do you know what a kiss is?"

"Two people put their lips together.

"What's the point of just putting their lips together?"

"Well—maybe I'd better show you." She put her arms around Nicole and put her lips on Nicole's, but Nicole didn't do anything. April pulled back and said, "We'll try it again but this time move your lips a little like I did and part your mouth so your lips match mine."

"Okay." This time Nicole was doing it as she should be and what she was experiencing was pleasing to her. They kissed for a long time and April decided Nicole had kissing learned and she pulled back.

Nicole said, "I could feel something like a low electrical current tingling all through my body. Is this what a kiss is supposed to do?"

"Yes, kissing is a prelude to sex or love making."

"I think I like this kissing, it was good. Can we do it again?"

"Ah—it was good, but no, we don't need to do it again. You'll have to wait for Gary."

"Will he know how to kiss like you?"

"Yes he'll know how. Often when couples are on a first date or have just met, the man sometimes will only kiss your cheek. Then the next time the kiss will be more passionate."

"Okay, I wait for Gary. I know what sex or love making is but will you show me this also?"

"Ah, no, you're on your own there. It'll come naturally for you. Just don't rush it."

That night April asked, "How many rooms have you reserved?"

"Just two. I was planning to spend the first night here so Gary and Nicole could get acquainted. Then when we leave they'll have another eight hours. I figure by then the awkward newness will be over."

"I hope you're right or you might be sharing a room with Gary."

The next day, April and Nicole went shopping again for clothes for them both, for the trip. And for Galen.

Back in Skowhegan, Gary was doing his own shopping and preparing to leave. Then on Friday morning, he locked the house and drove to Falmouth. He was anxious to meet his sister's friend Nicole. He could think of nothing else.

At 11 o'clock, he pulled into their driveway. "Nicole, my brother is here. Let's go out and meet him."

"Okay," and she followed April outside.

Gary took one look at Nicole and he said, "Wow," loud enough for her and April to hear. And this brought a smile to each of them.

"Hi, Gary."

"Hi, April."

"Gary, I'd like you to meet my friend Nicole Charles. Nicole, this is my brother, Gary."

He took her hand lightly in his and said, "Nicole, it is a pleasure to meet you."

"And I am also glad to meet you, Gary," April had her fingers crossed. So far so good.

"Where do you want me to leave my pickup?"

"Right there is fine. Bring your luggage inside."

"Where's Galen?"

"In his laboratory inventorying for two more A.I.'s."

"For the company?"

"Yes, and no more about that."

"Nicole, will you show Gary to his room and I'll go downstairs and tell Galen, Gary is here."

Nicole was wearing a light yellow asymmetrical skirt with a white blouse which accentuated her skin tone; almost the same color as American natives. Watching her walk as he trailed behind her—well all he could see and think about was Nicole and how beautiful she was. And friendly.

"Here's your room, Gary. Where do you live, Gary?"

"Skowhegan, and you, Nicole?"

"I have been in Boston, but I want to relocate. I have only been here with the Merrills for a few days.

"Are you tired, Gary?"

"I was up early but it is only a three-hour drive from home."

"Maybe we should go back to the living room," she said.

Galen was there with April, "I see you have met Nicole. It's too early for lunch. Would you like some coffee?"

"Yes."

April started to get up and Nicole said, "I'll get the coffee, April. How do you like your's, Gary?"

"No sugar and a little milk or cream."

Galen and April looked at each other, so slightly they each nodded their head. Not enough for Gary to notice.

"Tell us about this property."

"I found it listed on the internet and when I drove up to look at it, I fell in love with it. The wood has all been harvested a few years ago but they had done a good job."

While Galen and Gary talked about the camp, April went to help Nicole. "Did you find everything okay?"

"Yes, but how did I know how to make coffee? You never talked to me about cooking."

"Well, it must be in your program somewhere."

A few minutes later April and Nicole rejoined them, each carrying two cups. "Here Gary," and she gave him a cup and sat down beside him.

"Maybe you would like to come up to our camp sometime, Nicole."

"I would like to. Maybe when you guys start to work on it."

"Galen, how are we going to share the cost of everything?" Gary asked.

"How about I pay for the jet and you pay for the hotel and then we pay every other meal. How's that?"

"Are you sure? That private jet must be expensive. What are we flying in?"

"It's a rather new Gulfstream G700 with a long enough fuel range so we can fly nonstop to Nassau."

"Where will we be staying?"

"I had originally wanted the Aqua at the Hilton, but it is too far from the airport. So I decided on the Orange Hill Beach Resort. It is a five star hotel."

"When do we leave?"

"Tomorrow morning, Friday, at 6 o'clock. We should be there by 5 o'clock."

"Who owns the G700?"

"The Nassau Charter Company. We'll land about 11 o'clock, weather permitting and we leave Wednesday morning at 6 o'clock."

"I would feel better about this trip, Galen, if you let me pay for the hotel and meals."

"Okay."

They had soup and sandwich for lunch and then Gary said, "I think I'll go for a walk. Would you like to go, Nicole?"

"Yes, I would enjoy a walk."

April said as they closed the door, "It's working so far. I think they actually like each other."

"If this turns sour, I hope Gary will still be my friend," he said.

They walked down toward the shore and found a boardwalk to walk on. "What is it like where you live, Gary?"

"The town is spread out more than Falmouth and there are eight thousand people. Falmouth is more of a resort community where as Skowhegan is more industrial. It's a great place to live."

"Do your folks live in Skowhegan?"

"My mom and dad spent their entire lives in Skowhegan. They both were killed in an automobile accident ten months ago."

"Oh, I'm sorry."

"That's okay. I had a difficult time to get over it. My dad and I were close and April and Mom were close.

"What about your family, Nicole?"

"I was raised by an aunt in Boston. Here in Falmouth, things are not so crowded. The town is spread out more. There's space. I'd like to see your Skowhegan some time."

They walked along the boardwalk for a long time just talking and getting to know each other. "I've noticed," Nicole said, "that you and April's husband, Galen, are more friends than in-laws."

"They're staying out a long time," April said.

"Maybe they are getting along better than we hoped."

They found a place on the boardwalk where there was a bench seat overlooking the ocean. "Let's sit for a while," Nicole said, "and enjoy the view. Even though there are several other people here, this still is a nice place."

Just then a little boy threw a rubber ball for his dog and the ball rolled under their bench. The black lab ran up and stopped in front of them and Nicole said, "Hello, fella. You're a pretty dog," and the dog cocked his head to one side while looking at Nicole. "Oh, you want me to get your ball?" and the dog barked once.

Nicole reached under the bench for the ball and she held it out for the dog. Before taking it he licked her hand. Then he took the ball and ran back to the little boy.

"You know, Nicole, dogs are good at judging one's character. When he licked your hand, he was accepting you."

"Do you have a dog?"

"I always wanted one, but my mom was allergic to both dogs and cats.

"My sister said you were a receptionist at the Boston General Hospital. Are you still working there?"

"No. And what do you do, Gary?"

"I went to college and studied drafting and carpentry. Then I formed my own carpentry business and I had men working for me. Then last year while I was at our camp on Tomah Stream in Forest City, I found crude oil bubbling to the surface. My sister and I owned the camp and property jointly and she and Galen and I negotiated the sale of the property to an oil company.

"Since then I let my foreman, Don Hadley, have the company and I do his finish work when he needs help and the cabinets. I'd like to buy old houses and remodel them for sale. I enjoy building."

"Maybe I should get a dog. We should start back."

On the way back they held hands and Gary was thinking he had never felt skin so soft.

April was looking out a window when they walked into the driveway. "They're holding hands."

"I guess I don't have to wonder how they are getting along," Galen said.

While April and Nicole were making a light supper Galen and Gary sat outside in the spring air. There was a cool ocean breeze but they didn't mind.

"So?"

"So what, Galen?"

"So, how do you like Nicole?"

"I have only known her now for seven hours, but she is the nicest woman I have ever met. I can't get over it. She is so precise about everything she says, so I'm not left wondering. She is always smiling and happy. When I took her hand in mind, she didn't resist. In fact, she very lightly squeezed my hand. I wish I had met her before Millie. She is so easy to be around."

While April and Nicole were working in the kitchen April asked, "Well, Nicole, how do you like Gary?"

"I do. He is so easy to talk with. I feel like I have known him for some time. He isn't pretentious and he is interested in me. When he took my hand and held it, I could feel the excitement though my whole body."

"Nicole, don't let on that you are an A.I. Galen will do that in a tasteful way, okay?"

"Okay. I know one thing for sure."

"What?"

"I need to learn how to cook." They both laughed.

"Gary has Mom and Dad's house and he probably still has all of her recipes."

"Have you heard how the company liked the A.I. you sold them?" Gary asked.

"Yes. Not long ago we received a handwritten message from the Director and delivered by an agent, that the A.I. is working far beyond their expectations and they want two more."

"Wouldn't that be something to have A.I.s eventually running this country. They probably would be more honest than their human counterparts. Would lying and deceit come natural to an A.I.?"

"No, not unless the A.I. was programmed to lie."

"You know, Gary, there was an A.I. in China that was recently granted citizenship and another in Saudi Arabia. I saw them on television and no one would be able to tell they weren't human. Their movements and speech was exactly like that of a human being," Galen said.

"Wouldn't that be something if you could create a female A.I. that could make love."

"Yeah, that would really be something, Gary."

After supper they all stayed up for awhile talking. Finally Galen said, "We have to be up early tomorrow, so I suggest we go to bed."

Gary took Nicole's hand to help her stand and then he walked her to her bedroom door. Nicole was getting that electrical tingling all through her body again and she was hoping Gary would ask her to his room.

But he didn't. They stopped by her door and he kissed her cheek and opened her door and said, "I'll see you in the morning."

Nicole was thinking that it happened just as April had said it might.

Gary lay on his back for a while thinking about Nicole, "I have never met anyone like you Nicole."

* * *

April and Nicole made French toast with sausage. "I never could make French toast. These are very good."

"I have never had French toast before, and I think I like these," Nicole said.

They hurried through breakfast and cleaned up in the kitchen and Galen and Gary loaded their luggage into the S.U.V. and they were at the airport fifteen minutes early.

The G700 Gulfstream was parked off to the north side, "There's our plane." Everyone was loaded down with luggage and Gary noticed where April was struggling, Nicole didn't seem to have any problem. Galen had all he could carry also. "Do you need any help, sis?"

"April, tuck that one under my arm. I'm okay," Nicole said.

They boarded the plane and a flight attendant helped them store their luggage.

"Good morning folks, my name is Captain Richard Holmes.

The copilot is Micheil Gervais, a native of the Bahamas. We'll be wheels-up on time. According to the National Weather desk, we will have calm air all the way to Nassau.

"Drinks and coffee are available if you wish and there is one restroom at the rear of the cabin. Ms. Stewart, your hostess, will help you with anything," and he returned to the cockpit.

"If you'll take your seats please and buckle up, we will be underway."

The takeoff speed set them all back against their seats. Once they were airborne the Captain came on the intercom, "Ladies and gentlemen, we will be in a rather steep incline for a few minutes. We must be above 20,000 feet over Boston and New York airports. Our ceiling maximum is 51,000 feet, although for this flight we will level off at 40,000. Our cruising speed will be Mach 0.90 or 600 miles per hour. Sit back and enjoy the flight."

Once they could unbuckle their safety belts, they sat in the lounge area. "Would anyone want a drink or coffee?"

"It's too early for drinks, but I think we all would like some coffee and maybe a donut if you have them?" Galen asked.

Nicole was sitting real close to Gary. April was aware and she smiled. Happy for them both.

"This is a beautiful plane. What is this costing to fly roundtrip, Galen?" Gary asked.

"The cost isn't important."

"I wish you'd let me help."

"You are. You agreed to pay for the hotel and meals. Besides," real serious now, "I have never forgot, Gary, how you saved my life. None of us would be here now, if not for you."

"I told you, Galen, to forget it."

"How can one forget when one saves the life of another."

Nicole looked at the others and they all knew what they were talking about.

"Tell me, please," Nicole asked.

"I'll tell you, Nicole." And April told her all about that

day, while Nicole sat and listened very quietly. She understood it must have taken great courage at so young an age to risk his own life to save that of his friend. Something like this event had not been programmed into her inner computer. But after analyzing the information from April, she was able to make her own determination about Gary Newman. And she concluded he put the well-being of others before himself. She squeezed the inside of his thigh.

Nowhere in all of her programming had she been prepared for this. Then she said, "I wonder what your mother and father were thinking when they saw all three of you nude standing in front of the fireplace. That must have been quite a shock for them at the moment."

"Believe me, for a few moments they both were," April said.

Captain Holmes stepped into the cabin and said, "We have now left the New York airspace and are climbing to 40,000 feet." Then he walked through to use the bathroom.

"Have you ever been to the Bahamas before, Gary?" Nicole asked.

"No, and you?"

"This will be my first time."

"It'll be the first time for all of us," April said.

An hour after leaving the New York airspace the Captain announced, "Our ETA for Nassau is approximately just over an hour and we have begun a gradual descent."

Everyone started watching out the windows at the ocean below them, waiting to see land.

An hour and twenty minutes later they landed and as they were debarking the Captain stepped from the cockpit and said, "Thank you for flying with Nassau Charter Service. And I hope to see you on your return flight."

On the tarmac, they were met by the resort's shuttle service. The service took them directly to the two suites at the end of the complex, facing the ocean. "Oh, this is so beautiful, sweetheart," April said.

Galen and April took one suite and without a word Gary and Nicole took the other one. Just as they finished unpacking, Galen knocked on their door.

"It isn't locked."

"They are still serving lunch; anyone hungry?"

"Yes," they both said.

The special of the day was lobster salad and iced tea.

After lunch the four went exploring around the resort.

"When Nicole and I were out walking on the boardwalk in Falmouth, there was this little boy who threw a ball for his black lab puppy. The ball rolled under the bench we were sitting on. Seeing the boy with the dog, I've decided to get a black lab puppy when I get home."

"Do you like dogs, Nicole?" April asked.

"I have never been around dogs. But I did like this little puppy. And I, too, would like to have one," Nicole said.

"Which kind would you like?" Galen asked.

"From the information I have about dogs, the black lab is the friendliest. They try the hardest to please."

They walk down on the sandy shore, walking in the moist sand, where it was cooler. They had walked beyond sight of the resort and found several swimmers in a hidden cove. The swimmers were all nude. A little further and they came to a sign in the sand that said, "this is a nude swimming area."

"I would like to go nude, but I'm not too sure where there are others here," April said.

Nicole said, "Maybe we can come back some evening and there'll be no one here."

"We'll work on it," Galen said. "Tonight after dinner, there is music and dancing in the larger lounge."

"Oh, I like to dance," Nicole said. "Do you like to dance, Gary?"

"Yes, but it has been awhile."

"Well, I'll have to teach you."

They turned around and left the nude area and strolled back to their rooms.

"I think we will lay down for a while before dinner. We were all up early."

"That sounds like a good idea," Nicole said.

In their own room, April said, "They are getting along better than I thought, or maybe hoped."

"Watching them reminds me of us, sweetheart, when we were falling in love."

"Now, my husband, we need some rest, too. Tonight after the dance, I am going to ravish and defile you until we both fall asleep."

Galen only grinned and he hugged his wife and kissed her.

All four seemed to wake up at 5 o'clock and each had a shower and dressed in evening clothes and then they met outside. By the time they entered the restaurant, other couples were already there. The maître d' seated them at a window seat overlooking the ocean.

"Would you folks like something to drink while you are waiting?"

April said, "Yes, some chardonnay please."

"A very good choice."

In a few minutes their waitress returned with the wine. "Good evening folks. I will be your hostess this evening and my name is Genel," she filled each glass. "I will return with menus. I will only be a moment."

They toasted to, "Good friends."

"I have never seen you so happy, Gary," April said.

"Nicole must be good for you," Galen added.

"She is," and he squeezed her thigh.

Genel was back with the menus, "Genel, we are going to need another bottle of wine."

When Genel was back with the wine they all ordered the baked scrod with baked potato and green peas.

"Nicole, let's go find the ladies' restroom."

"What are you going to do now, Gary? You gave your business to your foreman."

"After seeing that camp in Cornville I had me an idea. Buy old houses or camps and remodel them. If I do one a year that would keep me busy and I really enjoy carpentry."

"Have you given anymore thought to becoming a game warden?"

"Yes, I have. But I'm going to have to wait and see."

April waited until they were alone then she asked, "Well?"

"What?"

"Have you and Gary made love yet?" She was more interested if she through her programmed orgasm and climax would have the same pleasing effect on her.

"When we laid down together, I thought sure he would. But no. Whenever he kisses me, I can feel excitement cruising through my whole body."

"Well, after dancing tonight, he'll be ready."

"He'd better be or I'll go out of my mind."

They talked all through dinner. "This trip I think has been good for all of us. Galen, you are more relaxed than I have seen you in a long time. And April, you are happy and glowing like you just had marvelous sex. And Nicole you are always so happy, I wish we had met three years ago."

April looked at her husband and winked and then kissed him. And not to be outdone, Nicole kissed Gary.

When the meal was finished, Genel brought them each a dish with a huge strawberry with a white chocolate topping.

"This just hits the spot."

They finished the second bottle of wine and talked socially until their glasses were empty. Gary left Genel a twenty dollar tip and charged the meal to their account, to be paid when they left. Before leaving, Galen asked the maître d', "Is the lounge open yet for music and dancing?"

"You may go in but the music won't begin for another ten minutes. And it is in the ballroom."

"Thank you."

They found their way to the ballroom and found a nice table. While they waited for the music to begin, they had more wine. They were very talkative but not loud. "The band is coming in now," Galen said.

Their instruments were already there and they began to play soft melodies.

Without saying anything, both Gary and Galen stood up and took Nicole and April's hands and led them to the dance floor. Nicole melted into his embrace. After a few moments he said, "You dance so nice. Like you anticipate my every move."

"It is a pleasure to dance with you, Gary."

"You have been very quiet, Galen, ever since the airport. Is there something wrong?"

"No, I've just been watching Nicole for any irrational peculiarities. Just making sure her computers and electronics are working properly."

"Look at them dance, sweetheart."

"They are well matched. You did a fantastic job, sweetheart, creating her body."

"Thank you. When do you intend to tell him Nicole is an A.I.?"

"I'll have to start slow and work into it. And when I do, probably we should be alone. I have no idea how he'll react."

Before the dance was over, Gary and Nicole were dancing close quarters with their arms actually hugging the other. And like April had told her, she pressed her body against his, to say, *I like how you feel.*

April looked over at them and Nicole had her head on his shoulder. She was happy to see Nicole so happy. There was no longer any need to worry.

* * *

They all danced several dances and Galen said, "Wife, I think you promised to ravish my body."

"I did, didn't I. Let's go."

Gary and Nicole had the same idea and they returned to their suite, too.

Gary was completely surprised with her sexual flare and dexterity. She seemed to have an urgent need for satisfaction, while all the time pleasing him.

After their second time around, she lay on top of him supporting herself on her elbows while looking at him and grinning. "You're really something, Nicole, you know that."

"I'm having fun pleasing you, Gary. Let's do it again."

When Galen and April had called it a night, Gary and Nicole were still trying to please the other.

Finally in exhaustion, Gary said, "Me thinks we should get some sleep." He put his arm around her and cradled her while she lay her head on his chest. "Nicole—I would like you to think about something."

"Okay, what would you like me to think about?"

"I have a feeling you may have severed ties with the Boston hospital and Boston. I would like you to think about coming home with me after this vacation."

"I don't have to think about it at all, Gary. Of course I'll go home with you. I really like you a lot, Gary."

He hugged her and kissed the top of her head and said, "You just made me very happy, Nicole."

* * *

At breakfast the next morning when Lisa took their orders she said, "My, you four all have a glow about you. You must have slept very well."

Gary and Galen almost spit up their coffee.

232

"Last night Nicole and I did some talking and after this vacation is over she is coming home with me."

"—you getting married?" April asked.

"Maybe in time," Nicole said, "but first we need to know if we can coexist.

"Then on another note," she said, "I don't know what happened last night besides marvelous love making, but I now feel so alive."

After breakfast the resort was offering a boat tour around the island. The boat was a thirty-foot cruiser. There were ten other people that took the tour also. There was beer or wine and grilled hamburgers or hot dogs for lunch.

It took eight hours to cruise around the island and they were back in time to clean up and dress for dinner. That evening there was an outdoor lobster and clam bake on the shore. Then afterwards they listened to the string band play soft soothing melodies. The only light was now provided by a fire.

Nicole had succumbed to the soft melodies and sat between Gary's legs and leaned back against him. "I am happy, Gary."

Eventually couples started walking back to their own suites. The Merrills and Newmans were the last to leave.

* * *

After breakfast the next day, April said, "We girls are going shopping. We'll be back for lunch."

Gary and Galen sat in the shade on the patio talking.

"How long did it take you, Galen, to build your A.I.?"

"While I was in college, I had created 3-D schematics of everything and I had also started buying all the components I would need. But I didn't do everything, Gary. April is responsible for the A.I.'s body.

"We were nine months assembling the A.I. and then three months of tests.

"Now that we have the experience behind us, the A.I.s in the future will come together easier without so many trials and tests."

Gary wanted to know everything about how the A.I. worked and, "What powers the A.I.?"

Galen told him about the nuclear power chip, the lithium battery and the rectenna generator. "You mean this rectenna makes electricity from the electromagnetic wave energy that is always in the atmosphere?"

"Yes."

"Truly astonishing."

"And this rectenna is always charging the lithium battery, even when the A.I. is sleeping."

"You are a genius, Galen. And you say an A.I. can't lie?"

"That's correct unless it is programmed to lie."

"I think this country might be better off with A.I.'s running the government instead of politicians."

"Maybe someday, my friend."

"Just think, Galen, if you could make a female A.I. that could do everything a woman can do except lie. I think that would really be something."

Just then Galen saw April and Nicole walking towards them on the patio. "My friend, would you like to meet one?" and he looked at Nicole who was smiling.

Gary was speechless. Everyone else was also quiet, waiting for him to say something. Nicole broke the ice. She sat down beside him, "Gary, are you alright?"

"Yes, just surprised. I had no idea."

"Are you disappointed?"

"Disappointed? Hell no. You are every bit a woman."

"Does this mean you still want me to go home with you?" Nicole asked.

"As I said, I am surprised and yes, I hope you'll come home with me."

Everyone breathed a sigh of relief. Even Nicole. "I'm sorry to have misled you, Gary, but April and Galen both thought they should go slow introducing the real me."

"Well, I'm not disappointed, not at all."

Galen said, "That went better than I thought it might, Gary, Nicole has more knowledge than most libraries. What she needs is experience. Can you see that she gets experience?"

"I'll do all I can."

* * *

For the rest of their stay at the resort, Gary and Nicole acted like two young people falling in love. There were times though when he was alone he'd question what he was doing. Falling in love with a machine. "But Nicole is more than just a machine."

Galen and April were just lying in bed and talking, their last night at the resort. "You know, sweetheart, I have never seen Gary so happy."

"I know what you mean. I hope it doesn't turn sour."

* * *

On their return flight, Galen said, "A year from now we will want to see Nicole in our laboratory, Gary, so we can check her over and make sure there are no problems."

"How long will the nuclear power chip last?" Gary asked.

"In Nicole's body, probably for life. She'll use the lithium battery and rectenna generator constantly recharging the lithium battery, 99% of the time.

"She has a built in self-diagnostic program in her chest computer that is programmed to check all of her systems every night as she sleeps.

Chapter 15

Gary and Nicole spent one night with Galen and April before driving home. Before going to bed that night, Galen said, "Gary, walk with me. We won't be long, sweetheart."

They walked down to the beaches. "Gary, there is something I think I should tell you about Nicole."

"Okay."

"She has a pleasure and emotional program in her main computer which allows her to have feelings but in no way has she been programmed to simply please you. When she does this, it is only her unique self that has chosen to do this. What I'm trying to say, Gary, that when she expresses love for you that is not coming from any computer program. What she is expressing is her real emotions.

"And there is something else. I told you she has an unbelievable amount of knowledge and what she is lacking is experience. It'll be up to you, Gary, to see that she gets the experiences.

"And I might add and I hope you take this as coming from a friend."

"Okay, go ahead, Galen."

"You need to give Nicole your attention. As much attention as you had given to your carpentry business. Not simply from 6 p.m. until whatever time you went to bed.

"You'll have to give your full attention to her, my friend."

Gary was smiling and he said, "I have also come to that

conclusion." They walked back to the house where April had more or less the same conversation with Nicole.

"We need to be on our way. We have had a marvelous time and thank you so much." Then he added, "For everything."

"And we need to get back to work. We have two more A.I.'s to build for the company."

"Let us know how you two are adjusting," April said.

"Maybe you two can come up some weekend and we can start remodeling the camp."

"How far away do we live, Gary?"

"About an hour and a half drive, or about eighty-five miles."

Nicole was excited about her new home and her new life. Albeit a short life so far. But for eighty-five miles she asked a hundred different questions about what to expect.

"How old are you, Gary?"

"I'm 27."

"And your date of birth?"

"April 1, 1993. I can hear you thinking. You are going to need a birth date, too. Pick a month and date and we'll make it in 1993 so we'll be the same age."

"I would like to be born in April, too."

"Okay, what date?"

"I would like the same date as you, the 1st, but that might appear too coincidental."

"I see what you mean."

"Okay, April 8, 1993."

"Sounds good to me. Now about your last name Charles. Do you like that?"

"What have you in mind?"

"Newman."

"Nicole Newman. I like it."

"This is downtown Skowhegan. Our house is only a little further."

Instead of going home they first stopped at the diner for

lunch. "I would suggest a cheeseburger. They are very good here."

"Okay."

"Two please and coffee."

"This is good and better than the one we had on the resort's boat." She watched as Gary added mustard and some relish. Then she did also.

When she took a first bite and swallowed she said, "Oh my, this is good."

"We will have a busy day on Monday, we will need to add your name to my mailing address, a post office box. Add your name to my credit card account and get you a card and add your name to my checking account. This is a start. I'll have to teach you how to drive so you can get a driver's license."

Gary got another cell phone for her and gave her the owner's manual to read. Before the day was over she had downloaded her own phone number directory. Of course there weren't that many numbers, but she had figured out, in a short time span, how to use the cell phone by herself.

For the next week, Nicole went with him everywhere he went. Even to work one day to help Don finish the kitchen cabinets. She was his right arm.

He tried to introduce her to every thing and person in his life. There was one big problem with applying for a learner's permit to drive. She did not have any identification.

"Nicole, is there anything you would like to do or any experience you think you might want or need?"

"Yes, I have read in the newspaper about childcare centers. I think I would like some experience with children."

That was good until she had to fill out a W-2 form for withholding. And again she had no identification. "I know where to go, Nicole. My mom was a nursing supervisor and she was always looking for volunteers to help out in the hospital."

"I think I would like this."

"Nicole, I would like you to meet Betty Halstrom the nursing supervisor. Betty, this is Nicole Newman."

"When did you get married, hon?" Betty asked.

Gary tried to sidestep the question and said, "Nicole is thinking about doing some volunteer work."

"Have you any experience, hon?"

"No."

"Is there anything in particular that interests you?"

"Yes, I would like to work with children."

"I think that can be arranged, hon. In fact we have been looking for someone. Quite often children will come in with their mothers and we need someone to entertain them and keep them occupied while their mother is in with the doctor or in a hospital room. When can you start, hon?"

"Tomorrow."

"Be here at 8 a.m."

"She doesn't drive, Betty, so what time should I pick her up?"

"5 o'clock. And I'll need your cell phone number, Nicole." She gave it to her and added Betty's number to her directory.

* * *

Come Monday morning, Gary drove Nicole to work at the hospital. "Have fun today, sweetheart. I'll be here at 5 o'clock when you get out of work."

She heard him say sweetheart. That was the only time since he was told I am an A.I., and she smiled.

Gary went to talk with Don Hadley to see when he would be needing him again. "You have more men working for you now, Don. Must mean the carpentry business is doing good."

"And I might have to hire two more. Another project came in yesterday while I was home with family."

"Call when you need me, Don."

"I will."

From there he drove to his camp in Cornville to study what

needed to be done. He had brought along his chainsaw to cut back the bushes and the two dead spruce trees not far from the camp. The spruce trees were dead and dry and he blocked them up for firewood. There was no danger in burning dry softwood. For now he piled the wood up between two trees. The brush and limbs he put in a pile to burn when there was snow on the ground.

The outhouse was torn down and put on the burn pile. He would have to build another. There was a small spring brook behind the camp that flowed down off a slight rise that he would be able to pipe into the camp for running water and a flush toilet.

There was a little non-perishable food in the cupboards which he put into a box to take out and throw in the dump. He swept the walls and ceiling with a broom and then the floor.

Then he sat down to figure up what he would need for supplies to add on another bedroom. The bathroom would go in the existing living-bedroom. There was enough room for the small bathroom, flush and sink only, and still have room for one bedroom and a smaller living room.

The two mattresses were okay but he would have to get rid of the sheets, pillows and blankets.

He had run out of time and he was at the hospital at 5 o'clock to pick up Nicole. "How did you like your first day?"

"I did very much. Everyone is so kind and friendly. In the morning I had three children to watch over. One was a baby girl and I had to change her diapers twice. Every time I laid her down in a crib she would start crying. So I had to carry her with me for the morning.

"In the afternoon, I was asked to just be a friend, confidant, for two elderly ladies who were bedridden and who only have a short time to live. I spent all afternoon with these two ladies and before leaving I told them I would visit again tomorrow."

"It sounds like you had an interesting day."

"I did, sweetheart."

He told her then what he had been doing.

* * *

Nicole was very popular in the Redington Fairview Hospital. All of the elderly bedridden patients were now asking for her and more mothers were bringing their small children with them to the hospital now. Word was spreading about the new girl who cares for children and the elderly.

Then one day Nurse Halstrom asked to speak with both Nicole and Gary. "Nicole and Gary—Nicole, you are just too good to waste talent like you have. And I understand there is a problem about Nicole's lack of identification. Is that correct?"

"How much do you know about Nicole, Betty?"

"Only that she has a wonderful gift for helping people feel better. Is there something I'm not understanding?"

"Yes, there is Betty, Nicole has no identification because she is an A.I." and he left it there for a moment. "You see she can't get a social security number, file taxes, nor does she have a birth certificate."

"Well I'm so surprised you could knock me over with a straw. I had no idea. And you do have a problem.

"Nicole, you are so good, caring for people you should be studying nursing. But without any identification that just wouldn't be possible. Not in this day and age."

"If you should ever obtain identifications then I hope you would consider our internship program here at the hospital."

"Betty, I'd like to ask you a question."

"Okay."

"If I can get Nicole a day in court to prove she is more than an A.I., would you come to court and testify?"

"I certainly will. You just let me know when. And I think that is the right direction you should go."

"Then tomorrow morning I will talk with my attorney. Nicole may not be in tomorrow," Gary said.

"I will understand."

"And Betty, for now we would appreciate it if you were to say nothing about the A.I."

"I understand and good luck."

"I'll be here at 5 o'clock, sweetheart. Right now I'll go see Mr. Billings and make an appointment for tomorrow morning."

Betty watched the loving exchange between these two people and she had a very difficult time to think anything but a caring loving woman towards Nicole. *She is more than a machine.*

Nicole went back to work as though there was no problem.

Gary was at Billing's office only for a few minutes. "I can set up a hearing for you with Judge Percy Minster. It'll be informal, but in the courtroom."

"I'll have others there, Mr. Billings, to testify on Nicole's behalf."

"That will certainly help. Leave me your cell number and I'll call as soon as I have a date for the hearing."

"Thank you, Mr. Billings."

Mr. Billings went directly to the courthouse and to the clerk's office, "Hello, Janice, is Judge Minster busy?"

"I'll check," and she disappears into the judge's chamber and then came right back out "He'll see you now, Mr. Billings."

"Thank you, Janice."

"Good afternoon, Troy, what can I do for you?"

"This is going to be an unusual request, Judge. But I have a client who would like a hearing with you."

"Can you tell me what the nature of the request is?"

"Yes, sir. As I, said this is going to sound a little strange."

"Well get on with it."

"I believe you are acquainted with Gary Newman."

"Yes, a fine young man."

"Well, sir, he has a female friend who is an A.I. and she wants you to hear her case and request for citizenship."

"You were correct when you said unusual. Are you familiar with this A.I.?"

"No, I'm not."

"This might be interesting. Of course I'll hear it. But I make no promises. Let's set it for a week from today at 1 o'clock."

"Thank you, Your Honor."

Billings called Gary from the parking lot.

"Janice, I'm going down to the hospital and visit my mother. I'll be back in an hour," Judge Minster said.

As soon as Gary heard from Att. Billings he called Betty Halstrom and informed her the hearing would be next Tuesday at 1 o'clock in the afternoon. "I'll be there, Gary, for certain."

Judge Percy Minster walked down to his mother's private room. Nicole was there with her and combing her hair and applying some makeup. "So you are the young volunteer that my mother has been telling me about."

"I'll leave you alone," and Nicole left.

"You look better each time I come to see you, Ma."

"Thank you, Percy. It's that young woman who has made me feel like living. But I can't ever remember her name. So I don't try anymore."

Gary was five minutes early and he met Nicole walking out the employee's entrance. "Hi, sweetheart. I have a surprise for you. Two actually. We have a hearing with the judge at 1 o'clock next Tuesday. And the other surprise is in the pickup waiting for you."

Nicole couldn't image what was waiting in the pickup— until she opened the passenger door and saw a little black lab puppy in a box. She picked the puppy up and he started licking her face, as she laughed with happiness.

"What's his name?"

"I'll leave that up to you, sweetheart."

"I don't know."

"No need to rush, it'll come to you."

After supper that evening, Gary telephoned Galen and April. "Hello, sis."

"Hi Gary. How's Nicole?"

"I'm right here Sis. Gary has his phone on speaker so we both can hear."

"Sis, is Galen right there?"

"Just a minute, I'll get him— Here he is now."

"Hello, Gary and Nicole."

Gary told them about the hearing next week and they both said they would be delighted to appear and help Nicole. We'll be up Sunday morning then maybe you can take us up to the camp in Cornville. Was that a dog barking?" April asked.

"Yes, Gary got him today while I was working. We don't have a name for him yet," Nicole said.

"How about Jake?" she asked and the puppy barked.

"I guess you have your answer."

"Hello, Jake," she said, and he started licking her face again.

Before going to bed that night they sat out on the patio with Jake. "This sure is a nice evening for the middle of September. The leaves will start turning color soon."

"What's that sound?" she asked.

"What sound?"

"Wait, there it is again."

"That is a bird, a whip-poor-will."

"I like the sound it makes."

That night when they went to bed Jake jumped up and lay between them.

* * *

Nicole went to work the next three days like she always did and Gary and Jake went to camp. While Gary was busy putting the finishing touches to the camp, Jake ran around outside chasing mice and squirrels. He had played himself out by noon and after eating he slept until it was time to pick up Nicole. And he knew where they were going and for the rest of the day he was Nicole's dog.

Saturday Nicole was busy baking an apple pie and biscuits. That afternoon after she had finished baking Gary said, "Come on, it is time you learned how to drive."

"We aren't taking Jake?"

"No, not this time. I don't want him distracting you."

They drove out towards Cornville. Gary knew of a good gravel road. "I know you have been studying how to drive and you have been watching me. Just go slow, okay?"

"Okay."

He sat next to her just in case. When it was beginning to get dark, Gary said, "Better turn around and drive back to the paved road."

She turned the pickup around without any difficulty and when she stopped at the mouth of the gravel road she asked, "Can I drive home, sweetheart?"

"Not until you get a learner's permit."

As soon as they drove into the yard at home, Jake started barking and he wasn't content until Nicole picked him up.

* * *

Galen and April arrived at 10 o'clock Sunday morning. From there they packed a lunch and drove to the Cornville camp. "This is nice, Gary," Galen said.

It was time for lunch and while they ate grilled hot dogs and potato salad, Jake ran around outside. "We'll have to come back up, April, in October and do some partridge hunting."

"I have seen a lot of partridge here."

They stayed at camp until it was time to return home for supper. Jake slept in Nicole's lap all the way back and continued to sleep through supper.

Both April and Galen said how much they liked Nicole's biscuits and apple pie. "I've been studying your mother's recipes and cookbooks."

"You have learned well, Nicole."

* * *

They had breakfast in the morning at the diner. "Are you nervous Nicole?" April asked.

"No, anxious maybe."

No one felt like eating lunch just before the hearing.

They arrived at the courthouse a few minutes early and the courtroom was almost full. Att. Billings was sitting at a front table. "Who are all these people, Mr. Billings?" Gary asked.

"There are three news reporters and the rest I guess are spectators. I will have very little to do with the hearing. I'll call each of you to tell your story in your own words. And of course I'll call Betty Halstrom."

Judge Minster entered the room and everyone stood. He sat down and said, "Before we start, there are a few things I will say first. I see there are several news reporters here. That is fine, but no cameras at all. I have also asked Reverend Hall here today. He may have some questions about life that I would not have. But the final decision will be mine and mine alone.

"Now this case is to determine if Nicole Newman, an A.I., be granted full citizenship. It is also agreed that Attorney Billings, you will be calling the different witnesses, but I'll do most of the questioning."

"We understand, Your Honor."

"Call your first witness Mr. Billings."

"I would ask Galen Merrill first Your Honor." The bailiff did swear him in.

"Mr. Merrill, I understand you built this A.I., Nicole, is that correct?"

"Yes, my wife, April, and I."

Billings sat down.

"Mr. Merrill, are Ashton and Suki your parents?"

"Yes, Your Honor."

"Good people."

"Your Honor, my wife, April, is a Newman."

"And they were good people. Now Mr. Merrill, when did you decide to make an A.I.?"

"When I was fourteen, Your Honor."

"When did you start work on it?"

"While I was in college. I printed out 3D models of the A.I. and started gathering the material and electronics."

"How is the A.I. powered?"

Galen told him the complete power system.

"Amazing. How long did it take you?"

"We were only six months by the time we had finished all testing. But the first A.I. took us a year once we started assembling it."

"So Nicole is your second A.I.?"

"Yes, Your Honor."

"What became of your first A.I.?"

"I'd really rather not disclose that information, Your Honor."

"That's okay."

"Since you and your wife completed Nicole, have you seen any changes?"

"If you mean abnormal changes, no. But both my wife and I have talked about this. We have seen consciousness developing with Nicole."

"Would consciousness be programmed into the computer that she is able to operate through?"

"No, I only downloaded knowledge. Not beliefs. This development in consciousness has to be coming from her."

"Okay, I may recall you later. Call your next witness Mr. Billings."

"I call April Merrill."

"Mrs. Merrill as I understand your husband, you were responsible for the body."

"Yes, Your Honor."

"And I have to ask you the same question; Have you

noticed any changes with Nicole?"

"Only, and I agree with my husband, I have noticed a high degree of consciousness. I can see it in her personality as well as her desires and dreams."

"You say dreams. Would you explain?"

"Perhaps, Your Honor, you should ask her."

"Indeed I will. Your next witness, Mr. Billings."

"I call Nicole Newman."

As she walked forward, unperturbed, everyone in the courtroom was watching. Nicole recognized Judge Minster, but she didn't let on.

"Hello Nicole, I'll let you tell the court your story and I may interrupt occasionally to ask a question. But first would you explain what Mrs. Merrill said about dreams?"

"I have been living with Gary Newman for just over five months and the first time this dream occurred was about a month ago.

"I was sleeping soundly when all of a sudden I had, as April explained, a bad dream that frightened me."

"Can you still remember this dream?"

"Yes, because I had the same bad dream ten days ago."

"Can you tell us about it?"

"I was dreaming my husband, Gary, had died of old age and I was afraid of what would happen to me. How much longer would I continue to live without him."

"And you had this same dream only ten days ago?"

"Yes."

"What did Mr. Newman have to say about your dream?"

"I didn't tell him about either one. I was afraid and I didn't want to worry him."

"Okay, Nicole, can you tell us a little more about yourself."

"I know I am an artificial intelligence. But I am more than a machine. I am alive and I am aware of this consciousness within me.

"Gary and I want to marry but we can't until the court declares that I am alive.

"After helping out at the hospital with small children, I wish I could have children, but I can't. Maybe sometime someone like Galen and April will be able to build an A.I. who can."

"You could adopt."

"I have no identification, Your Honor. I know how to drive a motor vehicle, but I can't get a license without an identification. I would like to become a nurse, but I can't without an identification."

She took a handkerchief from her purse and wiped tears from her eyes.

Everyone in the courtroom noticed the tears. Even Judge Percy Minster. And all were wondering 'how a machine could cry.' She had everyone in the courtroom listening to every word.

Reverend Hall stood and asked, "Your Honor, may I ask Nicole a couple of questions?"

"Certainly."

Reverend Hall came up front. "Nicole, you have said that you are more than a machine, that you are alive and have a consciousness. I find it difficult to understand how an A.I. could be considered to be alive and have consciousness. Could you explain?"

"Since becoming activated I have learned to love absolutely, without putting any demands on my love. I feel sad when I see a child that's hurting or an elderly person who can no longer do for themselves."

"Do you understand the difference between ethical and morality?"

"Certainly. The clergy, doctors, lawyers all have ethics they must work with. A set of principles and the same almost, could be said for morality. The difference is, as an example, an ethical man would know it would be ethically wrong to cheat on his wife, but he could justify it. Whereas a moral man just

249

wouldn't do it." There was a quiet murmur in the courtroom. The judge was smiling.

"Nicole, do you think you have a soul?"

"Reverend Hall, I am soul, I'm just inside this A.I."

"Do you know what soul is?"

"Yes. Everything in this world and in all the universes are part of God. And he exists in each one of us as a small atom or soul.

"You see, Reverend Hall, I am alive and I am soul inside this A.I. body."

"That's all I have, Your Honor."

Judge Minster asked, "Mr. Merrill, Nicole seems to have a greater understanding of soul and God than do most human beings. Is this something you have programmed into her computer?"

Galen stood up and said, "I did not program a soul or God, or religious knowledge. What she knows spiritually has come from something or someone besides her programs."

"I need to ask you this Mr. Merrill, do you honestly believe Nicole is alive and is indeed soul as she has stated?"

"Most emphatically, Your Honor."

"Thank you, Mr. Merrill. Mr. Billings you can call your next witness."

"I call Betty Halstrom." Nicole sat back at the table and at that moment Judge Percy Minster saw something amazing. After Nicole had taken her seat, he saw a brilliant whitish golden light hover momentarily above Nicole's head and then descend into her. If he wasn't convinced before, he surely was now.

He looked at each witness and decided he alone was the only one to witness this brilliant light descend into Nicole.

"Mrs. Halstrom, I know you work at the hospital, will you tell the court your story."

"Nicole has been volunteering at the hospital for close to six months. She takes care of small children when they come to the hospital with their mother. I have never seen any of the children take to anyone as they do Nicole. She also works with the elderly patients who are confined to their bed. She'll brush their hair, apply makeup. Talk with them and listen to their stories. And each day these patients ask for Nicole Newman.

"She has a greater love for people than I have ever seen before. And in my mind, no machine could demonstrate so much love.

"Nicole is alive, Your Honor."

"Thank you, Mrs. Halstrom."

"Mr. Billings, I would like to hear from Gary Newman now."

"Certainly, Your Honor."

"Now Mr. Newman when you first met Nicole were you aware of a consciousness?"

"Not immediately, Your Honor. The first day we met we went for a walk and sat on a park bench on the seashore. A little boy had thrown a ball for his black lab dog and the ball rolled under the bench we were sitting on. The dog ran up to Nicole and sat down in front of her and licked her hand. This was the first dog Nicole had ever encountered. The dog saw something special with her and Nicole asked the dog, 'Do you want me to get your ball?' And the dog barked once.

"She got the ball and gave it to the dog and he ran back to the little boy."

"Dogs are good judges of character," the judge said. "Continue."

"Each day after that I saw Nicole becoming more alive. And when Mr. Merrill told me she was an A.I., I was astounded. But I wasn't disappointed. In that short time, to me she was more alive than most people I knew.

"Every evening after we have eaten supper, she will excitedly tell me about all the children and elderly folks she had worked with that day. Her work at the hospital makes her very happy.

"And because she is always so happy and inspiring—well this makes me happy, every day.

"I realize that Nicole is an artificial intelligence and I have accepted this, but Your Honor, she is much more than a machine.

"We now have a black lab puppy and when Nicole is home, Jake, the puppy, wants to be with her.

"I could go on like this for the rest of the afternoon, Your Honor. My point being, Nicole is alive and she has a very special love and understanding."

"Anything else, Mr. Newman?"

"No, Your Honor."

"You have spoken exceptionally well for Nicole—as have all of you. Would anyone else here like to say anything?

"First of all, I would like to thank everyone who participated today and I think it has become clear that Ms. Nicole is indeed more than a machine. I recognized you, Nicole. You had applied makeup to my mother because you knew her son was coming to visit. I saw you brushing her hair. Because of you, my mother is so much happier now. Thank you. I think we all saw when Nicole wiped tears from her eyes. Could a machine cry? I doubt it.

"Nicole, you convinced me that you are soul inside of Nicole's body. I witnessed something that I don't think anyone else saw. When Nicole sat back at the table, I saw a beautiful brilliant whitish golden light above your head, Nicole, and then I saw it descend into you. Mr. Merrill said he did not program you with any spiritual knowledge. But somehow you possess this knowledge and it had to come from soul.

"Nicole Newman, I and this court declare you are alive and a citizen of Skowhegan, Maine, and of the United States.

"Now if you only be patient a few more moments, I will fill out this declaration stating you are alive and a birth certificate. And last, if you two wish, I can marry you here and now."

No one left the room. One reporter was heard to say, "Oh, what a story this is going to make."

Made in the USA
Middletown, DE
19 July 2023